For Hilary, Molly, Michael and Carmen
and my sister Irina

A short guide to old money

In this book I refer to small monetary values by their pre-decimalisation terminology.

Decimalisation – D-Day was the name coined for the momentous change – was introduced on 15 February 1971, but usage of pre-decimal terminology was maintained in everyday speech at least until the late 1970s.

Under the old currency, which had existed in Britain for centuries, the pound was made up of 240 'old pence' (denoted by the symbol *d*), with twelve old pence in a shilling (denoted by the symbol *s*) and twenty shillings in a pound. One shilling was commonly referred to as one bob. Some of the old silver coinage continued after D-Day as it had value in the new currency. A shilling, or a bob, became 5p and a florin, or two bob, became 10p. The new coins were ½p, 1p, 2p, 5p, 10p and 50p (where the 50p replaced the ten shilling note). The other coins (20p, £1, £2) have been introduced in later years, and the ½p abolished.

It was the morning of my tenth birthday when I experienced the first twinge of what I would later recognise as class envy. I suppose it must have had something to do with reaching my first significant age milestone that made me wonder where I came from and where my life was heading. I lived in a nice house in a safe neighbourhood, cared for by loving parents who regarded my welfare and education as their chief priority. They had steady jobs and we wanted for little. My childhood had not been blighted by alcoholism, drug addiction, poverty or crime and I was not ill-treated by malevolent teachers or abusive clergy. I couldn't help wondering where it had all gone wrong.

Our estate was one of prim, white-collar respectability. At the top of the hill was Pollokshields, a smart enclave of sanitised politeness and conspicuous silence, where broad, tree-lined drive-ways, populated with top-of-the-range cars gave way to forbidding sandstone villas.

At the foot of the hill was Maxwell Drive and beyond that the railway line which was the final frontier into the grim, industrial badlands of Govan, where most of my schoolmates lived. I remember that you could see the tops of the shipyard cranes – shadowy figures dominating the skyline like proud and depend-able sentries.

Our estate provided a buffer between two communities. That our world of fitted carpets, herbaceous borders and action slacks sat cheek-by-jowl with the mean streets of Govan was a little acknowledged reality. Its inhabitants' world was one of obscene graffiti, scrawled on the walls of tenement closes; of desolate backyards, punctuated by islands of rotting litter, rubble and the hardened excrement of dogs of questionable lineage; of outside toilets, whose smell hit you in the face with the force of a Peter Lorimer shot; of the acrid odour of frying, artery-hardening chip-shop fat, which hung in the air like a suffocating canopy and invaded your hair and the fibres of your clothing.

Everything about my childhood was comfortable, conformist and pedestrian – an unbending regimen of early nights, sensible shoes and short haircuts. I was dressed in functional, unfashionable clothes – mostly my sister's hand-me-downs – and I ate healthy, home-cooked meals. I was banned from watching television after eight o'clock and tucked safely between freshly laundered sheets by nine. Reading the women's underwear section of Mum's Kay's catalogue by torchlight was as rebellious as I got.

My Govan contemporaries, in contrast, led a dangerous, skin-of-their-teeth existence of late-night, do-as-you-please chaos. They spoke of strange, exotic experiences for which I could only yearn wistfully – Vesta chicken curries, high-waisters and the naked breast scene from *A Bouquet of Barbed Wire*.

I longed to be neglected like my friends, to be sent to the Criterion Sea Fish Bar on the Paisley Road to buy my tea and to dog school with the hungover complicity of my elders. I didn't see the dampness and deprivation in their lives. I looked on jealously at the laissez-faire attitude of their parents, exemplified by a rear-view shot of them sashaying down tenement closes on their way to the pub or the club or the bookies' or the bingo.

The things they complained about seemed, to me, exciting and edgy. I wanted to be woken in the early hours by police searching our home for stolen cases of Scotch and errant family members. If I was to be corporally punished I'd rather it was at a bus-stop or in a supermarket aisle where bystanders could tut disapprovingly at my parents' heavy-handedness. I wouldn't have regarded rowing, drunkenly chaotic parents as a liability the way Wally, my best friend, did. It seemed to me more of a financial opportunity. The drunker his dad got, the more he could steal from him.

Most of all I craved an interesting, impoverished family background. As far as I could tell, my forebears had all been grindingly respectable, God-fearing, middle-class types. Having a great-grandfather who was a baillie in the burgh of Renfrewshire was hardly adequate playground currency when you were competing against generations of gruel-fed, shoeless wretches from rural Ireland.

What I would have given for just one relative who had died in the potato famine or been terrorised by the Black and Tans. How I yearned to harbour long-held, spoken-only-in-hushed-tones resentment against the Catholic Church, for the way my auntie had been mistreated by an order of sadistic nuns. How I longed to sing, with sombre passion, about how *armoured cars and tanks and guns came to take away our sons* and actually have the faintest idea what I was going on about.

Because it was my birthday, Mum had promised to take me into town to buy my first suit. The fact that it was my cousin's wedding the following week, an occasion for which I would require a suit, was one of those happy coincidences in which my mother specialised.

It was a blisteringly hot day and I was sweating as we ran to catch the bus. Mum boarded first and the clippie hoisted me onto the rear plate as the bus pulled away. I asked if we could go upstairs. I liked to sit on the top deck, at the front, imagining that I was steering the ungainly old Routemaster round the twisting avenues, but Mum wouldn't hear of it because that's where the common people sat. And its up-*stairs*, not up-*sterrs*, she chided, correcting my pronunciation for the hundredth time that day.

I had to content myself with sitting downstairs, alongside the ladies from the big houses. They were perched on the rear seats, dressed in their weekend finery. Most would have already been to the hairdresser on the Paisley Road to have their finely sculpted beehives lacquered into place. They caught the fifty-nine bus into town at the same time every Saturday to spend the day shopping,

3

before meeting up for high tea at any number of the city's tearooms. A strategically placed bomb in the centre of Glasgow on a Saturday afternoon could have wiped out the country's entire stockpile of linen doilies.

Mum would pass the time of day with the ladies from the big houses but she didn't really like them. She said they looked down on people like us from the new estate. We sat opposite Mrs Yuill, whose husband played the organ at the church.

– Not the sort of weather you want the central heating on, she said to Mum, wearing the hint of a smile.

– Indeed not, Mrs Yuill, Mum replied.

– It makes you want to open the door of the deep freeze and let the cool air drift over you.

I pointed out that we didn't have a central heating system. Mum fixed me with an icy glare. I was about to add that we didn't have a deep freeze either when I felt Mum's elbow digging me in the ribs.

– Don't interrupt, she mouthed. It's common.

I spent the bus trip planning my choice of suit. Tony, my older brother, had been given money for his sixteenth birthday to buy what he wanted. He came home dressed in a wide-lapelled cream suit with lime green pinstripes and flared trousers. The outfit was rounded off with a black silk shirt, cream patent platform shoes and a white floppy cap like the ones the Rubettes wore.

When he walked in the door, Dad couldn't stop laughing. Mum was furious – she said he looked like a pimp – but that didn't mean she was going to stop him wearing them. Tony was her golden boy. He was the cleverest member of the family – definite university material, Mum said – and because of that, he could do no wrong.

I thought his outfit was the most fabulous thing I had ever seen, and I wanted one just like it. Tony had written down the names of all the best boutiques on Argyle Street where, he said, I should get Mum to take me. They all had groovy names like Threadz, Toggs and Glam Gear, but the minute we stepped off the bus she headed straight for Paisley's department store.

Paisley's was a traditional, family-owned store on Jamaica Street – the sort of place where you got dressed up just to shop in it. Located on several, mahogany-panelled levels, it was like a stately home with cash registers. The male sales assistants bore all the spit-and-polish, wax-tipped hallmarks of ex-military types, while the women staff – the genteel daughters of bank managers and kirk elders – looked like they were just killing time until their bridge club met.

There was nothing remotely democratic about Paisley's. It actively discouraged any upstartish notion that customers might have an opinion about what they were buying. You shopped there on the strict understanding that you were going to be patronised from a very great height. For my mother, it was always the first stop on any visit to town. Though she could rarely afford to buy anything, it gave her the opportunity to drop into conversation the fact that she had been there.

We made our way to Boys' Clothing where a fey officer type with halitosis measured me up before pronouncing on what was 'best for the lad'. I was dispatched to a curtained cubicle carrying a navy blue, single-breasted, pure wool jacket, which bore a remarkable resemblance to my school blazer, only without the badge, and a pair of grey trousers. When I returned, the assistant fussed around me, hoisting the jacket around my shoulders and pinching the trousers in at the waist.

– They're a touch on the generous side but the lad will grow into them, he stated in a tone which indicated he would broach no challenge.

To my dismay, Mum failed to demur and before I knew it, we were making our way towards the cash desk with the offending articles. Through gritted teeth, I tried to tell Mum that I hated them, that she was wasting her eight pound fifty and that I wouldn't be seen dead in them. I thought I was getting through to her but then the foul-breathed assistant intervened, asking me if I liked them. I felt my face flush with embarrassment. I wanted to say they were the most hideous things I had ever clapped eyes on but I was ten years old and he was an adult and respect for my elders was a principle too deeply ingrained to challenge.

– They're very nice, was all I could say.

For a birthday treat and, I suspect, because she felt guilty about the clothes, Mum took me to the Java Jive coffee bar on Buchanan Street for lunch. Tony said it was the hippest new place in town. I had a bottle of warm Fanta and a plate of cheese sandwiches with crisps and watercress on the side. Mum had a slice of cold quiche. The sweet trolley was wheeled to our table by a waitress dressed in yellow bell-bottoms and an orange-and-brown striped jumper with a heart-shaped hole cut round her belly-button. Mum had a meringue and I chose a vanilla slice filled with custard and topped with a thick layer of icing.

I was shovelling the last of it into my mouth when I nearly choked with shock. I sat frozen to the spot, my legs jolting involuntarily. I strained, peering closer to make sure I wasn't imagining it. I wasn't.

– M-m-Mum, I mumbled, that's Dixie Deans over there, drinking coffee.

– Who?

– Dixie Deans, 117 goals in 148 appearances for Celtic, including eight as a substitute.

Although I went to a Proddy school, I supported Celtic because they had won virtually everything as far back as I could remember. It meant being called a 'Tim lover' and a 'Fenian' but it was a small price to pay. Some of my classmates supported Celtic as well, until Rangers won the league the previous season, for the first time in a decade, then they started supporting Rangers, but I stuck to my guns. I didn't care what anyone else said, Celtic were still the best.

– OK, calm down, Mum said softly. Don't get over-excited.

– But he's here. In the same room as me, Mum. I can't believe it. I'm in the same room as Dixie Deans.

– Why don't you go and ask him for his autograph? she suggested.

6

My head felt light and, momentarily, I lost my peripheral vision. I thought I was going to pass out.

– I couldn't. I couldn't just walk over and talk to Dixie Deans.

– Of course you could. I'm sure it happens to him all the time.

She dug into her handbag and produced a pen and a piece of paper. I remained frozen to my seat.

– Do you want me to ask him?

I panicked. If there was one thing more mortifying than approaching Dixie Deans in a restaurant full of people, it was having your mother do it for you. I grabbed the pen and paper and steeled myself.

All the way home I cradled the autograph like it was a rare antique. I held it up to the light, scrutinised it from different angles and gazed at it with awestruck deference. That evening, I breathlessly recounted the episode. Something genuinely exciting had happened to me and it didn't matter that Dad and Tony were trying to wind me up about it. Tony wasn't interested in football and he was always taking the piss out of footballers for being thick.

– No-one's going to believe you actually met Dixie Deans, he laughed.

– Yes, they will, because I've got his autograph to prove it.

– That's what I mean. No-one's ever going to believe that he can write his name.

Dad and Sophia, my elder sister, were laughing like drains and Mum kept telling them to stop teasing me.

– Actually, I've got some good news of my own, she announced suddenly.

Everyone turned their attention to her.

– Oh, yeah, what's that, love? Dad asked.

– I got a letter from Cardonald College this morning. I've been accepted as a mature student to study psychology. I start next term.

For months Mum had been talking about how she wanted to

do a part-time college course, because she said she wasn't using her brain working at the Post Office. Dad couldn't understand why she felt she had to use her brain, as long as she was bringing money into the house.

I didn't see why anyone would want to go to college – it sounded just like school – but I couldn't help thinking Dad was over-reacting. He got angry every time a new college prospectus arrived by post and he complained about the mess whenever he found one stuffed behind a cushion on the settee or lying on the bathroom floor. But he made much more of a mess, leaving his old newspapers and dirty laundry everywhere. The prospectuses were just glossy little booklets that hardly took up any space at all.

When Mum made her announcement, Tony, Sophia and I all kissed her and congratulated her, telling her that she had done really well. We knew how much it meant to her. But Dad didn't say anything. He just sat there silently and continued to eat his dinner.

2

Aunty Betty was an unlikely cold warrior. To us she was the most indiscreet woman in Bonkle, but to Britain's security services, facing down the dreaded Soviet threat, she was a treasured military asset – a skilled black operative capable of spreading malicious and destabilising misinformation among the enemy in the event of a threatened nuclear strike.

In 1948 she set the modern benchmark for military-grade gossiping. In a controlled experiment at the government's weapons research laboratory at Porton Down, she was told 'in the strictest confidence' by her best friend, Ina, that the minister's wife was having an affair. The pair were locked in a hermetically sealed, lead-lined bunker fifty metres below ground level with no means of communication in or out, and yet, within half an hour, thirty of Betty's closest friends had the information.

I cast my eyes skyward and sighed. Tony had a million of these stories, each more fancifully embroidered than the last, and I never believed a single one. Someone of my tender years should have been a saucer-eyed sitting duck for his fables. My childhood self wanted to believe they were true, God knows I needed the excitement, but I just couldn't trust him. I couldn't trust anyone, not since the whole Santa Claus thing turned out to be such a grand lie.

I'd felt such a gullible fool, watching Dad furtively bundle a Raleigh Tomahawk from the back of the car into next door's garage on Christmas Eve. The following morning we all feigned euphoric surprise when, lo and behold, it appeared at the foot of my bed, sprinkled with glitter (reindeer dust) and bits of cotton wool (Santa's beard).

To his credit, Tony had tried to convince me that it was all a grotesque misunderstanding. Santa did exist, it's just that he wasn't able to make it to our house that year. He was on strike – out in sympathy with the miners – and besides, what with the whole OPEC crisis, how was he going to afford enough petrol to drive his sleigh all the way from the North Pole to Gower Street?

But by then the mask had slipped. Believing in Santa was an act of faith and, once questioned, it began to unravel like the cheap Woolworth's wrapping paper from the *Oor Wullie* annual which, I happened to know for a fact, had been lying stashed at the back of Mum's stockings drawer for weeks.

Until then I had been Tony's most consistently impressionable foil. For him it added an intriguing dimension to conversing with a sibling six years his junior, knowing that I could be hoodwinked effortlessly by whatever whimsy was passing through the transept of his mischievous imagination. After finding out the truth about Santa I was a twisted knot of cynicism, batting back each of his confections more astringently than the last.

Christmas was eight months ago but there still wasn't a day when I wasn't eaten up with the duplicity of it all. Even if the Santa thing had never happened, I doubt I'd ever have believed that Mr Gibb, two doors down, was really Evel Knievel.

For a start, he was about a century too old. Evel Knievel was chiselled and athletic and he wore white, star-spangled jumpsuits. Mr Gibb was lanky and stooped with thinning, grey hair combed back and Brylcreemed into place with parade-ground precision. He had a florid, parboiled complexion and a wardrobe that consisted entirely of shiny polyester suits and shirts from Brentford Nylons. Evel Knievel travelled the world performing death-defying motorcycle stunts. Mr Gibb worked in a factory in the Hillington industrial estate making paint for oil rigs.

– Tony, yer talking pish, was my considered verdict.

– Have you ever seen Evel Knievel without his helmet on?

I had to concede I hadn't.

– So how come he's Evel Knievel and not Evel Gibb? I demanded.

– He doesn't want his bosses knowing his true identity. He reckons that if the whole jumping-over-double-decker buses thing doesn't work out, he'll always have a job mixing paint down at Stenhouse & Barratt's.

Tony was sitting on the ledge of my bedroom window, smoking a Player's No. 6. His chin was resting on his raised knee while his other leg dropped carelessly against the white, stippled façade of the outside wall. It was the end of a long July day, during that short interlude when dusk and darkness are indistinguishable, when the moon is battling for supremacy with the retreating summer sun.

My brother habitually chose my bedroom in which to smoke because his faced onto the street and there was the danger that one of the neighbours would see him and tell our parents. The bedroom I shared with Sophia backed onto a network of small, uniformly manicured gardens, adorned with goldfish ponds, gnomes and stone-clad wishing wells. The driveways were populated with second-hand Ford Anglias and Datsun Cherries, wax-shined and scrupulously maintained by their proud owners.

We were one of the last families to move into the estate. It was the proudest day of Mum's life when she took possession of the house keys and was able to describe herself as an 'owner-occupier'. The builders' blurb for the new house had promised a 'modern, well-appointed, three-bedroom, semi-detached villa with a split-level lounge, new kitchen with appliances, fitted wardrobes and a patio garden'.

It was certainly modern, I'll give them that. Two years previously, the estate had been the muddy, dilapidated remains of a tyre factory. It was also factually correct to say that our house had three bedrooms, in that all were just about big enough to accommodate a bed, but physical separation of space was merely a concept, such was the flimsiness of the walls, no respecters of sound or smell.

Over the years, we would become intimately acquainted with our neighbours, their intrigues and manoeuvrings, their sanitary routines and their dietary preferences. They, no doubt, had a similarly detailed dossier on us but there was an unspoken rule that intelligence obtained inadvertently through the connecting walls was inadmissible in neighbourhood gossip.

While it was Mum's dream home, the rest of us were unconvinced. Dad moaned about the thirty-quid-a-month mortgage, the cheap fabric of the building – a fortnight after we moved in Sophia put her foot though the bathroom door during an argument about the provenance of a hairbrush. He moaned about the garden, whose thick clay soil didn't absorb water and which flooded every time it rained, and about the snooty neighbours who, he said, walked like they were softening up a caramel between their arse cheeks.

Sophia moaned about the lack of anything to do and the fact that none of her friends lived nearby. She also complained about having to share a bedroom with me. In our previous home – a rented tenement flat in Pollokshaws – all three of us had shared a room. Now we had an extra bedroom, Mum decided that Tony should have it. Sophia complained bitterly, claiming that she was fourteen and deserved some privacy, but Mum said Tony needed a quiet space for his studies. After he had finished his Highers, she promised, Sophia could have her own room.

I pointed out that Tony was two years older, so if anyone deserved his own room, it was him. Not that I was suggesting I'd rather share a room with Sophia, I was merely highlighting the weakness in Mum's argument. She said it was different for girls but she didn't explain why.

Through snatches of overheard conversation, I managed to elicit that Sophia was going through 'the change' but quite what that entailed was never explained. I racked my brain. What could it mean – change of heart, change of pace, change of clothes? I couldn't help but notice her physical development. Gone was the untamed boyishness of her youth, which had been replaced with a slimmer, elegant femininity. Her slightly chubby face had a new angularity and her flat, featureless upper body had acquired curves and bumps that now required accommodation in extra items of underwear.

It was also apparent that an increasing amount of the household conversation now revolved around Sophia's mood. Nothing was to be done to upset Sophia. Everything should be done to accommodate Sophia – though, of course, she still played second fiddle to the prodigal Tony.

As I lay in bed, I could see the silhouette of my brother's handsome, aquiline features against the night sky. He had changed too. He was mature now. It wasn't so long ago that we were inseparable, sharing the same interests and preoccupations. But he started growing away from me and I couldn't keep up. The more I tried, the more intolerant he became of my pitiful attempts.

He pinched the remains of the fag between his thumb and index finger and dragged hard on the last half inch of tobacco. Thin jets of grey smoke streamed from his nostrils as he flicked the misshapen filter and watched it fly in a high parabola, then crash land on the paving below. The following morning he would be up before Mum and Dad, scurrying about in the garden, collecting his discarded butts.

I always enjoyed it when Tony thought he heard the whining creak of a floorboard and frantically waved his arms like a windmill in a storm to disperse the clouds of smoke. When he was confident that neither of our parents was on their way upstairs he closed the window and returned to his own room.

The following day, after church, I went round to see Wally to show him my Dixie Deans autograph. In Govan, where money was in short supply, Wally's family had less than most. Fungus peppered the walls of their tenement flat in vast, impromptu murals. What was left of the wallpaper sagged forlornly, as though years of exposure to such a fetid environment had robbed it of the will to adhere to the walls. The living room carpet, permanently littered with empty Irn-Bru bottles and oil-stained motorbike parts, had a tackiness, which slowed your step. It was a felonious collage of brown and mustard hues, for which the designer responsible should have felt considerable remorse. Something smelled strongly of rotting onions, and my money was on the carpet.

Wally's dad was a wiry drunk who had the soggy stump of a Capstan Full Strength adhered permanently to his bony, tar-blackened fingers. Every night, with metronomic regularity, he staggered home from the local bowling club – where the subsidised drink was a quarter of pub prices – filling the streets with a criminally tuneless rendition of 'The Old Rugged Cross'.

That day, a Sunday, Wally's dad had been drinking all morning and was lying comatose on the sofa, killing time until the pubs opened.

As we sat on the floor half-watching *The Golden Shot* on their old black-and-white telly, I showed Wally my Dixie Deans autograph. Wally was a Pape so I knew I'd be on safe ground, but he didn't show the level of enthusiasm I'd been hoping for for. Instead, he glanced at it uninterestedly and mouthed some forgettable platitude. I shouldn't really have expected more. Wally was more interested in motorbikes than football.

Besides, his attention was now focused on Handbag and Holdall, two of his elder brothers, who were standing over the old man, crumbling an Oxo cube into his gaping mouth. They stifled conspiratorial laughter, willing him to wake up. Occasionally he stirred and coughed when one of the crumbs caught in his throat but, defiantly, he remained asleep.

After a while, they became bored, but Handbag had an idea. He rubbed part of the stock cube onto his dad's lips and chin and then roused Daphne, the family's obese and sickeningly malodorous mongrel bitch from a urine-stained cushion, which served as her bed. Daphne was dragged across the carpet, her legs buckling under the weight of her monumental behind, and her nose was pushed against the face of her drink-sodden master. She sniffed around his mouth and, recognising something edible, she began to lick, covering the bottom half of his face with a white film of canine saliva.

Once she had removed all traces of Oxo cube from his face, she began to probe the inside of his mouth with her searching pink tongue. We were doubled up with laughter, and yet, despite the din, old man Rafferty remained soundly in the Land of Nod.

Holdall decided to take more radical action to try to get a response. He lifted a box of matches that was lying at the foot of the sofa. He lit one and held it under his father's bare foot. The old man winced and pulled his foot away from the flame but then simply grunted, rolled over and continued to sleep. Holdall held the match under his other foot for ages until smoke started to rise from the hardened skin at the back of his heel.

Suddenly, his dad leapt up, clutching his foot and cursing the air blue. He stopped abruptly, swaying, confused and irascible, surrounded by laughing, baying tormentors like a bear in some degrading circus act. All the time his mouth chewed and, slowly, the expression on his face began to change from bewilderment to horror, as the taste of the Oxo cube registered. As the taunting grew louder he doubled over, retching and dribbling brown spit down his shirt and onto the carpet.

Now fully conscious, he reached for the closest thing to hand – a thick, rusting motorcycle chain – and lashed out. The brothers judged they had gone too far and made a beeline for the hallway, none of them stopping to observe social niceties, like ensuring the safety of their guest. I was left to follow in hot pursuit and, as I ducked behind the living room door, I felt the full weight of the chain crashing against it.

I was in the back yard, crouching next to Wally in one of the midden huts before I paused to draw breath. My heart was pounding violently. The others had run off in different directions and were nowhere to be seen. I was so terrified I could barely speak but Wally sat on the ground, resting languidly against a bin, laughing quietly to himself.

– Won't he kill you? I asked.

– Nah, said Wally dismissively, he'll never remember in the morning.

I couldn't help wishing again that my life was more like Wally's. There was a swaggering arrogance about him and his brothers that I wanted to emulate. Of course, Mum didn't want me associating with him because he was common. On occasion Dad stuck up for him, saying that he was just a harmless kid from a poor family, but Mum always won that battle.

Whatever thrall suburban respectability held her in, I didn't get it. I had just narrowly escaped bearing the full force of a ten-pound motorcycle chain thrown by a drunk whose feet had been set on fire. That was excitement. The most thrilling thing that ever happened in our house was when a soufflé collapsed. There was a thudding ordinariness about my life and no amount of fictional web weaving on the part of Tony or anyone else was going to change that.

3

We hadn't yet arrived at my cousin Billy's wedding and, already, the day had the makings of a disaster. A tension had been developing all morning, with a series of frosty exchanges between Mum and Dad, followed by an entirely silent car journey, and now we were lost.

Each of us had our own reason for not wanting to be there. I was dreading the first outing of my new suit – the one that made me look like I had raided Prince Edward's wardrobe. Mum was angry that Dad hadn't forced Tony to get a haircut (now eighteen months and counting since his last visit to the barber), compounding her embarrassment at being seen publicly with him in the controversial flared suit trousers, platform shoes and Rubettes cap ensemble. And Sophia was grumpy because she was always grumpy – something to do with the mysterious 'change', I presumed – and Dad was still simmering about Mum going to college.

All these grievances combined, however, failed to match the strain generated by five of us crammed into a Mini Clubman, driving around Coatbridge on a pissing wet afternoon trying to find the Church of the Sacred Heart with the seconds ticking down to three o'clock.

– For God's sake, Christine, why didn't you get directions before we set off? Dad demanded, driving us up yet another dead end.

– He's your bloody nephew, Robert.

– Why don't we stop and ask someone for directions? I suggested, thinking I was doing the right thing.

– No-one asked for your opinion, so keep your mouth shut, Dad snapped.

After another ten minutes of aimless meandering, we stopped and asked someone for directions.

It had been a full week since Mum's announcement about college, and Dad remained silently brooding. His reaction had surprised us all. He was always going on about how he'd never had a proper chance at school and that, if he had his time again, he'd stick in. Now it seemed his concern for the value of education didn't extend to Mum. After she had dropped the bombshell at the dinner table, Sophia and I were sent to bed early, but we sat at the top of the stairs listening to our parents arguing.

– What about your job at the Post Office? Dad demanded.

– Helen says I can go part-time, and with my student grant we won't be any worse off, Mum explained, I thought, quite reasonably.

– What about the kids? Who's going to look after them?

– The kids are at school all day.

– What about in the evenings, when you've got your nose in a pile of books?

– I can study after they've gone to bed, and you can always help out.

– Don't you think I've got enough on my plate? Dad demanded, his voice raising a decibel.

– I've done night classes before and there wasn't a problem then.

–That was just a hobby, Christine. It didn't affect your life. This is your life – me, the children, the house.

It went on like that for hours. Just when we thought Dad had run out of things to complain about, he forced Mum down another cul-de-sac of mangled logic. She could better him in an argument at the best of times and, usually, he would quit while he wasn't too far behind. But it was obvious there was nothing Mum could say, short of agreeing to scrap the whole idea, that was going to satisfy him.

We arrived at the chapel with minutes to spare and took our seats at the back, on the groom's side. It was a modern, functional building in the middle of a grim housing estate and it had garish, stained-glass windows whose biblical scenes looked like they had been designed by a Soviet committee. It was dominated by rows of wooden benches, many of which had been defaced by penknife carvings and graffiti. Its centrepiece was a painted ceramic statue of a hooded Christ. One of the outstretched, blood-stained hands had broken off, leaving a small wire stump. It occurred to me how different everything was from the sobriety of our own church.

Billy was the son of Dad's eldest brother, Christopher. After Christopher there was Vincent, who lived in America, then Frank and then Dad, the youngest of the four. This was the first time in years that we had seen any of them. Granny and Granddad had both died before I was born, and Dad never really kept up with the rest of his family. He rarely even talked about them. The only thing I knew about his upbringing was that he was born and raised in Leith and that he'd left school at fifteen to work as a commis waiter in a hotel in Edinburgh, where he met Mum.

I often wondered why we never saw any of Dad's side of the family. He said it was because they all lived in Edinburgh, which was too far to travel, particularly as he worked nights. Tony said that was bollocks, Edinburgh was fifty miles away and it would take us an hour to get there in the car. He said the real reason we never saw them was because Mum thought they were common.

Common-ness was a big thing with Mum. It governed every aspect of our lives and yet it had no consistent definition other than as an arbitrary set of conventions informed by her sense of propriety. Attempting to second-guess what was and wasn't common was never simple. Arriving late was common but so was arriving early. Talking loudly was common as was talking quietly. It was often difficult to pitch your voice at just the right level. Spitting, sucking loudly, whistling and eating with your mouth open were all common; in fact any oral activity was a minefield of potential social indiscretion.

Other equally common items included – in no particular order – tattoos, Catholics, blonde hair, platform shoes, British Home Stores, Val Doonican, HP sauce, *On the Buses*, untipped cigarettes,

Lena Zavaroni, football supporters, Wimpy restaurants and anyone from Maryhill.

I was at the end of our row of pews and so I could see all the way down the aisle to the altar. Billy kept glancing back nervously. I was struck by how young he looked. He couldn't have been much older than Tony. He and his best man were dressed in identical, standard-issue kilts and short black jackets with all the trimmings, their heavily lacquered rooster cuts, pasty pallor and rampant acne fatally compromising whatever romantic image they might otherwise have projected. There was a dispiriting drabness about the guests and it hadn't escaped my notice that, of all the children present, I was the only one wearing a suit.

The event was in marked contrast to the wedding of Mum's younger sister, Helene, which remained, by far, the grandest occasion I had ever attended. There, the male guests had worn grey morning coats, and the female brightly-coloured dresses with flamboyant hats. At the reception, the ladies were given little baskets of sugared almonds with sprigs of heather tied to them and the men got miniatures of whisky. Dad didn't drink, and so he gave his to me, saying I could start a collection. A year on, it remained a collection of one.

Suddenly the organist struck up the first notes of the bridal march and Billy's bride, Evelyn, appeared at the rear of the church, alongside her father. She was wearing a plain, white silk dress with no frills, which barely reached beyond her knees. She had a pained expression on her face, as if she was about to cry. As she passed our row, Mum whispered something to Dad about her stomach. Dad's face hardened and he whispered back, sternly, that this was not the time and she should keep her comments to herself.

When the bride reached the altar, the priest welcomed everyone to celebrate the joining together in marriage of the happy couple. There was no warmth in his voice and his face remained expressionless. He paused for an uncomfortably long period when only the shuffling of bottoms on seats and the occasional cough broke the silence.

– May the grace of our Lord Jesus Christ and the love of God and the fellowship of the Holy Spirit be with you all, he said solemnly.

– And also with you, the congregation muttered in unison.

I'd never heard people joining in like that at church before.

– Lift up your hearts, said the priest.

– We lift them up unto the Lord, said the congregation.

As I looked along our row, I was surprised to see Dad mouthing the responses.

– Let us give thanks to our Lord, the priest continued.

– It is right to give him thanks and praise, Dad replied, along with the rest of the congregation.

I leaned over to Mum.

– How come Dad knows the words? I asked in a whisper.

– I suppose because he remembers them from mass when he was a wee boy, she replied.

– What's mass?

– It's the Catholic Church service.

I couldn't believe what I was hearing. Dad, a Catholic? I sat in a state of shock, like Joe Bugner had just landed an uppercut on my chin. Why had no-one told me? Who'd have guessed? If Dad was a Catholic, that made me one as well, sort of. I could hardly contain my excitement.

I'd always wanted to be a Catholic, just like Wally. The stories he told us about St Bernadette's made the hairs on the back of my neck stand on end. Apparently, it was named after this woman who lived in the olden days, who kept seeing this ghost who looked just like Jesus's mum, Mary. Bernadette didn't run away when she saw the ghost, so they turned her into a saint. According to Wally, St Bernadette's was run by a priest called Father Byrne who made you do something called confession, which meant sitting in a box and telling him about all the times you'd thought about women in the nude. If you didn't, he could read your mind and he'd make you wash his car and run to Carter's, the newsagent's, for his fags. That was called penance.

With religion, like everything else in life, I was saddled with the boring, strait-laced alternative. Every Sunday, I was dispatched to the local Protestant church to listen to Reverend. MacIver droning on endlessly about tolerance, forgiveness and divine love.

Sophia and I were the only members of the family who still went to church on a fairly regular basis. Dad was strictly weddings and funerals. Mum attended occasionally, and Tony had stopped going altogether because Karl Marx said religion was the opium of the masses. Dad said he'd have changed it to the valium of the masses if he'd ever had to sit through one of Reverend MacIver's sermons.

To think that I'd spent all these years yawning in the pews at Pollokshields Parish Kirk when I could have been down the road at St Bernadette's marvelling at Father Byrne barking threats of retribution and eternal damnation. There was something exciting and dangerous about the Catholic Church. It had the cool menace of a Saturday night horror flick with all its sins and punishment. It had mortal sins, venial sins, capital sins, contrition, excomm-unication, penance and reparation. It also had great props – conception beads, scapular medals, holy water, communion wine – which Wally stole for his dad when he was an altar boy – wall crucifixes, mounted crucifixes, medallion crucifixes and more icons than you could shake an archiepiscopal pallium at. The Protestant Church had pews and hymn books.

If Wally missed confession, Father Byrne would go down to his school, pull him out of class by the ear and beat him with a stick. If I missed Sunday school Reverend MacIver always said Jesus would forgive me. Father Byrne drank the blood of Christ and issued warnings of souls being trapped in purgatory for eter-nity. Reverend MacIver judged the best drop scone competition at the Women's Guild annual fete.

After the wedding service, Mum made a point of commenting on how Billy and Evelyn had not posed for official photographs outside the church.

– Leave it alone, Christine, Dad said curtly.

We drove the half mile to the Coatbridge Knights of St

Columba Social Club where the reception was being held. Most of the other guests walked and, by the time they arrived, they were wringing wet.

The club was housed in a windowless, brick-built box on a piece of waste ground at the end of a long dirt track. As we entered by the reinforced steel door, we were hit with the bitter smell of alcohol and stale tobacco smoke. Inside, the yellowing walls were decorated with streamers and tinsel that looked like the limp remnants of a long forgotten Christmas party.

The guests were to be seated on benches along rows of paper-cloth covered tables – those invited by the groom down one side and those by the bride down the other – with a dance floor separating them. The tables were adorned with paper platters, piled high with sausage rolls, meat paste sandwiches and Scotch pies. There were also paper cups and bottles of Irn-Bru. As we took our seats, a waitress, not much older than me, told us that crisps were available at the bar.

We sat down at the same table as Uncle Christopher, Uncle Vincent and Uncle Frank and their wives. Billy and Evelyn were on the other side of the hall alongside her parents. When everyone was seated, Evelyn's dad – a thin, frail-looking man – stood up and said in a faltering, barely audible voice, that he wouldn't take up too much time, but that he wanted to wish the happy couple well and that everyone should enjoy themselves. All the men on our side jeered and heckled – principal among them Uncle Christopher and Uncle Frank – urging Billy to make a speech. Someone shouted something about the lead in Billy's pencil and everyone laughed. I figured they were just teasing him and that it must be good-natured but the guests on the bride's side, including her three fierce-looking brothers, scowled, and Billy sat, scarlet-faced, staring at the floor. Mum directed an acid-drop stare at Dad who shrugged, as if to plead innocence by non-association, as his brothers nudged and egged him on to join in the banter.

We had just started eating the sandwiches when Uncle Frank stood up.

– Right, who's for a bevvy? he asked the group.

Most of the men ordered half and halfs – whisky with beer chasers – and most of the women ordered Bacardi and Coke. Mum said she was driving and would have a tonic water. Dad tried to say he didn't want a drink but Uncle Frank was having none of it.

– Aw, come on, Rab. Ur ye a man or a moose?

Dad looked embarrassed and said he would have a pint of lager. When Tony was asked what he wanted, he hesitated.

– He'll stick with Irn-Bru, Mum said pointedly.

– Aw, let the lad have a beer, Uncle Frank implored. It's his cousin's wedding.

– He'll have Irn-Bru, Mum said more forcefully. He's sixteen, Frank.

Dad managed to nurse his drink for about an hour, by which time all the others at the table were on their fourth or fifth and were considerably less lucid. Uncle Frank's demeanour had become challenging, urging Mum to 'lighten up' every time she winced at his near-the-knuckle humour. Dad shifted on his seat and kept a nervous grin stapled to his face.

Mum sat next to Uncle Vincent and Aunt Sadie, who had travelled all the way from California especially for the wedding. The last time she and Dad had seen them was before I was born. Now naturalised Americans, they stood out from the other guests like well-hammered thumbs. Uncle Vincent looked well-fed, his rotund belly penned inside a pair of powder blue slacks by a matching, tight-fitting polo-neck sweater. Over that he wore a cream blazer and the look was accessorised with a pair of white moccasin shoes, a chunky gold necklace and a pair of matching gold sovereign rings, one on either hand.

Uncle Vincent had built up a successful used-car business in Santa Monica and, clearly, he had a healthy respect for his achievements. He spent a good deal of time telling anyone within earshot that you hadn't lived until you'd driven a 1949 Buick Roadmaster through the Sierra Nevada mountains and how he'd recently made a two hundred per cent mark-up on a 1972 Oldsmobile 442 convertible.

Sadie was entombed within a turquoise brocade kaftan with decorative gold piping. The only visible part of her was a shrivelled, sun-toasted, peanut-shaped head, which was topped by a thinning peroxide mane. She sat swigging long vodkas, adding conscientiously to a collection of lipstick-smeared, American cigarette stubs building in an ashtray in front of her, talking vociferously about 'the price of gas downtown' and her favourite 'mall, Stateside', in a strangulated accent which sounded like Stanley Baxter doing a bad impression of Mae West.

After the last of the pies and sandwiches were eaten and the plates cleared away, an unremarkable, single-tier cake was carried into the hall which Billy and Evelyn were persuaded to cut, doing so with as little ceremony as they could manage before shuffling back to their seats.

The man who ran the hall then clapped his hands briskly to get people's attention and announced that, due to unforeseen technical difficulties, the musical entertainment planned for the evening had been delayed. The unforeseen technical difficulties, it later emerged, involved a steaming drunk road manager and the unknown whereabouts of a Ford Transit van. It meant the members of Alice Band – a Smokey tribute act from Airdrie – were forced to make their way to the venue by bus, carrying their equipment on their laps. They eventually trooped in, wet and bedraggled, and assembled their equipment on a small elevation at the top end of the dance floor, immediately below a framed photograph of Pope Blessed John XXIII lying in state.

An uninspiring, but otherwise technically proficient, medley of Smokey hits followed. As the band struck up the opening bars of 'I'll Meet You at Midnight', Uncle Frank formed a delegation of one to the stage to ask if they might introduce some thematic variation to their set. The request did not appear to go down well with the Zapata-moustachioed lead singer – all of five feet three inches in his cowboy boots – who pointed out that they were playing in a 'poxy shithole', that their payment for the evening amounted to a case of McEwan's Export which, after the cost of their bus fares had been deducted, left them out of pocket, and that they would sing 'whatever fucking songs they fucking well wanted to sing'. Frank pointed out that the singer's microphone was still switched on and that his outburst had been relayed to all the guests,

The pair then retired to the back of the stage to continue their dialogue. Several times Uncle Frank squared up to the singer – or, more accurately, squared down to him – before being restrained by other members of the band, and several times the singer responded in kind.

Eventually Uncle Frank trooped back to our table to reveal that a deal had been brokered. In return for allowing the band to perform mostly Smokey covers, there would be an interlude where guests would be invited to perform their favourite songs to which the band would provide accompaniment.

After some initial suspicion among the other kids at the wedding, probably on account of my suit, it seemed that I had been accepted into the fold, and they invited me to join them in a game of 'The Poseidon Adventure' in which the underside of the long tables doubled as the hull of the doomed vessel. I declined, mainly because the Gene Hackman role had already been taken, but also because I was having too much fun watching the adults.

Dad had left our table and was standing at the bar with his brothers. Now onto his third lager, he was behaving in a way that was as unexpected as it was disarming, rocking back on his heels, blinking purposefully, slapping his brothers on the back and laughing uproariously even though no-one had said anything remotely funny.

Tony, meanwhile, had taken a close interest in one of the bridesmaids. They were locked in a corner of the room, their foreheads almost touching, engaged in intense discussion. Tony appeared to be doing most of the talking while she watched him intently, occasionally throwing her head back, her puffy, pink dress rippling with the force of her laughter. I could see Mum monitoring them closely, and she was clearly not amused. When she spotted Tony's hand rest on the bridesmaid's bare shoulder she told me to tell Dad she wanted him to go over and get Tony to stop being so 'familiar'.

– Tell your mother that he's a young lad enjoying himself and that she should do the same, Dad said.

– Tell your father he's no longer a young lad and he appears to be enjoying himself a bit too much, was her response.

I decided to pass on Mum's request directly to Tony but, as I approached, I overheard him telling the bridesmaid that Les McKeown, the lead singer of the Bay City Rollers, was dead. It was common knowledge at his secondary, he insisted. He had died in a freak accident two years previously after getting his tartan flares caught in an escalator. His death had been hushed up by the band's management, who feared the adverse publicity might lead to the Croydon Metropole cancelling their gig. Instead the Rollers' accountant, who bore a passing resemblance to McKeown, had been given a guitar and a feather cut and ordered to take his place.

Despite it being a really big secret, the other band members left clues lying around so that their fans would know the truth. On the cover of their album, *Shang-A-Lang*, 'McKeown' is standing in an upright position – an ancient runic death symbol – and if you played 'Bye, Bye, Baby' backwards you could clearly hear the voice of Stuart 'Woody' Wood singing: 'Likesay, Les is pure pan breid man, ken, s'nae real.'

The bridesmaid laughed like a drain. I was confused. Why did she find it so amusing? Even if, as I suspected, the story was one of Tony's tall tales, it was certainly no laughing matter. If, on the other hand, it was true, hers was a highly disrespectful response. Honestly, I just didn't get older people sometimes.

Soon it was time for the guests to perform their musical turns on stage, which turned out to be the best bit of the evening. I couldn't understand why anyone would want to make such a monumental spectacle of themselves, but there was no shortage of takers. First up was a short, inebriated woman with several teeth missing, who introduced herself only as Wee Jean. Despite the presence of the musicians, she insisted on performing an a capella version of 'Chirpy Chirpy Cheep Cheep' by Middle of the Road, but she was so tunelessly awful that she was booed off the stage before she got to the bit where she woke up this morning and her mama was gone. I had no idea who she was and assumed she was from Evelyn's side of the family. She was later exposed as a gatecrasher.

A brother of the bride, dressed all in black and with the vein-pulsing, meat-fed look of a gangster's enforcer, sang a slightly menacing version of 'The Shadow of your Smile'. It was the only moment in the entire evening that the guests were completely silent, as though they feared a demonstration of anything less than total deference would see them end the evening dead in a ditch.

Uncle Frank then mounted the stage, grabbed the mike and shouted *Hello Coatbridge!* to cheers of appreciation from his brothers. After the band had received instructions, they struck up the opening bars to 'Suspicious Minds' while he sang a drunkenly anarchic version of 'Her Latest Flame', though no-one appeared to notice the jarring discrepancy, least of all the band who, by then, had drunk most of their wages.

Sophia and I exchanged uncertain glances. We had never been anywhere like this before, and it was an adventure. I found it difficult to conceive that I was related to these people around me. I associated family gatherings with parties and lunches organised by Granny and Granddad or Aunty Helene and Uncle Barry. They were boring and sedate affairs, far removed from such raucousness, where eating, not drinking, was the focus of activity and where quietly piped classical music played second fiddle to studious conversation.

With everyone rapt by the scenes of musical carnage on the stage, no-one noticed that Tony had disappeared with the bridesmaid. It was Mum who first became aware that he was no longer in the hall and so she went off to look for him. A few moments later, she returned with a face like thunder.

She marched up to the bar and pulled Dad away. They had a heated exchange before Dad left the hall, cursing angrily. Mum returned to our table and told us to get our coats. Aunty Sadie asked if everything was all right, and Mum just said that it was getting late and it was time we were leaving. The next thing we knew Tony was frogmarched through the doorway, his face covered in lipstick and his shirt-tail hanging out of his trousers. The bridesmaid appeared behind him looking equally dishevelled and shamefaced.

The car journey home was another silent affair. Tony sat staring out of the window. I had no idea what had happened but I would quiz him about it later, when we got home. Dad sat in the front passenger seat with his head rolling around like it was being controlled by a puppeteer. Mum asked him if he was going to be sick, but he insisted he was fine and soon he was asleep. Sophia and I couldn't stop smirking.

Despite the atmosphere of disharmony, I didn't care. As far as I was concerned, the day had been nothing less than a triumph. I had learnt that I was half Catholic, which opened up all sorts of possibilities. I could now support Celtic with impunity, I could satisfy an increasingly unhealthy obsession I harboured to see the inside of a confessional, and I could breach the previously impenetrable code of papist jargon practised by my peers.

But, more importantly, I had borne witness to a side of my family that I didn't know existed – a side whose characteristics I couldn't properly categorise but what, I suppose, Mum would have referred to as common. I had relatives who had tattoos and bad teeth, who got drunk and abusive, and who smelled of cats. I realised that I no longer had reason to feel ashamed of my background. Some of my kin were so vulgar and inarticulate they would, almost certainly, give Wally and his brothers a run for their money. From that day, I vowed that never again would I feel patronised and condescended to by those less fortunate than myself.

4

It was the start of the new school year, and I was dreading going back marginally less than usual. Several of my friends lived in Shieldhall, a few miles away on the far side of Govan, and I hadn't seen them since last term. I wanted to hear everything that had happened to them during the holidays. I also had a couple of important items of news to impart.

When I woke, my freshly laundered uniform was already laid out at the foot of my bed. I wasn't surprised to discover that my 'new' blazer was, in fact, the jacket Mum had bought for me in Paisley's with the school badge sewn on the breast pocket. With the deftness of a fairground conjurer, Mum had managed to make my school uniform my birthday present.

The rest of the family was gathered around the dinner table for breakfast. It was a small, round, dark wood table which had been given to us by Granny and Granddad when we moved in. It sat at the top end of the living room, an area described by Mum as a 'split-level dining room'.

On a normal morning Mum would be out the door by half past six to start work in the Post Office by seven and Dad wouldn't be up much before midday because he'd been working late in the restaurant the night before. When Tony surfaced was anyone's guess.

But this wasn't any normal morning. As well as being the beginning of the new school term, it was the year Sophia started her O-Grade courses and also the first day of Tony's Highers year which, Mum kept reminding us, was the most important of his life, and when his future would be decided. Tony had been walking on eggshells since the wedding, keen not to put a foot wrong. I was still in the dark about what he was supposed to have done, and he refused to discuss it, so I remember thinking that it must be serious in the extreme.

There had been a couple of high-powered meetings between Tony and Mum in his bedroom, from which I was banned, but from behind the door I heard her tell him, in solemn tones, that it was time to forget about girls and to concentrate on his career.

This was also Mum's first day at college, and we were all keen to make a special effort to show her we supported her. Even Dad, who'd been particularly contrite following his performance at the wedding, appeared to be coming round to the idea. He'd prepared a big platter of French toast drenched in golden syrup, which we ate with strong, real coffee which Dad had brought home from the restaurant.

Sophia sought to capitalise on this new spirit of détente by asking Dad if she could have money to buy a ticket for the Bay City Rollers concert at the Apollo. The concert wasn't until November but Sophia had obviously anticipated resistance and was mounting an opening pitch in what was sure to be a protracted campaign of harrying and harassment.

– The ticket costs two fifty, which means, if I save my pocket money for the next ten weeks I can pay you back and I can also help Mum more around the house, which she'll need now that she's at college, and I know the concert's on a school night but I promise to do my homework before I go, and Celeste's dad has agreed to drive us there and back and drop me outside the door, which means I'll definitely be home by half ten at the very latest, so you don't need to worry about me being safe.

I had to admit it was a brilliantly executed delivery – a textbook exercise in parent badgering, closing off all possible avenues of objection before they could be opened and leaving Dad floundering in a sea of uncertainty.

– I'm not happy about you going to a concert with all these screaming hooligans. It's just not safe, was Dad's feeble attempt at a retort but we all knew that he was clutching at straws.

– But, Dad, I promise to be careful and do my homework before I go, and I'll be home by half ten. I'm usually still awake at that time anyway and if I was at home all I'd be doing is watching telly, and all my friends are going, Dad, and it's the biggest concert ever, and, aw, go on, Dad, say yes.

Dad was on the ropes as an onslaught of fair points and plausible explanations rained down on him.

– OK, we'll see, he replied, resorting to the standard parental cop out.

I was going into Primary Six at Maxwell Park Primary, which I had attended since Primary One. Although we had moved house, Pollokshaws was in the same catchment area, so I hadn't had to change schools. In fact it was now closer to home, about a ten-minute walk, at the far end of Maxwell Drive.

All the Catholics went to Our Lady of the Immaculate Conception which was about half a mile away from our school. It was a daily ritual that pupils from both schools met up in the morning for a game of football before classes started. It was always the same – Papes v. Prods – and played in our playground because it was bigger than the one they had at the Conception.

It was generally around twenty-a-side with no throw-ins, by-kicks, corners, fouls or offside. Tactics and positional play were considered unnecessary complications, and the passage of play usually involved a gaggle of bodies moving randomly around the playground with a ball trapped at the centre. The game lasted for thirty minutes or so before the Papes had to sprint along the road to make it to their school before the bell.

When I arrived, the match was in full swing, so I dumped my blazer on the ground, alongside a pile of others that marked out one of the goalposts, and I took to the field. I'd been playing for about five minutes when the game was halted abruptly because it was noticed that I kept passing the ball to the Papes.

– What the hell are you doing? demanded Billy Kemp.

– I'm playing for the Papes.

– Why?

– Because I'm a Catholic.

By this time a large group had gathered around us, and I was starting to wish I had chosen a less public forum to declare my sudden religious conversion.

– Why do you go to a Prod school if you're a Pape? he asked.

– My ma's a Prod but my da's a Pape. He knows all the words and everything.

There followed a collective, cacophonous murmur as everyone considered the implications of such a statement. His ma's a Prod but his da's a Pape? How could this be so? No-one had heard the like. After half a minute of rumination, it was denounced as a mutinous and seditious idea and decided, unanimously, that it couldn't be allowed to stand. Where would it all end? people asked. The issue was resolved when the Papes said they didn't want me in their team anyways because I was so shite.

When the bell rang, we lined up and waited for Mr McKechnie, the headmaster, to come out to assign us our new classrooms and teachers for the year. There was always fevered speculation about such matters, with generally baseless rumours flying thick and fast. Dougie McCann said his mum had met Mrs Gemmell, the school secretary, at the shops on the Paisley Road during the holidays and she said we were going to get Mr Boyce. If true, it was a major result as Boozebag Boyce was always falling asleep in the middle of lessons.

When it came to our turn we were given Room 30, which everyone was happy with because it was on the top floor and commanded a great view across the Clyde, to the Finnieston Docks. We were less happy when McKechnie announced that our teacher was to be Mrs Wutherspoon, an ageing and ill-tempered spinster with blue-rinse hair and a pungent body odour that managed to struggle, Houdini-like, through a heavy, daily application of Lily of the Valley. Sophia had Wutherspoon last year and said she was a total cow.

Our school was a soot-blackened, grey sandstone Edwardian building, whose bare, stone floors and high, green, distempered walls made it bitterly cold, even in August. Small pots of rat poison lay brazenly in every corner and the place reeked of strong disinfectant and coal tar.

As we crowded into our new classroom, eyes darted hither and yon, scanning the assembled ranks for any novel variations in standard uniform attire. Jebsy MacBride's shirt-tail hung languidly from the back of his blazer and his black school shoes were clearly beyond the regulation inch of platform sole – minor acts of rebellion, but hardly the last word in sartorial avant-garde.

Bifter was wearing his brother's hand-me-down blazer, which was so big that it reached his knees. He had cleverly improvised by tying his school tie in reverse so that the thin end was hanging down the front and the look was accessorised with a pair of wedges. He was clearly going for the Showaddywaddy, Teddy Boy look and, while he hadn't quite pulled it off, it was nevertheless a brave attempt.

Before long, everyone's attention was drawn irresistibly to Bobby Divers who had fashioned the biggest tie knot any of us had ever seen. The class was a sea of gaping mouths, held open in rapt admiration. It was huge. How had he possibly managed it? As Wutherspoon called for hush, whispered snatches of conversation passed from desk to desk. It was truly a magnificent feat of engineering, seeming to defy the laws of physics. At the very least, it would have required a quadruple wrap-around before the pull through, but how he had managed to achieve such an elegantly symmetrical triangle was anyone's guess. Word spread that he had spent most of the holidays perfecting the technique and, during the morning break, he would be in trap four of the boys' toilets offering individual tuition at two pee a go.

The first day of the new term was never very demanding, with little done in the way of teaching or learning. There was a lethargic mood, not helped by our municipal fathers' decision to send us back to school when the summer sun was still streaming through the classroom windows. No-one's mind was really on verb declensions and long division, least of all the teachers' who did little to disguise the impression that they would rather be somewhere else.

The first thing Wutherspoon did was to collect dinner and milk money. Despite repeated lobbying by me, Mum had refused to allow me to buy lunch at the local chippie or the City Bakery. Scoffing deep-fried half pizza suppers and Scotch pies on street corners was a requirement of upward social mobility at school. It was there that you were officially inducted into the in-crowd.

Needless to say, I was one of the unfashionable minority cast upon the dubious mercies of the school dinner hall, where flavour and nutritional value were regarded as dangerous and un-Christian concepts. Sixty pence bought you a weekly ticket into a looking-glass world of culinary psychosis where black was white and white was an unappetising shade of grey. Meat was regarded as a single, homogeneous entity – it was delivered to the kitchens in large tins marked MEAT – and to inquire into its provenance was like questioning the nature of gravity. Vegetables were similarly categorised. There was no difference between a carrot and a sprout after they had been boiled down for four hours and slapped on a plate alongside a mound of fossilised potato. Custard was regarded as one of the main food groups and was an ever-present on the menu, other than on those days that there was no pudding, when it was served as cheese sauce.

For ten pence, you got a weekly milk ticket. Milk used to be free for everyone until Margaret Thatcher abolished the right, earning her the nickname 'Milk Snatcher'. The teacher would go through the daily ritual of asking everyone who had paid for milk to come forward to collect their carton. She would then ask anyone who was under ten years old to come forward because, by law, they still qualified for free milk. Because the corporation always delivered too much milk, there would still be loads of cartons left over, so the teacher would then invite those who 'wished' milk to come forward. Anyone with half a brain would pocket the ten pence that their parents had given them and then 'wish' milk.

At dinner-time we all met up in the playground to swap stories about what had happened during the summer. Bifter and Chabs had nearly been savaged by Daft Davie. They tried reporting it to the police, but they were just told to beat it. Daft Davie was a one man killing spree waiting to happen, who roamed the streets of Govan talking loudly to himself. Adults didn't seem to realise just how dangerous he was. They would say *Hello, David* when he passed, as if he was the most normal guy in the world, and he would just smile at them and say something daft.

Chabs and Bifter told us they were passing Copeland Road subway station when they saw Daft Davie come out of the newsagent. They shouted *All right, Daft Davie?* at him for a laugh, knowing that he hated it, and he went mental, chasing them all the way to Cessnock like a crazed, frothing animal. They only managed to lose him when they ducked into the Crit and hid behind the queue. Who knows what he'd have done if he'd caught them? We all agreed that it was amazing Daft Davie was allowed to walk the streets.

Cuddihy then told us that he had bumped into the Prof. who he managed to con out of ten bob. I did a quick mental calculation to work out that ten bob was fifty pee. The Prof. was this crazy old guy who cycled round Govan on his rusting, ramshackle bike. He reeked of pish and wore the same clothes all the time – an ancient, brown tweed suit and a dirty white shirt, which was frayed at the collar and cuffs, with a tie. We called him the Prof. because he had a pair of tiny, wire-framed glasses.

If you got him talking, he would stand there for hours gibbering utter rubbish about the war and the Japanese and stuff like that. It was impossible to keep track of what he was saying, because the sentences didn't follow logically, and suddenly he would just shout random words which bore no relation to what he had been saying before. One time he was talking about some electrical machine or something and he just yelled *Testicles!* out of the blue while we all rolled around on the pavement in hysterics, slapping our thighs.

If there was a lot of us, he would get really edgy and his voice would get quicker and quicker until it looked like his head was going to explode. The Prof. had been around for years and he was totally doolally. Mum told me he was a poor soul and that we should leave him alone. She would freak if she found out that we had been teasing him.

Cuddihy said he skinned ten bob off him by telling him it was needed for the war effort. But when we asked him where the money was, he said he had spent it, and when we asked him what on, he got a bit vague, so I didn't really believe him.

The bell went before I had time to tell everyone my big news, but I was in no hurry. It seemed almost sacrilegious to drop Dixie Deans's name into a conversation about Daft Davie and the Prof.

After lunch the teacher handed out the textbooks that we would be using in the coming year. We were obliged to take them home and cover them with paper, to protect them. The kids from the well-off homes always covered theirs with swanky wallpaper or expensive brown paper while the poorer kids used old copies of the *Daily Record* or the *Evening Citizen*.

Then, everyone was led to the gym where we spent the rest of the afternoon watching films. A screen was erected at the front of the hall and a noisy, spool-to-spool projector at the back. We sat cross-legged, on the floor in the middle, while the teachers perched on chairs down the side, read their papers or dozed off.

It was never explained why we were being shown these documentaries about the bushmen of the Kalahari and the flight of the condor. They bore no relation to anything else that we were taught in the classroom and there was never any discussion about them afterwards. If we questioned their purpose, we were told they were 'educational'. But they were lost on me and by the end of the opening titles, I'd invariably have switched off, glazed over and set the theme tune to *Man about the House* playing in my head.

The exception was the occasional cartoon featuring Jiminy

Cricket, who, though by no means an A-list Disney character, was more entertaining than the course of the Yukaton or the Dayak people of Borneo. But even he appeared to have been nobbled by Glasgow Corporation school board, and there would, inevitably, be some underlying message about the value of grammar or hard work. We did our best to ignore that and enjoyed the fact that we were watching a cartoon while at school.

As we sat in the curtained darkness, I decided this would be an opportune moment to reveal my news, given that I had a captive audience. I was at the end of a row that included Bifter, Cuddihy and Chabs. I would have to do it stealthily, though, as talking during films was frowned upon by the teachers

– Guess who I met in the holidays? I whispered to Bifter, with one eye on Wutherspoon.

– Who?

– Dixie Deans.

– Yer arse.

– Straight up.

– Yer arse.

I produced the scrap of paper onto which the great man had attached his signature.

– What's that then, smarty baws? Scotch mist? I asked triumphantly.

While Dixie Deans played for Celtic, his talent transcended sporting rivalry. Even Celtic-turned-Rangers or even dyed-in-the-wool Rangers supporters like Bifter recognised that his autograph was a prized possession. He stared at it for several moments and then shook his head.

– It's a fake.

– Is not.

– Is too.

– Yer a jealous big bastard, Hamilton. It's Dixie Deans's signature. He gave it me in the Java Jive.

By now the others had caught wind of our argument and wanted to know what all the fuss was about.

– This lying shite claims that's Dixie Deans's autograph, Bifter said to Cuddihy, handing him the paper.

Cuddihy eyed it like he was a collector inspecting a rare banknote, holding it up and observing it from different angles. In the end, he offered no opinion on its authenticity, instead handing it to Chabs to allow him to conduct his own forensic examination. I began to panic. My most prized possession was out of my reach and I wanted it back.

– Give it back here, I demanded.

Chabs grinned maliciously and motioned as if he was tearing it in two. I felt tears welling up in my eyes.

– Give it back, ya bastard, I said, leaning across Bifter and Cuddihy.

Suddenly, I felt a blow behind me followed by a winding pain. I doubled up in agony and turned around to find Wutherspoon removing her pointed shoe from the small of my back.

– Stop yakking or you'll be getting the strap, she barked.

The others immediately sat up straight, faced the screen and pretended to be engrossed in the film. My back ached, and I could tell that I was going to have a bruise. Sophia was right, Wutherspoon was a vicious bitch.

Chabs still had the autograph at home time. As we left the school gates he held it above his head and kept running away every time I got near. He passed it to the others who took it in turns to wave it in front of my face, and then they pulled it away when I tried to grab it. This continued all the way along Maxwell Drive up to the railway bridge, which Chabs threatened to drop it over. I was becoming increasingly frustrated, my voice cracking as I told them I wanted it back. I was serious and, if any of them lost it or damaged it, I'd kick their heads in. I yelled with as much conviction as I could muster.

– Oh aye, you and whose army? Chabs sneered.

– My army, said a girl's voice in the distance.

We turned around to see Sophia coming over the brow of the

hill with three of her schoolmates. They were a formidable sight. It was incredible – Sophia had left the house that morning a demure, unthreatening adolescent in her pristine uniform. Now, less than eight hours later, she had transformed into a strutting, scarlet vamp, her face heavily made up, her skirt hoisted around her thighs and her tie worn around her head like a bandana. Her friends were dressed similarly and, as they approached, smoking cigarettes, Chabs and the others recoiled in trepidation.

Among them was Sophia's best friend Celeste, who had, for some time, induced in me an inexplicable confusion. I hated and mistrusted girls and had done so since I could remember, yet there was something about Celeste, with her golden-white hair and her soft, translucent face that obsessed me.

I observed her from afar, studying her mannerisms and sketching a portrait of her in my head. When she was at our house, I waited until she and Sophia were out of the room before picking up anything belonging to her – a coat, a scarf, a book – and examining it, sniffing it and holding it against my face.

I lay awake at night composing fantasy scenarios in which we were alone, and I would emerge witty and urbane, engrossing her with my easy charm and my winning turn of phrase. We would stroll together in effortless conversation, with perceptible electricity between us. Sometimes there was physical contact but it was grainy and ill-defined, like watching a television set without an aerial.

As the girls approached, Celeste ruffled my hair and I blushed.

– How's my wee boyfriend? she asked playfully. She was always making jokes like that which gave me a sickening sense of panic, as though she might somehow be able to tell what I had been thinking.

Chabs, Bifter and Cuddihy all cooed mockingly, and I could feel my face burn. Thankfully Sophia stepped in.

– What's going on? She asked, dropping her fag butt on the ground and stepping on it.

– They won't give me my Dixie Deans autograph back, I said.

Sophia turned to face Chabs who was doing his best not to look intimidated.

– Give it back, she ordered.

– It's only a game.

– Give it back, ya wee prick, or I'll boot yer baws, she said.

Chabs flushed with embarrassment. He walked towards me and handed me the papers, and Sophia's mates all laughed at the ease with which he had surrendered it.

– See ya later, Stevie boy, Sophia said as they began to walk on.

They were only a few yards away when Chabs decided he couldn't allow his humiliation to go unchallenged.

– Look who needs his big sister to fight his battles for him, he said.

Sophia stopped in her tracks and spun round, her face expressionless. Everyone froze. Slowly she walked the five or six paces toward Chabs, the clacking of her heels on the pavement ringing in our ears. She grabbed him by the tie and pulled his face close to hers. I thought she was going to head butt him but, instead, she planted a kiss, full on his lips.

After a few seconds, she let go of his tie, and he fell away, his face smeared in her bright red lipstick. As she strutted away, everyone, except Chabs, was helpless with laughter. I had my differences with my sister, and she could be a pain in the arse, but, at that moment, I was so grateful to her I could have burst.

5

The new school year marked the official start of the scrumping season. The lush gardens of Pollokshields were among the richest apple growing areas in the city, and the kids from Govan saw the act of relieving the bulging trees of their sweet harvest as a righteous act of economic redistribution. It would be another few weeks before the fruit was ripe enough to be worth stealing, but the intervening period, when the evenings were still light, would be used for preparation, when logistics were finalised and troops battle-hardened.

Everyone assumed a position in the raid team, which they were expected to keep until the end of the season. Wally appointed himself Big X – after the Dickie Attenborough character in *The Great Escape* – in overall charge of missions. He would decide which gardens to target, when we would strike, and he would also be responsible for divvying up the spoils at the end of each raid.

Chabs appointed himself Tunnel King – after the Charles Bronson character – responsible for working out the optimum route into each garden. Bifter pointed out that there was very little, if any, requirement for actual tunnelling, but the title was allowed to stand after a show of hands.

Bifter then said that, if Chabs was allowed to be the Tunnel King, he wanted to be the Scrounger, after the James Garner character, on the grounds that, if we needed something like a torch or a sack to hold the apples, he could scrounge it. Cuddihy demanded to be the Forger, after the Donald Pleasence character, claiming that he could forge false library tickets so that if we were caught and we had them in our pockets, they would throw our captors off the scent.

I said I wanted to be the Cooler King, after the Steve McQueen character, but Chabs objected, saying that was just stupid because there was no cooler to be king of. I accused him of still bearing a grudge because Sophia had winched him in front of everyone, giving him a big beamer. There followed a short debate, after which it was agreed by a majority verdict that I could be the Cooler King, but only if I was able to acquire a baseball and a catcher's glove, like the ones Steve McQueen had in the film. I said the best I could manage was a tennis ball and a sheepskin mitten, and there followed another short debate, after which it was decided that that would do.

Johnny Nae Da was roped in as the edgy man, whose job was to keep the edgy – or the lookout – and alert us to the sudden appearance of any residents. This would usually be done by whistling, or making a bird call. Johnny Nae Da wore thick glasses, was grossly overweight, and could barely run the length of himself without collapsing through exhaustion. His obesity and bright ginger hair marked him out as conspicuous. We might as well have posted a big neon sign in the driveway, which read APPLE THEFT IN PROGRESS, but he possessed that most essential quality in an edgy man – he was willing to do it.

Finding an edgy man was never easy, not least because it was the most unenviable job on a raid. Not only did you miss out on the excitement of sloping around in someone else's garden, filling your pockets with their fruit, you were also the most likely to be caught, given that you were the first and last line of defence. Then, at the end of the night, you were lucky if you got any of the apples.

Johnny Nae Da was happy to be involved in any capacity because he had no friends. Besides his comical appearance, he was the only person in our class from a single parent family, which marked him out as different and, therefore, a prime candidate for ridicule. His full nickname was Johnny Nae Da Wan Baw, because, as well as being fatherless, he had lost a testicle in an accident involving a glass coffee-table, but most people just referred to him as Johnny Nae Da – out of compassion, I think.

He tried to put it about that his dad was in jail for murder, but it was common knowledge that he really lived with a new family somewhere in the East End. It was said that Johnny Nae Da had half-brothers and half-sisters whom he had never met. He lived with his mum in a single end on Clifford Street. She was on the social, and they were so poor they made the Raffertys look like the Rockerfellers.

I did my best to be nice to Johnny Nae Da, but he wasn't the easiest person in the world to like. He reminded me of a film we had seen in the gym about locusts, which have to eat their own bodyweight every day to survive. I reckoned Johnny Nae Da must have eaten his own bodyweight in chips every day. I can't remember a time when he wasn't at some varying stage in the demolition of a deep-fried supper. I once went to tackle him at football and ended up having a half-eaten battered sausage smeared down my face.

Because of his weight, he sweated profusely and carried around a smell that would have bubbled paint, only partially masked by the perpetual whiff of salt and vinegar. There was one time, back in Primary Three, when he shat himself at the swing park. Because he was wearing short trousers, it started to slide down his leg, and he had to walk all the way home followed by a jeering crowd, poking him with sticks and calling him 'shitty shitty plop pants'.

Wally had done a provisional recce of the gardens that were known to house the best trees so that we could work out a battle plan. He was my friend, first and foremost, and I had introduced him to the rest of the gang. It wasn't usual for a Proddy like me to have a friend who was a Catholic. We met one day on the pitch 'n' putt course at Bellahouston Park and we just hit it off. We spent the rest of the day roaming about up the Cunyon, scouring Haggs Castle golf course for lost balls and generally having a laugh.

When other Proddies like Cuddihy, Bifter and Chabs got to know him, they liked him as well and accepted him as part of the group. On questions of scrumping strategy they knew his pedigree and accepted his judgement without question.

For the first few raids he decreed that we should concentrate on easy hits – a widow with a crab apple tree on Hamilton Avenue and, on Sutherland Avenue, an elderly couple who had a pair of cookers. In both cases the trees were close to the perimeter walls so we were able to raid them without having to set foot in the gardens. Neither variety was edible, of course, but they didn't go to waste. We took them down to the railway embankment and used them to pelt passing commuter trains, laughing at the terrified faces of the unsuspecting passengers.

A season wasn't a season without at least one raid on the garden of Shotgun Harry – a shadowy, vigilante figure, notorious among the Southside scrumping community. None of us had ever seen his face, and we knew him only by the personalised registration plate on his top-of-the-range Jaguar – H4RRY – but generations of pre-adolescents bore the scars, physical and mental, of the ruthlessness with which he protected his prized crop of Scotch Bridgets.

Most residents, if they spotted you in their garden, would emerge shouting threats that they were going to call the police – and many did – but Harry took pleasure in taking the law into his own hands. The first sign of his presence, as you picked your way through his foliage, was the whirr of an airgun pellet followed by a crippling, whipping pain as it embedded itself in your buttock.

Harry's garden was surrounded by nothing more challenging than a modest, easily scaleable privet hedge. We couldn't help but suspect that the lack of anything resembling security was deliberate, and that he enjoyed taking pot shots at his young invaders, grinning maliciously as we ran screaming from his premises clutching our bruised bottom cheeks.

For our main raid of the season we settled on one of the big mansions surrounding Maxwell Park. Living in the midst of these patrician citadels had never inured me to their sleek majesty. The biggest house I had ever been in was Granny and Granddad's in the West End, but these properties made that look like a tiny cottage. Set within expansive grounds, many on hilltops, they were grand and opulent, adorned with turrets, flagpoles, weather vanes and column-fronted entrances, which gave them the appearance of civic chambers rather than somewhere people would live. They had perfectly manicured gardens and many boasted indecipherable Gaelic names like Cruachan, Dadarraich and Sealladh Breagh, which added to their mystique.

We had chosen an impressive, neo-classical property on Glen-cairn Drive, which housed a small orchard of Russets in its substantial grounds. Jebsy MacBride's team had done it the year before and they had provided us with a full intelligence report.

The trees were located on a patch of open ground to the south-west of the main building and adjacent to an area of lawn. The easiest way to gain access was, unfortunately, also the riskiest – through the high, wrought iron gates at the front entrance, which usually remained open, even when neither of the two expensive cars was out. But after you were through them, you had to pass the front door which, Jebsy warned, was a major security threat.

The safest way of entering without being detected, he counselled, was over a perimeter wall to the rear of the building, which backed onto Colquhoun Lane. The wall was too high to scale and drop, so we would need a ladder. Once inside the grounds, we were advised to traverse the garden, commando-style, to avoid being spotted through a large bay window, which overlooked the lawn. Part of the orchard area was also visible from the window so we were told it would be sensible to concentrate on those trees occupying a blind spot to the north-east.

If there was the remotest sign that we had been rumbled, Jebsy recommended immediate abandonment of the operation. The grounds were patrolled by a giant, ferocious Alsatian, which had tried to maul him the year before, and he had only narrowly escaped certain death by fending it off with a rake. The lady of the house was a vicious witch who had chased them from the grounds, waving a large spade.

The most important thing on a mission like this was not to get caught. Stories concerning the terrifying fate of captured scrumpers were legion. It was said that the rich folks who lived in the big houses kept them imprisoned for years, using them as slaves.

There was one guy in our school a few years back called Eric Gillespie – everyone called him Dizzy – who was lost on a raid on a garden down in Newark Avenue. Everyone else had bolted after being discovered, and no-one thought to check what had happened to Dizzy. It was the last anyone ever saw of him.

He failed to turn up for school the next morning, and his family disappeared too. It was said they committed mass suicide because they couldn't bear to live without Dizzy. Tony said that was rubbish, that the family had been rehoused in Cumbernauld when the Porter Street flats were demolished. He said he saw Dizzy in town with his mum a couple of months later. I didn't know what to believe – Tony's version of events sounded plausible enough but it could have been another one of his tall tales.

As the self-appointed scrounger, Bifter had been instructed to go and find a ladder. He stared at us vacantly for a couple of moments before conceding that he had drawn a blank.

– What do you mean you've drawn a blank? Chabs demanded. You haven't even tried!

– I don't know anyone with a ladder, Bifter protested.

– You're the scrounger, that's your job.

– What about Kevin Kane? Wally suggested. His old man's a window cleaner. I've seen his ladder lying around their close.

Kevin Kane was in the year above Wally at the Conception and he had a reputation for violence. Being in the debt of some-one like Kane was a risk but no-one could think of a credible alternative.

There was something very unsettling about approaching some-one you knew had broken another boy's nose with a single kick and asking to borrow his father's ladder. He surveyed the motley collection before him with some scepticism and sighed heavily to let us know how much of an imposition we were on his time and patience. He was on the brink of telling us to piss off, but when Wally promised him half a dozen Russets and assured him that the ladder would be back within a couple of hours, he reluctantly agreed.

The ladder sat along the back wall of their tenement building, immediately below their ground-floor flat. We were instructed to wait until Kane had made sure his old man was busy. He would give three taps on the bathroom window as the signal for us to manoeuvre the ladder through the close, out the front entrance and along the road to the left in double quick time.

Everything went according to plan. It was no more than a couple of miles from Kane's place to Glencairn Drive, but it took longer than expected because we had to stick to side streets and drop the ladder every time we heard a car coming, in case it was the law, so it was dark by the time we got there. We crept along Colquhoun Lane until we found what we were sure was the right garden and hoisted the ladder against the wall as quietly as we could so as not to attract attention. Then we crouched down in a huddle to discuss tactics.

The idea was that all of us would climb up the ladder, sit on the wall and then lift it over to allow us to descend the other side. Bifter pointed out that, while we would be fine on the way in, when time was not at a premium, it could be problematic on the way out, if we were obliged to leave in a hurry with a snarling Alsatian snapping at our heels and a demented harridan whacking at our backsides with a giant shovel.

Everyone agreed that it was too risky for all of us to enter the garden, so we decided a task force of two should be sent in, with the rest stationed in the lane to keep the edgy. Johnny Nae Da was automatically exempted from frontline duties because he was the edgy man. It occurred to me that he was too fat to climb the ladder in any event, and I also feared his pungent aroma might attract the attention of the dog.

So, two from the remaining five would be selected to go over the top. No-one volunteered. Wally tried to claim that, as Big X, he should pick the members of the task force but he was outvoted. Instead, it would be decided by numbers. I turned my back and Bifter gave everyone a number, from one to five. I turned round again and scanned their eyes for any sign of a clue. There was none.

– Two and four, I said.

Chabs was two. He cursed instinctively and then tried to make out that he was really pleased to be going. The faces of the others cracked into smiles. No-one said anything, but I knew automatically that I must be four. I had chosen myself.

I was first up the ladder. When I got to the top I inspected the garden to get my bearings. The spotlights covered only the immediate area surrounding the house, and so most of the garden was in darkness. There was a greenhouse, which Jebsy had omitted to mention, and a couple of flower-beds but I was able to make out the lawn and, beyond it, the apple trees.

I climbed off the ladder and perched on the wall, and Chabs joined me. The ladder was too heavy for us to lift on our own, so the others hoisted it up from the bottom and gave it a heave, allowing us to pivot it over the wall and drop it onto the garden side. That was it, there was no turning back now. After all the talk and preparation, this was the real thing.

I had a sick feeling in my stomach and, momentarily, I was paralysed with fear. I was Charles Bronson, at the head of the tunnel in *The Great Escape*. The garden was the wooded area beyond Stalag Luft III, the wall was an electrified perimeter fence, and the house was a watchtower manned by armed Nazis.

I looked down into the lane and saw the rest of them giving me the thumbs up and, suddenly, I felt an overwhelming sense of obligation. This was not a time to freeze, I told myself. I had a responsibility to those people and a duty to come back with a jumper full of apples. I had to pull myself together. I had to overcome my feelings of self doubt. I remembered the pep talk given to Bronson by John Leyton.

Chabs looked as terrified as I felt. I offered what I hoped was a reassuring smile and held out my hand for him to shake.

– Good luck, he said, unconvincingly.

– See you back in Blighty, I whispered in reply.

We crept down the ladder and stood for a moment surveying the landscape, then I felt Chabs's hand grip my arm.

– Wait a minute. We're stranded, he said frantically.

– What do you mean?

– The ladder. The fucking ladder. How are we going to get it back over the wall?

I thought for a moment until it dawned on me that we couldn't. We didn't have a hope of getting it back into the lane unless we had several people lifting it from the ground, inside the garden, but all the others were on the other side of the wall. It was just like in *The Great Escape* when they realised they had dug the tunnel too short and the exit hole was still fifteen feet from the woods.

– Shite, was all I could think of to say.

– Yeah, shite, said Chabs. We're going to have to make a break for it through the front gate. I only hope it's open.

We decided to go ahead with the raid. If we were going to get caught, we might as well have some apples with us at the time, we reasoned. We began to crawl along the lawn on our stomachs. There had been a light shower earlier in the evening which made the grass smell sweet and fresh, but the pleasant aroma was offset by the sudden feeling of coldness as the rain seeped through my clothes.

In the distance, through the bay window, was a warmly lit room and I could see figures moving around inside. Suddenly a door opened and we heard a burst of sound – jazz music and people laughing and talking excitedly. Then we heard the sound of footsteps on gravel and a dog barking. Suddenly Chabs was upright.

– That's it. I'm off, he said, his voice quivering with fear. I'm not hanging around to be made someone's slave.

He bolted in the direction of the driveway. As he ran, the dog's barking grew louder and more frequent.

– Is that these bloody kids again? said a booming male voice.

I ran in the opposite direction towards the trees and ducked for cover. I lay face down on the ground for what seemed like an eternity, but was probably only a couple of minutes. The activity receded, the voices stopped, and I figured Chabs must have escaped. I remained frozen. I knew that it was pointless trying to make a run for it.

If Chabs had made it through the gates, they would almost certainly have been closed by now. My best option was to sit it out until things had calmed down, and then try to slip out quietly.

After a few more minutes of silence I became aware of movement nearby. I heard the sound of heavy breathing and then panting. I looked up to find a large St Bernard dog standing over me, its tongue hanging out, and large strings of saliva dripping from its jaws. It emitted a thunderous bark which made me yelp with fear.

– Don't worry. He won't touch you, said a female voice. As she approached, I could just make out her silhouette. She was tall and slim and wearing a cowboy hat. My heart was pounding so violently it was painful, and I was struggling for breath.

– Come on, get up, she ordered in a posh voice, which gave the distinct impression that she was used to getting her way. She led me towards the house with an arm casually cast around my shoulder. In the other hand she was holding a wine glass. I was terrified, convinced that she was going to make me her slave.

– I don't know why you kids have to skulk about in the dark. If you want apples, why don't you just come to the door and ask?

I was too nervous to speak.

– There's a barrel full of them next to the greenhouse. Take as many as you like and let yourself out by the front gate. I tried to say the same to your friend, but he scarpered.

She smiled and went indoors. I realised that I was shivering.

Apples were the last thing on my mind, but I felt it would be rude not to take her up on her offer. I grabbed a handful and ran to the end of the driveway. When I got to the lane, everyone had gone. No doubt Chabs had tipped the others off that we'd been rumbled, and they'd bolted. They'd be halfway home by now, talking about how I'd probably been taken into slavery and would never be seen again. I caught my breath and ran as fast as I could all the way home.

It was later that night, while I was lying in bed, still sweating about the experience, when it suddenly occurred to me that we'd left behind Kane's dad's ladder in the garden. My heart leapt at the realisation. I barely slept, worrying about what it would mean. Kane was known as one of the best fighters in the whole of Govan, and his gang had a reputation for casual and indiscriminate violence. He didn't need a reason to kick your head in, but now he had one, he would be relentless in hunting us down.

My one saving grace was that he didn't go to my school and he barely knew me. He didn't even know my name, for all I knew. But it was certain that Wally would dob me in, rather than taking the rap himself, saying I was the last to leave the garden and it was my fault the ladder got left. Then Kane would come after me, for sure.

I figured I had two options – either I could go on the run or I could return to the scene of the crime to recover the ladder. I felt hunted – like David Jansen in *The Fugitive* – only a psychopath with steel-tipped boots was pursuing me, rather than an obsessive copper, and I was chasing a ladder, rather than a one-armed man. I shivered with fear. Life was becoming more exciting suddenly, only not the way I had hoped.

6

Sunday dinner at Granny and Granddad's house was a family tradition going back as far as I could remember. The tradition was that we never went. The occasion was the focal point of their week, when they gathered together an eclectic group of friends and plied them with fine food and wines.

It had long been a bone of contention with Mum that Dad steadfastly refused to spend his precious weekends – being bored witless by the weirdos, misfits and hangers-on who made up her parents' social set.

On the odd occasion when he was press-ganged into going, he remained detached from the crowd, silent and stolid, as though the remotest sign of participation might expose him to some deadly virus. In the end Mum decided the recriminations that inevitably followed his being there were more troublesome than having to explain his conspicuous absences and so she no longer made an issue of it.

Instead she went on the odd weekend, accompanied by Tony, Sophia or me, who all thought it as much of an ordeal as Dad. More often than not, Tony and Sophia managed to talk their way out of it but, predictably, my voice was never heard and I was dragged along, no matter how strongly I protested.

We weren't allowed to refer to them as Granny and Granddad when they had friends over – they were Vera and George. They lived in a smart terraced house in the West End, on the edge of the university campus where George worked as a lecturer in medieval history. Vera was retired after a career in academic publishing.

Their home was warm and affluent with dark, polished

wooden floors and intricately corniced ceilings. Every available space housed a bookcase, packed with intimidating tomes, and the high walls were adorned with paintings by their favourite artists like the Surrealists and the Glasgow Boys. Pride of place in the hallway was a Peploe watercolour.

By one o'clock the lounge, whose generous bay window commanded an impressive view across the Botanic Gardens, was a dense fug of tobacco smoke and malt whisky fumes as bursts of exaggerated laughter erupted from the chattering crowd. I had no other experience of people like this. They were like characters from one of Vera's Art Nouveau posters in the bathroom – confident and elegant, dressed in psychedelic chiffons and silks, they gesticulated expansively, waving their Black Russian cigarettes and pontificating upon matters which made no sense to me whatsoever.

Mum was always nervous to begin with, but it didn't take her long to settle and she would laugh and joke in the company of some remnant of her upbringing. Among the regular attendees were those I liked, those I feared, and those who, frankly, baffled me. The most fearsome was Gretchen, a willowy old chain smoker who had greasy, grey hair and a mouth like a docker. She drank more than everyone else put together and was generally asleep before pudding. She was the only woman I knew who swore, but more surprising was that no-one appeared to turn a hair at her exotic language.

Gretchen was always angry, usually at some perceived inadequacy on the part of her husband, Macon. As to a road accident, my eyes were irresistibly drawn towards her, my fascination tempered with the stomach-churning fear that she might catch me staring and turn her wrath upon me.

At a certain moment, all the guests were summoned to the dining room where they gathered around a long teak table to spend the rest of the afternoon tucking into a rich roast dinner, continuing their incomprehensible discussions.

On this occasion, over the confit of smoked salmon and prawns

Marie Rose, Giles and Mignon, a husband-and-wife team of diversity consultants, held forth. In an emotional outburst Menzies, an emeritus professor of something or other, dismissed their conclusions as 'facile' and 'naïve' before being told by his wife, Eleanor, to make that his last glass of claret.

As the rack of lamb with Pommes Dauphinoise arrived, Minty and Bryce – who had given up their jobs as university lecturers to run an anarcho-syndicalist farm in Balfron – were predicting something unintelligible to my young ears. Vera said she had never heard such tosh and that, if they were to continue to avail themselves of her hospitality, they should have the decency not to spout such drivel.

As we tucked into pavlova with seasonal fruits, Bernie and Fran, who ran a council-funded theatre workshop in the East End, denounced all men as a word I didn't know and claimed the problems of the world could be solved by the eradication of something or other I couldn't understand.

Bernie and Fran were the only women who never brought their husbands to Vera and George's lunches. They wore dungarees, shaved their heads and they smoked roll-ups. Dad said they were queer and I could see what he meant. They were definitely a bit odd.

By the time the coffee and petits fours arrived, the room had splintered into half a dozen competing discussions. Smoke filled the air again as the guests swirled puddles of Armagnac around large balloon glasses and sought inspiration from the ceiling. I was beyond the point of boredom but I was made to remain at the table until the meal was finished.

It was now a week since the apple raid on Glencairn Drive, and there had been no communication with Kane. Rather than calming my nerves, with every passing day, tension heightened, as I imagined, with ever more creative embellishment, the fate that awaited me when we finally came face to face.

The scrumping team had all met up behind the Co-op the morning after the raid for a debriefing, with the issue of the ladder top of the agenda. Wally suggested the best course of action was simply to ignore the problem and to hope that it went away. His proposal was carried unanimously by a collective mumble of consent.

As the only member of the raid team who attended the Conception, Wally intended to dog school for the foreseeable future, to avoid the possibility of bumping into Kane. If any of us did meet him in the street, it was agreed that our favoured tactic would be to absolve ourselves of responsibility by blaming all the others.

Following the discussion of the ladder, I, as the last member of the team to leave the garden, was pressed for a full report of what had transpired. The story I had presented became somewhat inflated in the telling, and I had to make sure that I remembered every detail so that I didn't trip myself up in future tellings.

I had told them about how, after Bifter abandoned me in the garden, I was cornered by a ferocious, frothing Alsatian and how, as I tried to make a run for it, the sinister owners of the house, who looked like Norman Bates and his mother from *Psycho*, had given chase. I told how the man grabbed me and covered my face with a cloth soaked in chloroform to sedate me while the woman tried to shackle me with chains and ankle cuffs.

My listeners stood open-mouthed as I recounted how it took both of them to hold me down because I struggled so strenuously. How I felt myself becoming drowsier and drowsier and that I was almost unconscious. But then I felt a boulder under my hand. I lifted it and brought it crashing down on the man's head.

As blood gushed from the crack in his skull, the woman backed off, frightened that I would do the same to her. The dog was snapping at my heels but I picked up the chain and swung it around, clipping his nose which sent him scurrying to the other end of the garden. I then turned and fled. But even as I was climbing over the wall, the woman was trying to haul me back into the garden. I kicked out and caught her square in the face with the heel of my sand shoe and then managed to scramble over the top and drop onto the roadside before sprinting all the way home.

– God, I reckon they would have locked you up you for sure if they had caught you, Chabs said after my faultless account.

– I don't know, I said casually. I reckon they had a dungeon, and that's why they were trying to manacle me. I reckon they wanted to use me as a slave.

Mum was deep in conversation with her sister Helene, who was at the dinner with her husband, Barry. Both of them were high-flying lawyers. Helene was a couple of years younger than Mum and had no children, but she was my godmother which, she said, was the next best thing. She was always playing around with me and teasing me. She was the most affectionate person I knew – she would always want you to hold her hand or sit on her knee although I was way too old to do that by then.

She was keen to hear all about Mum's college course. I could tell Mum was pleased at the attention, but she played it down and kept bringing the conversation back to Tony and how well he was going to do at university.

– He's got conditional offers to study law at Glasgow and Edinburgh. He needs four As but that's a formality. He's the best in his year by a mile. His teachers can't praise him highly enough. They say he has an intellect beyond his years. He went through a phase of saying he wanted to be a writer, but I told him, law is a profession, writing is an indulgence. You can still be a writer and have a profession to fall back on.

– That's marvellous, Christine. Tony's a credit to you, said Helene. But what about you? Tell me all about your psychology course.

– Oh, it's nothing. It's just a further education class to keep my brain active, Mum insisted.

– It's not nothing. It's great that you're stretching yourself, Helene said, touching Mum gently on the back of the hand. And then, once you've finished that, there's no reason why *you* shouldn't do a degree.

– Oh, I could never go to university, Mum said, blushing.

– Of course you could.

Gretchen, who was seated opposite Mum, had been asleep since the starter course, but had now awoken and was lighting a cigarette. Several of the guests glanced at her in bleak antici-pation of what she was about to say or do. Macon, who was in conversation with Bryce, ignored her. Gretchen reached for the nearest bottle of wine and filled the glass closest to her before taking a large swig. Then she fixed her eyes on Mum.

– So, Christine, how's that dreary fucker of a husband of yours? she asked loudly.

Conversations halted momentarily before resuming. Mum's face flushed.

– He's fine, she said quietly, without turning round.

Undaunted Gretchen continued her interrogation.

– Is he still working in the catering industry? Really, I can't understand why anyone would want to work in a restaurant, pandering to the random whims of the great unhosed.

All the guests tried their best to carry on with their conver-sations, but there was the unmistakeable clunk of strides being put off. Granny, who was at the opposite end of the table stood up.

– Gretchen, come with me. There's something I want to show you.

– Oh, do fuck off, Vera, I'm talking to Christine.

Grandma persisted.

– No, really, there's something I think you'll be interested in.

Reluctantly Gretchen rose to her feet and followed Vera from the room.

After dinner was over, Mum and I stayed behind, along with Helene and Barry, to help with the washing up. Now that the guests had departed, I was permitted to call Vera and George Granny and Granddad again. Helene was washing, and the rest of us were drying and putting the dishes away in cupboards.

– I'm sorry about Gretchen, dear, Granny said to Mum. She

really is getting beyond the pale. That is definitely the last time I invite her for lunch.

– Don't worry about it, Mum said.

– No, there's really no excuse. Everyone is losing patience with her. She's not normally so obtuse, but it's the drink that makes her like that. We've been telling Macon for years she's got a problem.

– Really, Mum. It's all right.

There was a momentary silence, and I saw Granny and Granddad swap glances.

– So how *is* Robert? Granny asked.

– He's fine, Mum said curtly.

– And his job?

– His job's fine too.

– Any sign of a promotion?

Mum was drying the last of the dishes and she threw her dishtowel down on the kitchen table.

– Look, don't pretend that you care, Mum.

Granddad, who had been quiet for most of the afternoon, looked flustered.

– Stay calm, Christine, we're only trying to take an interest, he said.

– Oh really? Well, you never have before so why start now?

Dad had never got on with Granny and Granddad, we all knew that, but this was the first time I had seen Mum openly acknowledging the fact. Tony said it didn't take a genius to work out they had nothing in common. He said Dad came from a family of workers, while Mum came from a family who liked to talk about workers. Tony said Mum and Dad had very different backgrounds and what perplexed him was why they ever got together in the first place.

They met when Mum accompanied Granny and Granddad to an academic conference, held in the North British Hotel in Edinburgh where Dad was working as a waiter. Their memories of what transpired were markedly different. The detail of their courtship had become fluid and changeable, its chronology and tone dependent on who was recounting it. The only unshakeable certainty was that within months of meeting they were married. They were both sixteen.

When Mum was telling the story, they had fallen hopelessly in love at first sight, their eyes locking across a crowded room, like Natalie Wood and Richard Beymer in *West Side Story*. She was at the chairman's dinner with her parents, wearing her first ever ballgown, in the days when she still had a figure.

Dad was one of a small team of waiters serving four hundred guests, but he kept finding excuses to come over to her table. Whenever he passed, she felt a flutter of excitement in her tummy. He was tall, slim and dashing, with a dark complexion and a thick head of black hair cut just like Tony Curtis's. He was nervous around her, which made his performance clumsy. Then he spoke his first words to her – words she remembered to this day.

– More veg?

The following morning he came into the hotel hours before he was due to start work and hovered around the reception desk in the hope of bumping into her. When she saw him, her heart skipped a beat. He asked Granddad for permission to take her on a walk down the Royal Mile, to show her the sights, and Granddad agreed.

Mum and Dad spent the day dancing, metaphorically, around one another with the coy flirtatiousness of exotic birds. A chill wind swirled around Salisbury Crags, but she was basking in the warmth of his smile, and, when he told her that she was the most beautiful girl he had ever seen, she melted.

Despite their living in different cities, he pursued her with remarkable ardour, showering her with the modest gifts he could afford. They were like George Peppard and Audrey Hepburn in *Breakfast at Tiffany's*. Because Mum was still at school, studying for her Lowers, their relationship was frowned upon by Granny and Granddad who allowed her to see him only once every few weeks.

She met him off the midday train on a Saturday, and they

wandered the streets, hand in hand, looking in all the shop windows at things they couldn't afford. They took in a matinee screening of whatever film was showing at the Odeon or Green's Playhouse, featuring the big stars of the day like Sophia Loren, Jack Lemmon and Cary Grant. They sat rigidly, holding hands, their hearts pounding, trying to summon up the courage to kiss. Later they went to Sloane's tearoom where they ordered two fish teas, with bread and butter and a pot of tea, before Dad caught the six o'clock train home.

They were young, they came from different backgrounds, and they had little money, but they were in love. Despite the disapproval of her parents and her peers, Mum encouraged Dad's advances. After a few months they eloped.

Then there was Dad's side of the story. He was run off his feet, working at one of the busiest functions of the year and Mum – a mouthy wee lassie in a powder puff dress, kept pestering him for more veg. She followed him round the room with her eyes, glaring at him in a funny way that made him feel unnerved, which meant he kept tripping and dropping things.

The following day he came into the hotel early to meet one of the chamber maids, who he had been dating. Mum was hanging around in the reception area and she tried to attract his attention. He feared she had a mental disorder and he ignored her. Later, when he was out walking down the Royal Mile, he met her again. He was convinced that she was stalking him and warned her that, if she didn't leave him alone, he would phone the police. She told him he was the rudest person she had ever met, like Margaret Lockwood in *The Lady Vanishes*, and she wouldn't stalk him if he was the last boy on earth.

Somehow – he couldn't remember the detail – they ended up courting. He came through to Glasgow most weekends and they wandered the streets with Mum pestering him to buy her things he couldn't afford. With nothing else to do, they went to the pictures and, rather than endure whatever rubbish was playing, they sat in the back row smooching and petting, drawing complaints from the usherette and other cinemagoers.

Later they sat in whatever pub was prepared to serve them, usually the snug bar in the Corn Exchange, where Dad drank halves of lager and Mum port and lemon, and they split a packet of Chesterfield cigarettes while they got half cut. Then they headed off to one of the big dancehalls like the Barrowlands or the Locarno where they jived until the early hours of the morning when Dad hitched a ride along the A8 back to Edinburgh.

After they got married they were forced to live in Granny and Granddad's house because they couldn't afford a place of their own. Dad found a job in a hotel in Glasgow, and Mum, despite strong opposition from her parents, left school so that she could earn some money to support them. She had a succession of low-paid jobs, as a waitress, an office clerk and a shop girl.

According to Dad's version of events, Granny and Granddad disapproved of him and distrusted him from the outset. He was never made to feel welcome in their house and he couldn't wait to get out. Eventually he and Mum managed to save enough money to pay for the deposit on a rented room in Partick.

Soon after, Tony was born and Mum had to give up work to look after him, and so they became even more hard up. They lived in the cramped room where they slept, ate and hung their washing. Dad said it reminded him of Michael Caine and Jane Asher in *Alfie*. Granny and Granddad offered to help out financially, but Dad wouldn't hear of it. His view was that, if they didn't accept him for what he was, he didn't want their money.

It didn't sound like the most romantic of beginnings to their life together. Dad's memory was sketchy on the precise reasons why he and Mum got married but he likened it to the scene in *Spartacus* where Kirk Douglas is captured by the Romans and sold into slavery.

Mum was silent for most of the car journey home. Our conversations were never that long, and comfortable silences were commonplace, but I could tell she was unusually preoccupied. When we emerged from the Clyde Tunnel, she stopped at a café and bought a packet of cigarettes, which was also unusual as she rarely smoked. She got back in the car and lit one.

– Have you noticed me and your Dad arguing more, recently? she asked when we were back on the road.

– No, not really, I lied.

Mum looked at me and smiled.

– You know it's nothing to worry about, don't you? Mums and Dads argue all the time. It doesn't mean anything.

Never a truer word was spoken. I could have listened to their verbal exchanges for days and still been none the wiser about what it actually meant. Whenever I had an argument with Sophia, I knew there would be a bone of contention, which would prompt claim and counter-claim, and that there would be a resolution, generally after no more than a few minutes.

The previous week, for example, she accused me of stealing her Mud single – that was the bone of contention. There followed a claim – she accused me of being a thieving wee gypsy bastard – and a counter-claim – I alleged that she was a lying big poxy cow. She pushed me over, I punched her in the stomach, prompting her to pin me to the floor, sit on my chest and squeeze my right nipple until I had capitulated, admitted the theft, apologised and returned the disputed single – the resolution.

Arguments involving Mum and Dad contained none of those guiding principles and little or no structure. They meandered aimlessly and indefinitely, peaking and troughing at seemingly random junctures without ever getting to the point. Trying to comprehend their disputes was like listening to the shipping forecast – all the words were, more or less, recognisable but meant nothing in the order they were spoken.

At least the shipping forecast comprised simple statements of fact – low forties 994 moving slowly south-east and deepening 990 by 0600 tomorrow – but when my parents argued, normal rules of linguistic engagement didn't apply. Questions were answered with questions, answers given to questions that had never been posed and statements made when, clearly, the opposite meaning was intended.

Take the previous week. Dad had been working late and he didn't arrive home until the early hours. Then one morning, over breakfast, he kept going on about how busy the restaurant had been. Mum hadn't said anything, but I could sense she was building up to something.

– Did Vivienne have to work late as well? she asked suddenly.

– What's that supposed to mean? Dad countered.

– It's supposed to mean, did Vivienne have to work late as well? Mum said in a quiet, measured tone.

– Vivienne was the woman who ran the bar in the restaurant. I liked her because she always gave me a bottle of chilled Coke with a straw in it when I was waiting for Dad.

– Yes, she did. Everyone had to work late, Dad said.

– That's a shame.

– Don't start, Christine.

– Don't start what? All I said was that's a shame.

– Why is it a shame? Why is it a shame that Vivienne had to work late and it's not a shame that I had to work late? Dad shouted.

– There's no need to raise your voice, Robert.

– I think there is a reason to raise my voice. I don't need this aggravation on my day off. If you've got something to say, then say it.

And so it went on for most of the morning and, at the end of it, I was still at a loss to explain what it had all been about.

As we drove home I found that I was actually looking forward to going to school the following morning. It was the only place that seemed to offer sanctuary now from the perpetual rows at home. Even hanging around in the streets was no longer safe, given the ever present threat of being accosted by Kane.

7

Wally was my best friend but I began to feel I was seeing a bit too much of him. Every day when I came home from school, I found him seated in the Proffy opposite our house, waiting for me. If it had been anyone else, I could have taken them into the house to share a pint of milk and a packet of custard creams while we watched *The Saint* on telly, but I knew I'd never get Wally past the door because Mum disapproved of him. So I had to agree to do something with him until teatime or else hang around, being monosyllabic, in the hope that he'd get bored and leave, which he never did.

The Proffy was a small patch of grass surrounded by railings, which housed a large electricity box. It was so-called because it had a sign, which said 'Ball games are prohibited' which no-one could pronounce and everyone ignored.

As we sat picking the heads off dandelions, I noticed that, even by his own shabby standards, Wally looked unkempt and neglected, and he was giving off an offensive, musty smell. His clothes were creased and ingrained with dirt and sweat and his eyes were tired and defeated.

Wally came from a big family. His real name was Paul Rafferty but he earned the nickname because his eldest brother, Davie, bore a passing resemblance to Richard Bradford, an actor in the 1960s television series *Man in a Suitcase*. At the shipyard, where he worked, Davie became known as Suitcase. When word got out in the neighbourhood, his younger brothers were dubbed, in descending order, Briefcase, Holdall, Handbag and Wallet, shortened to Wally.

– You look like crap, I told him.

– So would you if you'd slept in the middens, he replied, matter-of-factly.

– Why were you sleeping in the middens?

– The old man locked me out of the house after I stole his fags. I'll tell you, I'm going to kill the old bastard one of these days. I'm going to whack him over the head with a shovel until he's dead.

I asked him if his mum and brothers had done anything to help.

– Och, the old dear's useless, he said. She doesn't want to rock the boat in case he starts on her. My brothers were all up the town, at the dancing. I had to wait till three in the morning for them to get back and sneak me into the house. I was brass monkeys. I thought I was going to perish with the cold. It stinks in the middens with all the rubbish and the rats running about but there was nowhere else for me to go.

I didn't know what to say. I felt sorry for Wally and I wanted to help, but I couldn't tell him to come and sleep in our house because Mum would never allow it. I was embarrassed because I could see him looking at my house and probably thinking how I had this great, cushy existence where nothing ever went wrong.

Although Wally used Kane as an excuse for not going to school, I knew he didn't really need one. For most truants, dogging was an occasional luxury they permitted themselves a handful of times during the school year. For Wally, it was a way of life. It was usually some time after the Christmas break when he'd decide that he'd had enough of formal education for that year, but it was barely two months into the new session and already he had given up.

There were the inevitable warning letters – ignored by his dad, who couldn't read, and by his mum, who was too ineffectual to do anything about it – followed by the home visits by truancy officers. But none of that made any difference to Wally.

I was astonished at how blithely he was able to take on authority and triumph. By his own admission, he sat through these meetings displaying effortless remorse, wrong-footing even the most resolute interrogator. Such was his coy, butter-wouldn't-melt deference, he managed to convince them that his idle indifference to education was in the past. Whatever it took to turn around his life, he would do it. Gone was the old Wally, and the new one had arrived: punctual, conscientious and wearing a beatific smile.

He had perfected the art of telling the corporation pen-pushers precisely what they wanted to hear, and they had barely returned to their Formica-lined offices before he was back to his old ways. The only exception was when the frequency of his absences merited a visit from Father Byrne, whose bilious fury was enough to coax him back into the classroom, if only for a few days.

Wally had talked me into dogging only once, when we were in Primary Three, and I found the experience so traumatic that I never repeated it. I had a crippling sense of angst as we wandered the lifeless, daytime streets and I couldn't escape the stomach-churning sense of guilt, knowing that I was somewhere I shouldn't be.

It was like in *Torn Curtain* when Paul Newman played an American spy, cast adrift behind the Iron Curtain with nothing but his wits to rely on to escape the pernicious clutches of the baddies. Worse was that I was Julie Andrews in the scenario, dragged into a dangerous plot, not of my own making, where my every move was monitored by the faceless forces of state control, as I played pitch 'n' putt in Bellahouston Park, hung around the Cunyon for a bit and went down to the civic dump to see if anyone had left anything of interest. They hadn't.

This was how Wally spent his days and he negotiated a well-practised routine like a seasoned, factory floor clock-watcher, until it was time to go home. I scaled ever greater heights of paranoia, scanning every horizon for members of the secret police, government informers, double agents and people who knew my parents.

Wally's absence from the Conception was chalked up as another short step down the road to academic oblivion. Mine, in contrast, was conspicuous against an otherwise blemish-free attendance record, and when Sophia, stopped in the corridor by my class teacher, was unable to explain my unexpected non-attendance, alarm bells began to ring. My crudely forged sick note failed to convince the powers-that-be that my absence was legitimate – it was pointed out that adults don't correspond in orange pencil – and the whole sorry affair ended ignominiously, with four of the strap and no pudding for a week.

As we sat in the Proffy, I couldn't wait to talk about something else. I was glad when Wally mentioned that he had seen an advert for a second-hand bike, posted in the hardware shop window, and that he wanted to go round for a look.

The seller lived at an address in Fleurs Avenue and they wanted fifteen quid. Wally was always going on about how he wanted a bike – he had coveted my Tomahawk since last Christmas, always asking for a shot. He would never have been able to afford fifteen quid – stealing that amount was beyond even him – but it was worth showing an interest on the off chance we might get a test ride.

Wally was obsessed with pushbikes. He saw the fixation as an apprentice phase until he was old enough to obsess about motorbikes, like his older brothers. To the Raffertys the combustion engine was a primal preoccupation, two-stroke engine oil more elemental than breast milk. They conversed in a members-only vocabulary of leather-clad, axle-greased jargon, meaningless to the uninitiated and uninterested. Their home was an Aladdin's Cave of disused parts from a thousand and one forgotten, concealed and misappropriated conveyances, all lightly coated in a black cocktail of brake fluid, WD40 and Swarfega.

Detached engine casings sat alongside spark plugs, head fasteners, spindle covers, valve springs, tappet adjusters, barrel base studs and manifold sprockets. The only reading material that graced their home was an abundance of well-thumbed motorbike magazines, which lay discarded in corners, beneath tables and chairs and behind the television set. Why they bothered to purchase these publications was a mystery, because they dismissed their contents as the ramblings of naïve and moronic amateurs, lacking their own profound aesthetic judgement and technical insight on all matters motorcyclical.

I had become an expert in my own right, by osmosis, after spending dozens of hours hovering around broken machine carcases in their backyard, stifling yawns as they engaged in Byzantine debates concerning the relative merits of Kawasaki and Honda, Yamaha and Triumph.

Then Wally dropped a bombshell. He said he had bumped into Kane in the street, and he was spitting fury that his dad's ladder hadn't been returned. Their next-door neighbour – an elderly spinster – had seen us removing it and had told his old man we were ages with their Kevin, maybe a bit younger. Kane insisted to his dad that he knew nothing about the ladder, but he didn't believe him.

– What does he expect us to do about it? I asked.

– He wants us to go back to the house and get the ladder.

My heart pounded with the shock of his statement as my mind raced through the possibilities. If we had to return and one of the others was caught, then they would realise the discrepancies in my story about the raid. There was no Alsatian, no *Psycho* couple, no blood-spattered life and death struggle.

– We can't. I mean, did you tell him I was nearly captured and held as a slave in their dungeon? I asked, sensing my voice was faltering.

– I tried. I told him there was no way we could go back. It would mean certain death. But he said that was our problem. He wants his dad's ladder back, and if he doesn't get it, he says he's going to kick your baws up and down Paisley Road.

– *My* baws? Why mine?

– 'Cos I told him you were the last one out of the garden. It was your responsibility.

I knew that was the strategy we had agreed, of brazenly incriminating our closest friends to save our own skins, and I had no doubt that, had I encountered Kane I'd have dobbed the others in quicker than you could say 'yellow chicken', but somehow, being on the receiving end, I couldn't help but feel a sense of sickening betrayal.

– Oh, thanks very much, Wally.

Before we arrived at the house with the bike for sale, Wally told a joke that Suitcase had picked up at the shipyard. It was all about a poof having a wank. I had no idea what Wally was talking about, but, given that it was set in a bedroom, I guessed it was dirty. I paused briefly, to be sure that he had delivered the punch-line, before laughing uproariously.

– Oh, that's a good one right enough, I said.

– I told Bobby Divers that joke at the Cunyon – he was dogging too – and do you know what? Wally asked rhetorically. He didn't know what a wank was. Can you believe that?

– Didn't know what a wank was? I repeated. Jesus Christ, imagine that.

– Yeah, he was laughing his head off, and I goes, do you know what a wank is, Bobby? And he goes, yeah, of course I do, it's the same as a shag. Can you believe it, the same as a shag?

– Imagine that, I said.

Fortunately we had arrived at Fleurs Avenue, and I was able to change the subject before he discovered that I didn't know what a wank was either. Or a shag.

– Here we are. What number did you say it was again? I asked.

– Forty-eight.

The seller lived in a sheltered housing block. Wally's heart immediately sank, believing the bike would be owned by a pensioner and would turn out to be some rusty old relic. We decided to press on regardless and chapped the knocker. A diminutive, elderly lady answered. She had grey hair and a kindly face and she was smartly turned out. While her faculties might not have been all they had been, her eyesight and sense of smell were acute enough to wince at the presence of Wally.

– We're here about the bike, he said.

The woman eyed us suspiciously, but then smiled.

– Of course, she said. Why don't you come and have a look?

She led us along the side of the house into the back garden where the bike was resting against a wall. It was a red Raleigh Colt, a few years old but in good enough condition.

– I kept it here for when my grandson came to visit but he's outgrown it and I've got no use for it now, she said.

I nodded and tried to look interested but Wally was down on all fours running his fingers over the cantilever brakes and checking that the wheel spokes were intact.

– Can I take it for a ride? he asked, without looking up.

The old lady baulked at his directness, but was clearly too polite to make a fuss.

– Well, all right, but as long as one of you stays behind.

Wally manoeuvred the bike down the garden path without a backward glance, as the old lady looked increasingly ill-at-ease. I assured her he was trustworthy and an able cyclist, and she looked a little reassured. She asked me if I was thirsty, and I said I was, so she went inside and emerged a couple of minutes later with a glass of lemonade and a Breakaway biscuit.

– My grandson has just started secondary school, you know, she said as if it was a major achievement.

– Is that right? I said, stuffing the biscuit into my mouth.

– He lives with his mum and dad in Yorkshire. He used to spend summers here and we would go on day trips to Loch Lomond and to Ayr beach. But he's too old to do that now. He's got his friends and he likes to do his own thing.

I smiled and nodded. After some more stilted conversation, Wally had not returned and the old dear started looking at her watch.

– Are you sure your friend will be all right? She asked nervously.

– Oh aye, riding a bike's second nature to him. He'll be back in a second, I assured her.

There was another long spell, mostly spent in silence, and Wally was still nowhere to be seen. I figured we must have been waiting for an hour. I racked my brain for something to say, to fill the void, but I couldn't think of anything that I would have in common with an elderly woman. I couldn't stand the thudding silence anymore.

– Baked any good cakes lately? I asked.

She shot me a withering glance and ignored the question. Embarrassed at the feebleness of my conversation I tried to rescue the situation by changing tack.

– We've been having some sunny weather in these past few days, don't you think, missus?

The woman looked at her watch.

– I'll give him another five minutes and then I'm phoning the police, she declared.

I felt a rush of panic. I offered to go and look for Wally, but that only angered her further.

– You certainly will not. I'm not falling for that one. You'll stay here with me, as a witness.

My heart raced and my skin felt tight around my face. I too began to question if Wally would return. Until then I was certain he would, but now I had doubts. Surely he wouldn't take off like that, leaving me in the lurch? Surely he wouldn't? Would he?

After another few moments, the woman signalled she'd had enough and ordered me into the house. She led me through a cramped kitchenette, in which the clawing stench of boiled cabbage hung in the air and fresh laundry dripped from a pulley onto the linoleum-covered floor. She ordered me to stand in her dark, musty lounge in which a bowl of wax flowers, coated in a thin film of dust, sat perched on a dark wood sideboard. A black cat lay curled on one of two wing-backed chairs, which were draped with yellowing linen antimacassars and flanked a small electric bar fire.

She made a grand gesture of picking up the telephone receiver and held my eye for a few seconds.

– I'm serious. I will phone the police unless you tell me what's going on.

At that moment the implication of her words dawned on me. She thought that Wally had made off with the bike and that I was complicit.

– I don't know what's going on, I pleaded.

She placed her frail, bony finger in the ninth hole of the telephone dial and began to turn.

– I'm not joking, she warned.

– Honest, missus, I'm telling you the truth. I don't know where he is.

At that moment, I caught a flash of red out of the corner of my eye. I looked through the window and saw Wally, free-wheeling onto the pavement and up the garden path. I had to stop myself lunging at the old dear and dragging her hand away from the telephone.

– Here he is, missus . . . he's back . . . look . . . out the window, there he is . . . see, he's back . . . he's back, I shouted, breathlessly.

I ran into the garden as Wally was dismounting. He leaned the bike against the wall and stepped away from it.

– Thanks, but I think we'll leave it. I've got a few others to look at and, to be honest, the price is a bit steep, he said coolly.

The old dear could barely contain her anger, but at the same time she was obviously relieved to have the bike back.

– All right, I've had enough of your time wasting. Just get out of my garden.

– Thanks for the biscuit and juice, I said, attempting some small gesture of amelioration.

– Just get out of my sight or I'll get the law onto you, she said, sweeping her hands towards us. Honestly, I don't know what young people are coming to. There's no respect.

I persevered.

– Look, I'm sorry, I didn't . . .

But she cut me off.

– Away! Be off with you and don't come round here again.

Wally was unrepentant on the walk back. He kicked a stone all the way along Maxwell Drive as though he was trying to smash it. I asked why he had taken so long. He said he'd taken it up to the Seven Hills where he met Frankie Mackenna on his Raleigh Budgie and they spent ages seeing who could do the biggest jumps. I asked him why he had taken so long and he just said he lost track of time.

I asked him how the bike was to ride but he just said it was all right and carried on kicking. I knew something was wrong. Bikes were one of two subjects guaranteed to get him talking at length and he had nothing to say.

– It looked in pretty good nick to me, I said.

– Who cares what nick it's in, he said angrily. Or any other bike for that matter. I'm never going to get one, so what's the point of talking about them all the bloody time?

By the time we got to the foot of Gower Street it was teatime. I offered to meet up with him after tea for a game of heidie kicks in the Proffy, but he said he wasn't in the mood. He was tired and hungry – he hadn't eaten today yet, so he was going to scrounge four bob from his ma for a chip roll and a bottle of ginger at the Crit. We said our goodbyes and, as I watched him trudge forlornly over the railway bridge, I had a lump in my throat and a consuming feeling of sympathy and I remember thinking, for the first time, that maybe being Wally wasn't so great after all.

8

The physical appearance of our neighbourhood seemed to be changing with every passing day, and there was a mood of transition which left the unshakeable impression that things would never be the same again. The municipal tennis courts on Maxwell Drive, which ran along the bottom of our street, had been cleared, and in their place, a new Co-op supermarket had been built.

A sign went up in the window advertising for shelf-stackers at five bob an hour. Dad encouraged me and Tony to apply but Mum over-ruled him. She said I was too young to get a job and she didn't want anything to divert Tony from his studies. Tony was clearly relieved, but I was disappointed at a missed opportunity. Loads of the Primary Seven guys worked at the Co-op and they said it was really easy to blag stuff because the supervisor was never around. Chabs's big brother ate a whole Artic Roll in less than a minute, while he was loading up a pallet in the freezer room, and he had a headache for the rest of his shift.

Work had also started on a new motorway, on the site of the dozen or so public football pitches which ran end-to-end along the northern side of the railway track. Netless goalposts and the occasional slug trail of fading whitewash were all that punctuated the giant muddy bog which, on Sunday mornings, was transformed into a sea of faded football strips as hungover pub teams sought to outdo one another on the field of play.

Mum never allowed us near the pitches when games were in progress, because of the industrial language and the potential for violence. Sectarian tensions simmered beneath the surface of many of the ties, and there were tales of referees being knee-capped, razors being pulled on opponents, and even players being shot at by spectators.

The people who lived in the brown houses on Maxwell Drive were livid that their homes would now back onto a motorway, as well as a railway, but Mum was delighted because, she said, it would provide another barrier between our estate and Govan.

Now the pitches were being churned up by bulldozers and were strewn with tons of scaffolding, concrete blocks, cranes and builders' huts. Giant concrete cylinders, which were to provide the columns for the raised approach to the Kingston Bridge, lay end-to-end, forming a network of tunnels, which, for the purposes of our games, had been recast as a wartime underground bunker.

The flats on Porter Street, where Dizzy Gillespie and Jebsy MacBride lived, had been demolished to make way for the motorway. They were a series of functional blocks, situated in overgrown and dilapidated grounds, each comprising four storeys and cloaked in graffiti. Their hallways were cold and squalid and they had a strong smell of disinfectant, which didn't quite manage to mask the stench of the urine that was habitually administered across the walls and in the concrete stairwells.

The flats were around twenty years old, new in comparison with the Victorian tenements, but flimsy and substandard. They hadn't presented much of a challenge to the wrecker's ball. A gentle nudge had been enough to send them crashing southward.

The former residents hadn't exactly been dragged kicking and screaming from their homes. They were off to begin new and more comfortable lives in peripheral towns like East Kilbride and Cumbernauld. They departed without fanfare, or even a backward glance, like evacuees from a volcanic eruption, their homes left as lava-cast monuments to their final moments in them.

Doors had been left unlocked and carpets, furniture and even personal possessions abandoned. Clothes remained draped over radiators and half-empty tea cups were stacked haphazardly on draining boards. Ashtrays sat piled high with the pinched stubs of cigarettes.

These ghost homes had become a playground for us, which we explored like archaeologists mining relics from a forgotten civilisation. Each room was a treasure trove of possibilities, each new find had a back story to be imagined and interpreted.

In one flat, we found a collection of dusty photographs, postcards and cheap crockery all bearing the imprint of John F. Kennedy, and we speculated that the family who lived there had been involved in his assassination. On the mantelpiece was a now dysfunctional cigarette lighter in the shape of a flintlock pistol which, Chabs suggested, was proof of a gun fixation. We considered taking the evidence to the police, but decided against it on the grounds that, if they weren't prepared to take seriously our warnings concerning Daft Davie, then we shouldn't go out of our way to help them.

In a plastic carrier bag in another flat we found a dog-eared magazine, no bigger than a paperback book, which told a story in photographs. It began with a man arriving at his car, parked on a busy street, being served a parking ticket by a lady traffic warden. The man pointed to his watch to indicate that he hadn't been away for long.

On the next page, the pair had moved inside a lock-up garage, and the man was pouring the warden a glass of whisky. She was seated on the bonnet of his car. Then he climbed on top of her and they started to kiss, like Burt Lancaster and Deborah Kerr in *From Here to Eternity*. But then it wasn't like *From Here to Eternity*. They took off their clothes until they were naked and they got into strange and improbable positions, like they were playing nude Twister.

I had seen women's tits before in the newspapers on display in the local library. We used to tear out the page threes and keep them until the librarians got wise to it and shooed us away when they saw us approaching.

But this was the first time I had ever seen a real, naked, human fanny. My first impression was that it was a bit of a disappointment – it was just a big mound of hair. On the next page the woman was kneeling down in front of the man and there was a little black circle covering her mouth and his willie.

Everyone sat in stunned silence, crowded around Bifter who was turning the pages. Suddenly Cuddihy started laughing and Chabs followed and, before long, everyone was rolling around the floor in hysterics. I joined in although I didn't really know what I was supposed to find funny.

– That's the best shag mag I've ever seen, Wally said.

– Nah, I've seen better than that, said Cuddihy.

My ears pricked up. I wasn't aware of any shagging going on but then I wouldn't have recognised a shag unless it was pointed out to me. I tried to grab the magazine from Bifter so that I could take a proper look, but he pulled it away.

– Ah, ah, finders, keepers, he said, stuffing it down the front of his shorts. I'll have a proper shufty through this later on.

I felt stupid and frustrated. This had been my big chance to find out what a shag was at first hand. The photographic evidence had been there before me, and I had missed it. If I was to make a scene now, I might betray my ignorance so I decided to let it go.

In another flat, we found a telephone, still connected to the exchange and we spent hours dialling random numbers in the hope of reaching people in far flung corners of the earth. The furthest we got was Wolverhampton where an angry woman said she'd ring the police.

Cuddihy showed us something his big brother had done, where he phoned someone and asked to speak to Mr Walls. When they said there was no Mr Walls there, he asked to speak to Mrs Walls. When they said there was no Mrs Walls there, he asked if there were any Walls at all. When they said no, he asked how they kept their ceiling up. That was a good one.

After a few weeks of excitement and intrigue at the flats, the demolition crews arrived. They started by removing all the contents, then the floors began to disappear, making our visits increasingly hazardous, until all that remained were the exterior walls. Finally, the bulldozers moved in and turned them to rubble.

The area was cleared and a section fenced off to house all the materials that would be needed to build the motorway. There were timbers of every shape and size, copper pipes, cladding, insulating materials, metal bolts and couplings, giant nails and screws, and an assortment of plastic pipes and wiring.

We spent some time sweeping the perimeter, gathering intelligence for a possible raid. It had a security guard who patrolled the place at night, along with two dogs, but, during the day, it was empty for long periods, between the arrival and departure of the lorries, which visited to load up with supplies. At those times, the large gates at the entrance remained open and unmanned.

We arranged to meet round the back of the Co-op on a Saturday morning, when the depot was at its quietest. We planned to launch a commando strike – in and out in a few minutes – as the longer we delayed, the greater was our risk of being caught.

Chabs and Cuddihy were assigned timber. Given the size of the chipboard and plywood sheets, it would take two people to carry them. Wally was on metals – pipes, nails, screws, bolts, brackets etc. – and Bifter was given plastics. I was on soft materials, such as claddings and foams.

Ideally, we would have liked an edgy man on duty, but Johnny Nae Da had cried off, pleading a verruca. He sounded convincing enough, but we all suspected his heart was no longer in the edgy game, and discussions were already taking place to recruit a replacement for next year's apple raiding season.

We arranged to take all the materials that we liberated to the disused railway station at Dumbreck and store them in the old ticket office until we needed them. We had, as yet, not given any thought to what they might be needed for – our policy was to steal first and ask questions later.

Come the appointed time on Saturday morning everyone was present, except Wally. Suddenly he swung around the corner on a pushbike. Everyone stood admiring his new acquisition – a well-maintained, second-hand red Raleigh Colt.

– Nice wheels, Cuddihy said.

– Yeah, the old man had a win on the horses and decided to treat me, Wally said nonchalantly.

He caught my eye and held it, challenging me to contradict him.

– Didn't know your dad played the geegees, I said. Thought he was more of a dogs man.

Wally smiled weakly. I rehearsed in my head what would have transpired after I had left him the other night, the night I had felt such pity for him and his luckless, impoverished existence.

He would have returned to Fleurs Avenue and sat a safe distance from the old woman's house, keeping watch until the lights were out. He may have smoked a few cigarettes stolen from his father while he waited. Then, when he was convinced the coast was clear, he would have made his way into her garden, probably via a circuitous route of other people's properties, making certain he hadn't been spotted. Of course he wouldn't have been – he was far too clever for that. And without making a sound, he'd have spirited the bike away.

I knew that he knew how reprehensible his actions were – stealing from an old woman – otherwise, why was he not prepared to admit to the others what he'd done? I couldn't bring myself to smile back.

– Stroke of luck, eh, Walls?

With everyone now present, we finalised tactics. Our last remaining task, before moving in, was to memorise false names and addresses, which we would give in the event of being caught. We set off with a swagger – these, after all, were the moments of excitement that you lived for.

This was the real deal – like David Niven, about to enter occupied territory in *The Guns of Navarone*. I had a sick feeling in my stomach at the thought of what lay ahead, but I didn't let on to the others. After my supposed near-death experience on the scrumping raid on Glencairn Drive I was still riding the crest of a massive wave of public approval and I couldn't compromise that by showing any signs of weakness now.

After we crossed the bridge on Gower Street, we hunkered down in the long grass of the railway embankment overlooking the depot and kept watch. A lorry, collecting scaffolding rods, had just departed, and another arrived to load up with underground drainage pipes. After a lifetime, it drove off, leaving the site deserted.

Wally left his new bike lying flat in the long grass, and we made our way down from the rise. When we were sure there was no-one around, we entered by the gate, swarming across the yard to our various areas of interest like ants commandeering a sugar factory. There were whoops of excitement at the range of gear that was there for the taking. Chabs and Cuddihy piled several sheets of timber on top of one another and were out of the place within a minute, carrying them like ambulance men with a stretcher.

From another corner, I heard the clunk of metal as Wally piled anything he could lay his hands on into a sack, which he had found lying around. When he tried to lift it, though, he found that it was too heavy, and he was forced to offload some of the haul. Bifter was juggling several plastic socket bends and junctions as he departed. I had found a large roll of thermal insulation padding, which I was trying to manhandle across the yard.

Suddenly, a truck swung through the gates, blocking my path. Three men sat in the cab, and several others were standing on the trailer behind. I froze, terrified, and felt my heart pounding. My mouth contracted with dryness. I let go of the roll and tried to sprint around the vehicle but the driver opened his door to block my path. He jumped out and grabbed me.

– Right, I want your name and address, he said angrily. I'm sick to death of you thieving little bastards.

My mind went blank. I had been rehearsing a false name all morning and now I couldn't remember it. I stared at him for a few seconds, but I could see he was growing impatient.

– Come on, what's your name? he demanded.

– William Watson, I said, blurting out the first name that came into my head.

I panicked. William Watson was a boy in my class. He was big. If the cops turned up at his door, word was bound to get back that I'd landed him in it and he'd give me a doing.

– Wanson, I said, correcting myself. William Wanson.

The driver looked at me suspiciously.

– William Wanson, he repeated, writing the name down on the scrap of paper. That's a first. Address?

Again I couln't remember my false address. It had been Something Crescent.

– Crescent, I said, hoping that would buy me some time until I was able to recall the more crucial detail.

– Aye, what Crescent's that, sonny? he bellowed.

– Crescent Road, I stammered.

– What number?

– A hundred.

– Right, so let me get this straight. You're William Wanson of one hundred Crescent Road? he said, betraying the impression that he wasn't altogether convinced of the veracity of my answers. I have to tell you, William Wanson, I've never heard of Crescent Road.

– Oh, it's just over the hill there, up the road and along a bit, I said trying to sound convincing.

The others in the van were pressing him to leave, so, reluctantly, he told me to scarper. I ran as fast as I could without looking back, faster than I'd ever run before, until I thought my lungs would burst.

Avoiding the old railway station, in case I was being followed, I headed over the bridge and along Maxwell Drive in the direction of Nithsdale Road. When I was sure that no-one was on my tail, I slowed to a trot and, finally, to walking pace. I continued to walk, with no intended destination – a nervous instinct kept me moving.

Suddenly, I heard my name being called from a distance. My heart missed a beat, but when I turned around I saw it was Wally, on his bike. He caught up with me and told me what had happened to him. The truck had been driving down Porter Street just as he and the others were heading in the opposite direction. They'd been forced to drop all the gear they were carrying and make a dash for it. Everyone headed in different directions, and

Wally was sure they'd all escaped. He had gone back to the railway embankment for his bike.

I told him how I had been captured and practically tortured for the names and addresses of everyone in the gang but that I had stood firm and refused to yield. How the driver had me, bound and gagged, in the truck and was set to take me to their headquarters where, he said, they had more persuasive methods of getting me to talk. But then, when they were loading up, I'd managed to work my hands free from the ropes and had made a run for it.

– Who knows what they'd have done if I hadn't escaped, I said, breathlessly.

– They could have used any number of torture techniques, Wally said with evident authority. They could have kneecapped you like the IRA do. That's where they take a hammer to your kneecaps or, if they want to make it slower and more painful, they use a Black & Decker to drill from the back of your leg through the kneecap.

– One of them did sound like he had an Irish accent, I said.

– Well there you are then. Sounds like you had a very lucky escape, my son.

We walked on a bit in silence.

– Or, it's possible they could have used torture techniques from the Japanese prisoner-of-war camps, Wally continued. Like water torture or sticking a boiled egg up your arse.

– I don't think any of them were Japanese, I said.

We decided it would be best if we headed for the Cunyon to lie low for a while until we were sure the dust had settled. I climbed onto the seat of the bike and Wally gave me a backy.

The Cunyon was an area of wasteland situated on a hill, which ran from the top end of Hamilton Avenue all the way down to the railway track. As with our estate, it provided a buffer between the big houses of Pollokshields and the high flats at Dumbreck. Vastly overgrown, it occupied several acres of thick grassland, which had been neglected for so long that the grass stretched high above our heads. It was navigable along a single, twisting, tree-encumbered path, which opened out onto a patch of scrub-land known as the Seven Hills, after a series of hardened slag heaps, which doubled as bicycle ramps for Evel Knievel-type stunts. Actually, there were more than seven, but the Nine Hills didn't have the same ring.

We found a clearing and sat down. It had been raining, and the ground was damp, but I didn't care. My legs were quivering so much that I had to take my weight off them. Wally lit a fag, and I chewed on a long grass.

After we'd exhausted every last detail of the morning's abortive raid and speculated about all the possible repercussions, I raised the issue of the stolen bike. As expected, my diagnosis had been correct in virtually every detail other than the bullishness with which Wally was prepared to defend his actions. I left him in no doubt that I disapproved but I wasn't prepared for the force of his rebuttal.

– So if stealing's such a big sin, how come it's OK to steal from the motorway yard? What about apple raiding? That's steal-ing as well, he countered.

– That's different, I said.

– How's it different? It's all stealing. What's the big deal?

– The big deal is that she was a nice old lady who never did you any harm.

– Och, yer talking pure shite. Why should I care about her?

– Because she trusted us.

Wally looked at me, bewildered. If he understood what I was saying at all, he wasn't showing it.

– What are you talking about, she trusted us? She had a posh accent and she lived in a nice house. When do you think the last time was that she slept in a midden? Her poncy wee grandson probably gets everything he wants. The fact is she had something I wanted, so I took it. She wasn't even using the bike, she's not going to miss it, so why should I lose any sleep over it?

I couldn't think of an answer. He had a point about apple

raiding and the motorway yard. There was also the small matter of the lead we'd stolen from the church roof last winter and sold to the scrappy, but since Wally hadn't raised it, I wasn't going to either. Somehow all those things seemed more like an adventure than committing a crime. If it was crime, it was victimless, or at least, if there was a victim, it wasn't one that had grey hair, who gave you biscuits and ginger.

As we were talking, we heard the sound of voices. We froze, daring the other to move. Slowly we got up and looked around. I started heading for the path, but Wally grabbed me. He whispered that we didn't know what direction the people were coming from so, whatever way we went, we could be headed straight for them.

Instead we crawled into the rough and crouched behind a bush. As we waited, the voices grew louder and it became obvious it was a man and a woman. Then they stopped talking, and all we could hear were their footsteps. They entered the clearing where Wally and I had been sitting, but, instead of rejoining the path, they headed into the rough, across the clearing from where we were hiding. We heard the woman giggle as they disappeared into the bushes. There was a brief, muffled conversation and then everything went quiet.

After a few moments of silence Wally motioned for us to leave. We crept out of our cover and back into the clearing without making a sound. As we were leaving we heard a wailing sound. We stopped and listened. It sounded like the woman was crying.

– Do you think she's all right? I whispered.

– I bet she's getting a shagging, Wally said.

I couldn't believe my luck.

– Let's go and have a look, I said.

– No chance. If the guy sees us, he'll kick our heads in, Wally said.

I thought for a moment. I knew he was right, but equally I knew that I couldn't let this opportunity pass me by. This might be my last chance to find out what a shag was before my ignorance was rumbled by my peers. I edged closer, picking my way through the foliage and lifting branches from my face as quietly as I could.

In the distance I saw the couple on a flattened-out patch of grass, which they had fashioned for themselves. I inched closer and could hear her moans grow louder and more frequent. They were lying flat out. He was on top of her with his trousers around his ankles. She had her skirt hoisted above her waist.

There was a hypnotic quality to the rhythm of his bare white bottom as it rose and descended with increasing frequency. I inched closer to get a better look and stood, transfixed.

I became aware of a feeling of euphoria overwhelming me. It was similar to the sensation I got when I was in Celeste's company, only deeper and more profound. It made my body tingle all over and my mind empty of all thoughts other than the minute detail of what was going on before me.

I felt a build-up as though this was all leading to some event of monumental importance, but I didn't know what and I didn't know when it would happen. Suddenly I felt an unbelievable high, which lasted for only a few seconds before giving way to a prolonged, cathartic rush like I was pissing my pants. I was experiencing the greatest feeling of my life and nothing else seemed to matter. Then I felt disorientated and unbalanced and I thought I was going to keel over.

Someone touched my arm and I jumped with fright. It was Wally, again entreating me to leave but, at that moment, wild elephants wouldn't have moved me.

I continued to stare at this mesmerising spectacle that, it seemed, was being performed solely for my delectation and education. Then something caught my attention that I hadn't noticed before, prompting me to shift my gaze from what was going on beneath the man's oscillating buttocks. There was something about the jacket that engendered a flicker of recognition – a wide-lapelled cream jacket with lime pinstripes. For the first time I looked at the man's face and I realised it was Tony.

9

The moment the bell sounded for home time, Wutherspoon made her usual, half-hearted attempt at crowd control, reminding everyone what she had set for homework and urging us all to leave the room quietly. The spontaneous eruption of chatter and the deafening screech as chairs were pushed from desks along the wooden floor drowned out her exhortations.

Witnessing the sudden, excited release of energy unleashed by forty seething ten-year-olds, after a day of compulsory spelling and multiplication tables, was like watching the face of a drowning man break the surface of a still pond and gasp for air.

I had slipped on my sand shoes ten minutes before the end of the lesson to hasten my departure and, by the time the bell had stopped ringing, I was halfway down the stairs. Within a minute, I was out of the building, sprinting homeward along Maxwell Drive like a whippet in a hurry.

It was Guy Fawkes Night, but my mind was on fireworks of another kind. After months of canvassing, harrying and lobbying, I had finally convinced Mum that I was old enough to attend my first football match – albeit with Tony acting as my chaperone. Celtic were playing Boavista of Portugal that night in a European Cup Winners Cup, second round, second leg tie, having drawn the first leg nothing each in Opporto a fortnight before.

Without wishing to overstate it, I believed my entire existence had been a rather unsatisfactory rehearsal for this single moment, when I would take my first, tentative steps into the revered sporting citadel that was Celtic Park.

I would finally bear witness to the sublime genius of Dixie

Deans in real time, in colour and in the flesh. I would stand amid a heaving throng of fellow travellers and pay awestruck homage to my heroes in green and white. I felt like a salivating carnivore who, after a lifetime subsisting on cheap cuts, was about to dine on prime fillet steak.

I arrived home to find Mum in the kitchen with Suzanne, a classmate from college. Mum was making dinner, and they were both drinking red wine. Mum rarely drank wine and never in the afternoon. I'd heard her talking about Suzanne before, in fact she seemed to occupy an increasingly prominent role in her conversation, but I had never met her. What struck me was how youthful she looked. She must have been almost as old as Mum because she had children who were ages with me and Sophia, but she was trendy and glamorous, just like Faye Dunaway.

She had been trying to talk Mum into joining her and a group of friends who were going to see John Martyn play at the college union. I had never heard of John Martyn and I had no idea what a college union was, but it sounded exotic and sophisticated.

– I'd love to come, but who would look after the children? Mum asked rhetorically.

I'd never looked at any of Mum's friends the way I was looking at Suzanne. They all appeared leathery and matronly, and they wore the same sexless uniform of pastel-coloured, tightly-tailored skirts, short jackets and flat shoes, with their hair ubiquitously held back in a stiff beehive.

Suzanne wore a pair of faded blue denims that hugged her tight bottom and fanned out as they descended towards her sandal-covered feet. Her toenails were painted pillar-box red. A loose-fitting cotton blouse flapped loosely around her tummy, the buttons unfastened to her breastbone revealing a bit of bra. She had wavy locks of chestnut hair, tied and held in a bun with a biro above her delicately sculpted face, which frequently broke into a wide, heart-stealing smile.

She was fetching cooking ingredients as Mum required them, and, as she knelt down to ferret in a ground-level cupboard for a tin of tomatoes, I glimpsed the tops of her fleshy breasts. She stood up and handed the tin to Mum, and, with her other hand, fastened two of the buttons on her blouse. In that single gesture, I knew I had been caught staring.

– What about your eldest, why can't he look after the children? she asked.

– That's all very well, but who would look after Tony? Mum replied as she chopped an onion. I need to be here to keep an eye on him to make sure he's studying. His prelims are in January, and he hasn't done a stroke of work.

– That's three months away, Christine. Give the boy a chance. Besides, you can't watch over them twenty-four hours a day. And I'd say you could do with a break. When was the last time you had a night out?

Mum and Dad rarely socialised and almost never together. When we were younger, they occasionally went out in foursomes with one of Mum's friends and her husband, or one of Dad's workmates and his wife, to the pictures or to a dinner dance, but they invariably returned home discussing some argument or mishap that had marred its success.

– I don't know, Mum said. I can't remember.

– What about Robert, why don't you ask him to babysit? Suzanne suggested.

– Oh, I could never do that, Mum said.

– Whyever not? My husband looks after the children all the time.

– Oh, I just couldn't. Robert would never do anything like that. We just don't have that kind of relationship.

– Well, it sounds like he needs to be dragged into the 1970s.

Ever since the episode at the Cunyon with Tony, I found it difficult to look at any female without thinking of *that* being done to her. Something strange had happened to me which I couldn't rationalise. I felt like I had peed myself, and, anticipating awkward questioning from Mum, I rinsed my Y-fronts through in the bathroom sink before depositing them in the laundry basket.

I obsessed about what I had witnessed, alternately denouncing it as a corrupt and sordid practice limited to my brother and the traffic warden from Bifter's shag mag and speculating that it might be more widespread. Perhaps everyone was at it – Mrs Gemmell, the school secretary? Reverend MacIver's wife? Mrs Yuill? Wutherspoon? Oh God, surely not Wutherspoon? Mum? Granny?

Merely giving such thoughts headroom filled me with a shivering sense of self-loathing but when my gaze rested on Suzanne, I experienced some of those same warm, comforting sensations. As I retrieved a milk bottle from the fridge to pour myself a glass, I stared deeply into her dark brown eyes and the memory came flooding back of the scene I had witnessed, with Tony grinding rhythmically on top of the girl whose hair cascaded across the damp grass . . .

– Watch what you're doing, you stupid boy, Mum shouted as the milk splashed across the floor. And close your mouth. You look like you're catching flies.

Suzanne had left by the time Tony arrived late home from school. He proceeded to fanny about, ironing a shirt and coiffing his hair in front of the mirror, just to piss me off. He knew how important this match was to me, and I could tell from his malicious grin that he was determined to wind me up.

Tony had little interest in football now. He had watched Rangers a few times when he was younger and briefly played for the school team, but then his attention switched to music. He built up a respectable collection of LPs and he went to see the Small Faces and the Sensational Alex Harvey Band at the Apollo before that interest gave way to his current passion for politics.

A detailed knowledge of football, music or motorbikes was an essential requirement if you were to have any degree of credibility at school. Occasionally another area of expertise was put before the court of public opinion and judgement passed, but it was rarely favourable.

Recent successes had included Angus Dickie's ability to name every item of field artillery used in the Second World War and Stephen Munro's amazingly detailed knowledge of the making of *Enter the Dragon*. Others given a positive approval rating included Tam Connolly (serial killers), Jamie Cameron (venomous insects) and Rab Quigley (disabling an opponent with a single blow to the larynx).

But for every expert in Mafia-style assassinations or Japanese martial arts, there were the traditional music buffs and the collectors of souvenir thimbles. It would have been easy to feel a modicum of pity for these otherwise personable souls whose single character flaw happened to be a talent for macramé or a fascination with sub-equatorial flora. But there was no room for sentimentality – they existed as objects of ridicule, to be ostracised and dispatched to the furthest reaches of the playground, where they would spend the rest of their schooldays considering the error of their risible predilections for woodwind instruments and postage stamps of the Eastern Bloc.

Tony got away with an interest in politics because he was older. But there was more to it than that. He got away with it because he was Tony. If anyone else had turned up at school displaying an abnormal familiarity with incomes policy and the balance of payments deficit they would have been given their underpants to play with while their head was used as a lavatory brush.

Tony was above all that. He wasn't the biggest guy in the secondary – he wasn't even the biggest guy in his class – but no-one dared challenge him because they risked being at the wrong end of one of his verbal volleys. By the age of sixteen, he could outwit most of the teachers, a skill that made him popular and feared among his peers in equal measure.

After he had finished his lengthy grooming process, he finally agreed that we could leave. We walked over the top of the hill onto Nithsdale Road to catch the fifty-nine into town. We would get off at Hope Street and walk across to Argyle Street where we would catch one of the buses that would take us along the Gallowgate, past the Fruitmarket and the Meatmarket, into the heart of the East End.

Alone together, I realised how ill-at-ease I still felt around Tony after the Cunyon incident. I had beat a hasty retreat as soon as I realised it was him with the girl, but my biggest concern remained that he might have seen me watching. If he had, he hadn't said anything, but it was a strange experience, not being able to look straight in the eye someone I had known all my life, or to hold a conversation with him that wasn't stilted and disjointed. I felt sure that he must have noticed the awkwardness which had entered our relationship but, again, he didn't say anything.

We stood in silence until the bus arrived. We sat on the top deck so that Tony could have a smoke, and he started telling me a story about Mr Seaman, his English teacher, whose nickname was Spunky, for reasons that were never properly explained to me.

– Spunky was having a go at Wallington today, going on about how useless he was, Tony explained. He's standing at the board, all cocky-like, and he goes, If you look up 'stupid' in the dictionary, there's a picture of you, Wallington.

Spunky was known as a bully who picked on the slower pupils and tried to humiliate them in front of the rest of the class. That kind of behaviour was acceptable if it was one pupil doing it to another, but when a teacher was involved, it fostered a spirit of classroom solidarity.

– So, quick as a flash, I says to him, Wallington wasn't the one who had to look up 'stupid' in the dictionary.

I laughed out loud.

– Bastard gave me six of the strap. Was worth it though, seeing him take a beamer like that.

Wallington ended up failing all his O-Grades and getting a job on the production line at WD & HO Wills, the cigarette factory in Dennistoun. It was later discovered he was dyslexic.

While my brother's keen intelligence made him a hit with his classmates, it was becoming a source of increasing tension at home where Dad resented his position as family sage being usurped by an upstart less than half his age.

I couldn't help feeling sorry for Dad. By his own admission, he hadn't had a proper education, but he was used to voicing his opinions frequently and forcefully in the comfort and safety of his own home, without being challenged. Dad voted Labour because he'd always voted Labour, although many of his convictions didn't coincide with the party's policies. He supported the rights of workers over the rights of bosses (while simultaneously believing that unions had become too powerful); he was suspicious of foreigners; and he believed a woman's place was in the home. While the subjects upon which he pontificated – at the table, or while drowning out television newsreaders – were wide-ranging, they invariably reflected one of these three positions.

Now, with Tony as the self-appointed arbiter of our ideological purity, every utterance Dad presented as a statement of fact had to be supported by evidence, every statistic sourced and every opinion justified. Our living room became an adversarial chamber of ill-tempered debate. While the detail of what was discussed passed me by, it was clear that Dad was almost perpetually on the back foot, arguing from a position of relative ignorance, and he inevitably resorted to accusing Tony of spouting idealistic claptrap and of being an arrogant little sod.

By the time the bus reached Eglington Toll, Tony was in the middle of a story about how Billy Gemmell, a guy in his history class, had grown women's tits after eating sherbet dib dabs. It bore all the hallmarks of a Tony classic but it had broken the ice so I allowed him to continue.

Gemmell, whose wee brother Alec was in my year at the Primary, had lived in the flats in Porter Street until they were demolished, and then the family moved away to a three-bedroom semi- in Irvine new town. Or so I thought. According to Tony's version of events the family had moved abroad. He claimed Billy was rushed to the Victoria Infirmary one morning last year after waking to find that he had developed a full set of female breasts.

The medical staff ran a series of tests and discovered high levels of a chemical in his body found only in sherbet dib dabs. The makers of sherbet dib dabs offered the family a million pounds and a lifetime's supply of bras to hush up the scandal so they took the cash and emigrated to Canada.

– So how come Deek Devlin doesn't have women's tits and he's never done eating sherbet fountains? I asked.

– It only works with sherbet dib dabs, Tony countered.

– It's the same sherbet. They're made by the same company. Tony thought for a moment.

– The chemical is in the lollies. Sherbet fountains don't have lollies, they've got liquorice.

As we walked through the centre of town, the emergence of Celtic supporters began as a trickle, with occasional flashes of colour appearing randomly from buses, pub doorways and side streets, like the first pieces being laid in the construction of a giant jigsaw.

The further east we travelled, so the picture took more shape, with increasingly frequent sightings of hats, scarves and flags until, half a mile from the ground, in every direction, was a mass of emerald, white and gold.

By that stage, the traffic had ground to a halt, and it was quicker to walk than catch another bus. The air was heavily charged, and I was breathless with nervous anticipation. We were early – it was still forty-five minutes before kick-off – but everyone seemed in a hurry, as though to proceed at a normal walking pace was to disrespect the enormity of the occasion.

Brightly decorated ice-cream vans and hot dog stalls lined the route, and singing by drunk but good-natured fans lent a carnival atmosphere to proceedings. In the distance, the floodlit stadium illuminated the night sky.

The ground had a bygone age feel, like a Victorian workhouse, with long queues of chain smoking men snaking back from the stiff, grinding turnstiles. Tradition held that boys were lifted over in return for a small consideration to the operator. This was a European tie and, officially, tickets had to be bought in advance, but we still saw boys being lifted over.

From the moment we stepped inside the ground, we were helpless flotsam on a sea of bodies, crammed into a space designed for half the number. I had never experienced anything like it, caught on a wave of human momentum, dragging me in one direction and then another.

There was little point in taking a stand against this irresistible tide. All I could do was go with the flow, gripping tightly onto Tony's arm so as not to become separated from him.

Across the pitch was the stand, the only modern part of the stadium, where the club's directors and their fat cat hangers-on sat smoking large cigars and looking self-satisfied. But this was where the real live football experience was to be had, on the long sweeping terraces where the fans stood, shoulder to shoulder, packed like sardines.

Eventually, after the last of the fans had filtered through the gates, and there was some respite from the crush, we tried to find somewhere to watch the game. We settled on a spot at the edge of the traditional Celtic end, which didn't give us the best view but saved us from the worst of the overcrowding.

A potent cocktail of smells filled the air, from the food sold on the terraces by uniformed vendors – greasy Scotch pies and Bovril – and the stale alcohol on people's breath. As time passed, and the drink passed through its normal channels, it gave way to the overpowering odour of urine.

What struck me was the unreconstructed maleness of everything. With so many men gathered together in one place, normal rules of human engagement didn't apply. People belched, farted, vomited and relieved themselves on the terraces, and I heard swear words that I didn't know existed. The conversation was uniformly negative and aggressive, as though to say anything positive about anything – even the performance of the team – was fanciful and effeminate.

Tony needed a pee but couldn't bring himself to do it on the terracing, so he decided to brave the crowd again to seek out the toilets. I didn't need, which, I was later to discover, was an almighty blessing. The toilets were dark and clammy, with all the charm of a Turkish prison. The first instinct of most who patronised the facilities was to piss. Worrying about where they pissed was somewhere lower on their list of priorities. By the time Tony arrived, well before kick-off, the place was awash with urine, and the basins and toilet bowls were overflowing.

While he was away, I was temporarily adopted by a middle-aged couple who must have noticed how terrified I looked. They were sober, which set them apart from most of those around them and the woman was, conspicuously, one of very few at the game. They smiled at me, and I smiled back.

– The troops are out in full force tonight, the man said.

– Aye, right enough, mister, I said, trying to sound suitably informed about such matters.

– Where are ye from, sonny? the woman asked.

– Pollokshields.

– Oh right. Don't know that area. Where's that then?

– Southside.

– Ah. What school do you go to then?

I thought for a minute.

– Our Lady of the Immaculate Conception , I lied, not wanting them to know that I went to a Proddy school. They looked harmless enough, but you never knew who was listening in.

Just at that moment Tony returned and saw that they had been looking out for me.

– Thanks for doing that, he said. It's his first match.

At that moment, I could have killed him.

*

With my usual, impeccable timing, I had taken an interest in football, and decided to support Celtic, just as the club was coming to the end of the greatest run of success in its history. They had just won the last of nine league championships in a row – a world record. This was the first year in a decade that they hadn't qualified for the European Cup, the continent's top trophy. Jimmy Johnstone, Celtic's greatest ever player, and Billy McNeil, their greatest ever captain, had recently left the club and Jock Stein, their greatest ever manager had been involved in a near-fatal car crash from which he had never fully recovered.

But from the moment the team ran onto the park that night and 60,000 fans erupted in a frenzied harmony of passion and commitment, I knew that I had found my spiritual home. The ground felt like a giant, protective blanket, and suddenly all the negatives – the drunks, the filth, the dilapidated surround-ings, the fact the club's golden age was at an end – no longer mattered.

Celtic won 3–1, Dixie Deans scoring five minutes from the end to seal the team's passage into the quarter-finals. Even Tony admitted it was a great match and he had enjoyed himself. On the way home we bought Mars Bars and a bottle of Irn-Bru and discussed each of the goals in minute detail.

He said the crap food, the run-down terraces and the drunken crowd was all part of the football experience. You had to suffer a little because there was no salvation without pain, no proper appreciation of pleasure until you had experienced hurt. If the price of winning league championships and European cups was standing in a decrepit stadium, ankle deep in navvies' piss, then it was a price worth paying.

– Supporting a football team teaches you the two most valuable attributes: loyalty and a sense of justice, he said. Once you choose your football team, it's with you for the rest of your life. How you respond is a test of your loyalty. You won't be judged on the commitment you show during the good times, when the team is winning and the stadium is full. It's how you respond during the bad times that matters – the lean years, when the trophy room is bare.

I listened intently and I felt our relationship was back where it belonged. Adults were always talking about high-minded stuff but Tony was the only one who could make it meaningful and relevant.

I didn't care what he got up to in the Cunyon – that was his business. All that mattered was that we were friends again, and it had all been made possible because of football. That was the beauty of the game. It meant that whatever problems you were faced with, whatever issues threatened your peace of mind, they could always be overcome by ignoring them and talking about football instead.

By the time we got off the bus at the top of Gower Street, it was almost eleven o'clock. The only time I had been up later was at Hogmanay. Already I was looking forward to the morning, when I could tell Dad all about the match. But when we arrived home, he was already back from the restaurant, sitting in the living room with Mum, drinking tea. They both looked serious, like something very bad had happened.

10

It was the first time I had heard the word 'redundancy'. It sounded like such an adult word. Even when it was explained to me, I didn't understand it. How could someone not have a job? A job was what you got when you left school. Everyone had one. Well, everyone except Johnny Nae Da's Mum, but she had angina.

My immediate reaction wasn't unfavourable. If redundancy meant having Dad around to cook French toast every morning, it couldn't be all bad. But then Tony pointed out that, if Dad wasn't working, he wasn't earning and if he wasn't earning, there would be no money to pay for French toast, or anything else for that matter, including tickets to see Celtic.

The development presented Sophia with a potentially significant setback in her campaign to get Dad to pay for a ticket to see the Bay City Rollers. It would have been enough to convince most people that they were flogging a dead horse, but Sophia wasn't most people. Her reaction was an object lesson in never-say-die endurance – of relentless buttering-up and manipulation.

Sickeningly, but ingeniously, she offered to take a cut in her pocket money to ease pressure on the family budget. She even said she would look for a Saturday job. Carter, the newsagent, was always looking for paper boys and girls, and every little would help. Of course she knew full well that Dad would never hear of it. His view, as he often reminded us, was that men worked and women stayed at home. The thought of Sophia wandering the streets in the early hours, delivering newspapers, was unthinkable. Dad kissed her on the cheek, thanked her for her consideration, but said that wouldn't be necessary. She beamed triumphantly.

Feeling under pressure to make some small gesture of my own to boost the household finances, I offered to rein in my food consumption – vegetables in particular – and to cut down on my use of toiletries, but Mum said we weren't that hard up.

It was Saturday afternoon, and we were all having lunch together. Dad was looking sheepish, like he had something controversial to say.

– If I don't get a job soon, you might have to think about giving up college and going back to the Post Office full-time, Christine, he said.

Everyone looked at Mum.

– Well, that's a bridge we can cross when we come to it, she said calmly.

– We're there now, Christine. My redundancy money won't last forever.

Mum stood up and started to clear the dishes away.

– Let's not get ahead of ourselves, Robert. You only lost your job last week.

Dad was flustered, like he was about to lose his temper.

– Children, go to your bedrooms, your mother and I have things to discuss.

– It's one thirty in the afternoon, Tony pointed out.

– Well, go outside and do something.

Tony stayed to argue it out, but I couldn't bear the thought of another row, so I went into the garden with my jar of conkers. They'd been soaking in malt vinegar for a fortnight, and the time had come to begin the process of drying them and stringing them on a shoelace in preparation for the season ahead.

Sophia appeared behind me and told me how impressive they looked, which immediately made me suspicious.

– I bet you'll win lots of matches with that big one there, she said, betraying a ludicrous ignorance of the sport. The big ones had a greater surface area and were, therefore, more prone to splitting. It was the small, tough ones that won you matches.

– What do you want? I asked her.

– Why should I want anything? Can't I just pass the time of day with my favourite brother? Don't be so suspicious.

After another few moments of pointless chit chat she finally revealed her motive. She wanted me to go somewhere with her. She wouldn't tell me where or the reason why, only that there was someone she wanted me to meet, which made me even warier. Sophia never requested my company and she had certainly never sought to parade me in company.

She dragged me across the road to the Proffy where Gordon Cummings was waiting with his wee sister, Lyndsey. I'd seen Sophia walking home from school with Cumbo a couple of times, but I never thought anything of it. She was always hanging around with boys. Lyndsey was in my year at the Primary, but in a different class. I knew her to look at – she had sat on the coach seat in front of me on the school trip to Troon last year, and I often saw her playing with Samantha Henry and Joanne Moffat outside her house on Maxwell Drive. But I'd never spoken to her – in fact I'd barely given her a second thought.

Sophia grabbed me by the arm and stood me, toe-to-toe, with Lyndsey.

– She fancies you. Do you want to be her boyfriend? she asked matter-of-factly.

Lyndsey flushed with embarrassment and turned away.

– I do not, she protested.

– Shut it, Lyndsey, said Cumbo. She does too. She told us she does.

I didn't know what to say. It was certainly the most humiliating experience of my life, and my heart was pounding like a Lambeg drum on an Orange Walk. My face burned with such intensity that I could feel my ears glow.

– Well? Do you want to go out with her or not? Sophia demanded.

– No, I do not, I blurted out, indignantly.

Sophia and Cumbo both sighed loudly. Cumbo turned to face me, his shoulders dropped and he smiled, then he put his arm around me. I liked Cumbo. He had a reputation as a bit of a hard man, but the only time our paths had crossed before was when he did me a favour. The chain had come off my bike outside the Co-op and he helped me put it back on.

– Look, let's start again, he said, squeezing my arm in a matey sort of way. Me and your sister . . .

– Sophia, I said, trying to control my breathing.

– Yeah, Sophia. Me and Sophia are going for a little walk through Bellahouston Park. Then we might go up Gino's for milkshakes and pancakes. With golden syrup.

I nodded as if I had the first clue about where this conversation was heading or why it should have anything to do with me.

– We've invited Lyndsey and, since she fancies you . . .

– I do not fancy him, Lyndsey protested.

– I said, shut it, Cumbo ordered, his tone immediately changing from matey to sinister. Since she fancies you, we thought you might want to come along to keep her company. And, of course, we'd treat you to a milkshake and pancakes. With golden syrup.

He stood staring at me, wide-eyed and expectant. Lyndsey was facing the other way to hide her obvious mortification.

– So, wee man, what do you say? Are you in or are you out?

I was faced with a dilemma. Until then, I had spent my life avoiding girls. At school, boys and girls were kept in separate playgrounds, and in the classroom, where we were given the freedom to mix, no-one did. The golden rule was that you shunned girls, in any forum, in any context, because they represented the antithesis of everything that we boys held to be worthwhile.

It wasn't just that they were boring, annoying, stupid and untrustworthy, or that they couldn't climb a wall or a gate or a fence or a tree without getting their tights caught. It wasn't just that they couldn't run in a straight line or that, whenever they tried to play football, they defiled the beautiful game, turning it into a grotesque parody, like a cross between yoga and performance art.

It was more fundamental than that. Being in the company of a girl was a dereliction of maleness. Girls existed as a rejection of everything that boys stood for, and their presence alone was enough to contaminate those essential principles of masculinity.

Boys played loud music, they didn't bathe for weeks on end, and they regarded nose-picking as a spectator sport. Shoes were worn to be scuffed, trousers to be split at the crotch and pants to be stained with bodily filth. If something was worth picking up, it was worth dropping and breaking. Anything with a resale value was there to be stolen, sensitivities existed to be trampled upon, and disputes were settled with fists, not words.

The only boy in our class who had broken the golden rule was Mark Crawford, who had disgraced himself – and his sex – by taking a shine to Susan Patterson. He bought her a quarter of pick 'n' mix at Woolworth's, scribbled his initials on the bag and left them inside her desk. When word of his romantic infatuation got out, it spread like wildfire and his reputation was shot.

Ostracised by his closest friends, sacked by his gang, he couldn't have found a marbles game if his life depended on it. The biggest tragedy was that the whole thing backfired on him spectacularly, because Susan Patterson scoffed all the sweets like a fat bitch and then told him she didn't fancy him anyways.

I had seen the devastating, feminising influence of girls at first hand, on Tony. One minute he was a normal, soap-averse boy, listening to Queen, putting his feet up on bus seats, picking detritus from between his toes and sniffing it. The next he was up to his neck in bubble bath, window-shopping for gonks, humming Carpenters' songs and doing *that* up the Cunyon.

Under normal circumstances I would rather have sold Dixie Deans to Rangers than spend a moment in the company of Lyndsey Cummings, but milkshakes and pancakes had been mentioned – with golden syrup – and I was about to learn the importance of two new additions to my vocabulary, pragmatism and compromise.

When we arrived at the gates of Bella Park, Sophia and Cumbo disappeared inside the walled gardens. Cumbo said they were going to have a wander around to look at the flowers and stuff, and that Lyndsey and I would just be bored so we should stand outside. For some reason Sophia found this very funny indeed.

We couldn't see them behind the walls but we could make out snippets of their conversation. Cumbo must have been the funniest guy in the world because Sophia spent the whole time giggling maniacally at everything he said. Sophia kept saying No and Stop it, because she Wasn't Ready.

After a while they must have disappeared to the other side of the gardens because we could no longer hear them. Lyndsey and I stood in deafening, pulsating silence, avoiding one another's gaze and shuffling our feet. After what seemed like an eternity, Lyndsey spoke.

– I don't fancy you, by the way, she said.

At that moment, and despite every instinct I harboured to the contrary, my heart sank a little.

– Aye, I know, I said.

There was another long silence. Bored with drawing pictures with my shoe in the gravel, I coughed up some phlegm to see how far I could gob it.

– They only said that to get you along – that I fancied you, she added.

– Oh, right, I replied, not quite sure what she was talking about.

– My mum wouldn't let Gordon out unless he took me with him. Him and Sophia cooked up this plan to get you to come along to keep me out of their hair.

– Oh, right.

I looked at Lyndsey properly for the first time. I had to admit she was pretty. She had a petite, perfectly formed nose, dotted with a few freckles, and her face was framed by a bob of light brown hair, with a fringe cut slightly above her eyebrows. She looked smart in a white knitted jumper with a panda bear pattern on the front and a tartan skirt.

I considered how I would have looked to her. I was wearing a pair of brown nylon trousers and a pea green Simon shirt.

Both were hand-me-downs from Tony and had clearly seen better days. Over the Simon shirt I was wearing one of Sophia's old cardigans which was a mustardy yellow and full of holes. On my feet was a pair of torn black plimsolls. My fingernails were black and bitten, and my hair was uncombed. I hadn't had a bath for three weeks. Suddenly I felt a pang of self-awareness and an irrational desire to improve my appearance.

After another long wait, Sophia and Cumbo emerged, arm in arm, from the gardens and we set off for Gino's. They proceeded at a snail's pace along the Paisley Road, frequently stopping to whisper to each other and share jokes, so we ended up miles ahead of them.

Lyndsey said she was fed up with her brother because all he ever thought about was girls. She couldn't understand why any girl would want to go near him because he was so irritating. I hadn't expected her to say that. I told her I agreed; that my brother was the same. I couldn't understand why anyone would want to hang about with girls all the time. I hated them and I was never going to get married to one. Realising my gaffe, I said I didn't mean her and I hadn't meant to cause any offence. She said it was OK, that she understood.

Sophia and Cumbo finally caught up just as we were approaching Gino's. In a previous incarnation Gino's had been a traditional Italian café – with seated booths, Pyrex cups, typed menus, fried egg rolls and large jars of boiled sweets – until its owner decided it required a facelift. Now it had the garish showiness of a fairground ride. The walls were a psychedelic collage of bright swirling colours, and a long pink bar ran the length of the back wall, lined with optics containing bottles of radiant milk shake concentrate. Orange and red, cloud-shaped Perspex signs advertised the various delicacies on offer.

In front of the bar was a row of candy-striped, PVC-topped swivel stools, bolted to the floor. Those which hadn't been pockmarked with cigarette burns were slashed and oozed grimy, yellowing foam. Behind the bar the eponymous Gino stood at a griddle, unshaved and dressed in a dirty white tunic and toque, smoking a cigarette while tossing pancakes unenthusiastically. There was a toxic aroma of overheated cooking oil mixed with stale tobacco smoke.

The place had the look and smell of a 1950s American soda fountain as imagined by a lugubrious Scots-Italian whose zest for life had long since been trampled underfoot by the twin realities of financial hardship and clinical depression. But I was oblivious to its shortcomings. It represented a level of sophistication unparalleled in my social experience. Eating out was not something we did as a family. Eating out, unaccompanied by my parents was a novelty, which no amount of ketchup-stained, grease-soaked, schlock décor was going to diminish.

I ordered a strawberry milkshake and a pancake with golden syrup and vanilla ice-cream. The pancake arrived without garnish or fanfare, a triumph of minimalist, bottom-line conscious portion control. The milkshake came in a tall frosted Pyrex glass with two paper straws. I rolled the pancake with my fingers, mopped up the syrup and wolfed it down. Then I scooped up the ice-cream and the last of the syrup with my spoon before draining the milkshake, through the straws, in two long, audible sooks.

I was the first to finish by a metric mile. Sophia and Cumbo had hardly touched theirs because they had spent most of the time giggling and touching each other. Lyndsey hadn't eaten very much of hers, and she must have been conscious of me staring at her plate, because she asked me if I wanted some. I felt guilty but said yes, anyway, and helped myself to a couple of large mouthfuls.

I had expected her conversation to be all about dolls and flowers and boring stuff like that, but she had some good stories. She told me about the time her dad slammed the car door on her hand by mistake and it went up like a big purple balloon. She lost the nails from two of her fingers. It took three weeks for them to become dislodged completely and, in the meantime, one of them became poisoned and spewed gallons of thick, yellow pus.

She also told me how a friend of a friend of her cousin adopted a stray puppy when they were on a camping holiday abroad. It followed them everywhere, and, at the end of the holiday, they couldn't bear to part with it so they decided to bring it home with them, smuggling it through customs at the ferry terminal. It was a friendly wee thing that slept at the bottom of their beds, and they even let it lick their faces. It was only when it got sick back home and they took it to the vet that they discovered it was actually a Turkish sewer rat.

I was so disgusted that I nearly sicked up my pancakes and milkshake all over the floor of Gino's, but I had to admit that was one of the greatest stories I'd ever heard. And I'd been told it by a girl.

Cumbo made a big deal of paying the bill, like he was some kind of Hollywood hot shot or something, and Sophia swooned at his largesse. Lyndsey whispered to me that he had been saving up his pocket money for weeks to impress her, and we laughed. Cumbo shot us a withering stare.

As we walked home, we compared notes about school. I told Lyndsey how Wutherspoon had kicked me in the back, leaving a big bruise. She said Miss Black, her teacher, was just as bad. Like Wutherspoon, she was an old spinster, who wore long, heavy woollen skirts with thick, grey stockings and white ankle socks. She was only five feet two but she was one of the most vicious teachers in the school. If she saw you talking or chewing, she picked her moment to creep up behind you and flick your ear with a ruler.

When she belted you, she took a run-up to get extra power behind it, and, whereas most of the other teachers used the single end of the strap, she used the rat's tail end, which had three prongs and was more painful. She knew all the tricks like licking your palms so the strap slipped off easier and she would make you dry your hands with chalk dust beforehand.

Lyndsey said Black had whacked Samantha Henry across the arse with the crook end of a hockey stick for reading a copy of

Jackie behind her desk during class. A couple of weeks later they were walking past her car, which was parked outside the school gates, and they noticed that the doors were unlocked. Samantha Henry got inside and peed on the driver's seat.

Cumbo and Sophia were dallying again, and, by the time we had reached Bella, they were so far behind that we couldn't see them, so we stopped to let them catch up.

While we were waiting, Lyndsey told me how she could do the splits because she was double-jointed, so I asked her to show me. It was the most incredible thing I'd ever seen. She was sitting flat on the ground with her legs splayed in opposite directions. No matter how hard I tried, I couldn't do it. Even with Lyndsey pushing down on my shoulders, I couldn't get my bum any closer than about a foot off the ground.

We were both giggling like mad at my feeble attempts, and I finally gave up and rolled over on the grass. She tried to haul me up to try again, but I was laughing so much that we both fell over. My sides hurt and there were tears rolling down my face.

I sat up and rubbed my eyes, and, when I opened them, Bifter and Cuddihy were standing over me, staring in bewilderment. They must have been on their way to play pitch 'n' putt because Bifter had his lucky nine iron with him. There was a long, tortured silence as they looked at me and then Lyndsey and then me again.

– What's all this then? Cuddihy asked, his lips curling into a malicious grin.

I was so mortified I could hardly bring myself to speak.

– Eh, this is Lyndsey Cummings, I mumbled.

– I know who she is. She's Cumbo's wee sister. The question is, what are you doing with her?

– Nothing, I said.

– Well, it doesn't look like nothing to me. You were rolling around in the grass with her.

– I wasn't rolling around in the grass, I said defensively. She was showing me how to do the splits.

– Oooh, they cooed in unison, showing him how to do the splits!

– Why was she doing that? Cuddihy asked. Is she your girlfriend or something?

Bifter laughed nervously, as though he was enjoying my discomfort but feared that the truth might almost be too painful to endure. It occurred to me that my body language was all wrong and that it was putting me at a disadvantage. I was sitting next to Lyndsey, which said, metaphorically, that we were together. Cuddihy and Bifter were standing over me, which gave them the appearance of having power over me. I needed to regain the initiative so I shot to my feet and stood alongside them, facing Lyndsey, who was still seated.

– No, she's not my girlfriend, I spat, indignantly. I don't even like her. She's a stupid girl. The only reason I'm with her is because her brother's winching Sophia, and he bought me pancakes and milkshake at Gino's. She's been bugging the hell out of me all day, but I said I'd look after her.

Bifter and Cuddihy exchanged glances and raised their eyebrows.

– Gino's, eh? Bifter said. What flavour of milkshake did you have?

– Strawberry, I replied.

– What did you have on your pancakes?

– Golden syrup and ice-cream. Vanilla.

– Not bad, said Cuddihy.

We turned our backs on Lyndsey and it was as if she was no longer there. I walked the boys over to the pitch 'n' putt course and stood chatting to them as they waited in the queue. By the time they'd paid their green fees and moved onto the first tee, Cumbo and Sophia had arrived, so I said I'd see them later.

We walked the rest of the way home in virtual silence. The mood between Lyndsey and me had changed, and, despite my attempts to start several conversations, I couldn't prompt anything from her other than single word responses.

I hoped Cumbo and Sophia might start to hang back again, so I could try to explain to Lyndsey that I didn't really mean what I'd said. I did like her. In fact she was the first girl that I'd ever talked to properly, but if I hadn't pretended to hate her, my life wouldn't be worth living.

But for the first time that day Cumbo and Sophia kept pace with us. He kept cracking coy and annoying gags about how well Lyndsey and I seemed to be getting on together, which only made things worse. Lyndsey pursed her lips and stared straight ahead.

When we arrived back at the Proffy, Cumbo tried to drag Sophia behind the electricity box for a final winch but Dad was out in the driveway, washing the car and I could see him keeping his beady eye on them. As they were saying their long goodbye, finally I summoned the courage to say something to Lyndsey, but when I looked up she was already halfway down the hill.

At a stroke my life had just become more complicated. Now I had two people I would have to avoid – Kane and Lyndsey. I knew I was bound to bump into her sooner or later, at school or in the street, and I didn't know what I would do or say.

11

M um bought a pair of jeans. I'd never seen her in jeans before – she'd hardly ever worn trousers – but she went into town one day and came back with a pair of flared Falmers from Chelsea Girl. Then she changed the way she wore her hair. It had been stacked in a beehive for as long as I could remember, and then, out of the blue, she got a feather cut. Sophia, Tony and I gathered round her, admiring her new look and we got her to do a twirl. It was amazing – a new haircut and a pair of jeans made her look ten years younger.

Her mood changed as well, but not for the better. Where her new look was fashionable and flamboyant, her demeanour became withdrawn. She spent most of the time reading. Every night, after we'd eaten dinner and the dishes were washed, she retired to her bedroom with a book. Not college books, but novels she read for fun, borrowed from the library during her weekly visits on Friday afternoons.

I could no longer remember the last time that Mum had sat with the rest of the family in the living room, watching television. It annoyed Dad that she always had her nose in a book. He accused her of being anti-social but she just said she enjoyed being on her own sometimes.

She started playing records as well. The only evidence of any previous interest she'd shown in music was a small collection of dusty mono LPs, which she'd bought before she was married and which sat, untouched, in a cardboard box beneath the stairs. They were sung by people I'd never heard of, like Lonnie Donegan, Marty Wilde and Dickie Valentine.

Now she borrowed records from Suzanne and played them

on the red, vinyl-covered record player which sat under the telly, while she did the housework and cooked. They were all a bit folky, by singers like Joni Mitchell, Bob Dylan, Neil Young and James Taylor. Dad, whose musical tastes began and ended with 'The Impossible Dream' by Matt Monro, said they were depressing dirges, but Mum said she could listen to what she liked.

It wasn't particularly cool to listen to the same music as your parents, but I liked this stuff, particularly 'No Secrets' by Carly Simon, which I played over and over, memorising the lyrics and trying to make them fit the events of my life.

There was a song called 'The Carter Family', all about a family who lived next door for almost fourteen years and then they moved away and she missed them terribly. I thought it eerily reminiscent of the time the Gardners moved away from our street. They hadn't lived next door, they were three houses down and they were only there for two years, not fourteen. Also, they didn't have a daughter called Gwen with whom I had become inseparable from rag dolls through brassieres. In fact, they didn't have any children, they had a black-and-white cat called Muffin, but I felt quite sad when they left all the same. Mr Gardner worked as a printer at DC Thomson's and he used to give me piles of old comics that hadn't been sold.

My favourite song was 'You're So Vain' because it was loud and raunchy and spoke of exotic things like Lear jets and a total eclipse of the sun. It included a line – I had some dreams, they were clouds in my coffee – which I pondered over long and hard. It was funny and meaningless at the same time.

I guess it just means that she had some problems going on in her life at that particular time, Mum said, when I asked her about it.

It was sad and unsettling to see Dad, who'd never been without a job, confronted with an excess of time he didn't know how to fill. It was like he'd forgotten the rules of living and he was having to learn them all over again. He stood up, sat down, moved from room to room, began random tasks on a whim and dropped them with equal urgency. Holding a sustained conversation was beyond him. There was always something more important on his mind, and, through it all, he seemed overcome with an inexplicable guilt, as though submitting to inactivity would prove his undoing.

During his first few weeks of unemployment, he was up before everyone else in the mornings, making breakfast and helping us to get ready for school. He even offered to walk me to the school gates. I told him I'd managed to find my own way there since I was six, but he looked so hurt that I agreed a compromise. He could walk me part of the way on the strict understanding that, if we were spotted by any of my friends, he would make out that he was on his way to the newsagent's to buy his morning paper.

He spent his days in a frenzy of cleaning, gardening, shopping and household planning. He washed every dish, polished every window and laundered every item of clothing in the house. He pointed walls that didn't need pointing and unblocked drains that weren't blocked. The house was cleaner than it had ever been; crevices that we didn't know existed were located and dusted and there was an all-pervading smell of lemon and bleach.

In the evenings he pored over the classified job adverts in the *Evening Citizen*, circling those he thought might be suitable and making copious notes. When it came to sending off for details and filling in job applications, he relied on Mum, because he said she was better at words than him.

Despite having no income, he refused to sign on. He ignored Mum's pleading that he was entitled to claim the dole and that he'd spent years paying National Insurance contributions in preparedness for an eventuality like this. There were people better off than him who wouldn't think twice about claiming, she said, but he stood firm. None of his family had ever signed on, and he wasn't about to become the first. He'd rather starve than lay himself open to accusations that he was a scrounger.

After a couple of failed job interviews, defeatism crept into his mood. He said things had changed since the days when everyone had their pick of jobs. It was to do with the recession, which meant no-one had any money to spend in restaurants. Tony said how it was all to do with the ownership of the means of production, but Mum said he wasn't being helpful and told him to be quiet.

– Why don't you work for yourself, Robert? she asked, out of the blue.

The room fell silent as we awaited Dad's response. None came.

– Well, why not? You're always going on about how you hate working for other people and how you'd like to start your own business. We could sit here waiting for you to land a job, going through your redundancy money, or we could invest it and try to make it work for us.

Mum was right about Dad wanting to start his own business. He was always dreaming up money-spinning ideas which he assured us would make him a million if only he had the capital to get them off the ground. There were the patents which no-one else had thought of, like self-foaming shaving brushes and reversible Y-fronts, and the things which had gone out of fashion, which people would go crazy for, if only someone had the vision to reintroduce them – winkle pickers, plus-fours and chewing tobacco.

Tony couldn't let an opportunity like this go without making a few suggestions of his own. He told Dad he could earn a fortune selling the Ronco Button-o-matic to Pearly Kings and Queens and exporting the Boot's facial hair trimmer to Turkey where, he said, there was twice the potential market because the women were as hairy as the men. He asked Dad if he'd recognised an, as yet, unexploited cultural link between Germany and Cumberland on account of their mutual partiality for big sausages. He said it was only a matter of time before retailers in Penrith diversified into Edelweiss and Lederhosen and that Dad should jump on the bandwagon before he missed the boat.

Dad eyed him suspiciously and, for a few moments, we thought he might take the suggestion seriously. Then, his faced cracked into a smile, and he chased Tony round the living room before trapping him on the sofa and tickling him until the pair of them collapsed with laughter. We all joined in the hilarity. I was really happy that night.

From that moment, Dad's mood improved. It was like he'd made a leap of faith, and, once his mind was made up that he would start his own business, he was like a new man. Mum remained a restraining influence, keeping him grounded and focused on what was realistic and achievable.

Dad figured that, because he had worked in restaurants all his life, it was logical that his new business should be some kind of catering outlet. Mum pointed out that selling cooked food meant first buying the equipment necessary to cook it, and, since his funds were limited, perhaps he should temper his ambitions. There were also hygiene rules to be learned and followed, which seemed like excessive bureaucracy for someone just starting out.

She made the point that, since it was coming up to Christmas, he could start by selling things that people would buy as presents. The quayside was full of cash and carry warehouses selling things he could make a profit on selling at a stall at the outdoor markets.

It didn't quite fulfil Dad's romantic vision of high finance and entrepreneurship, but he accepted he had to start somewhere and entered into the spirit of his new venture with good grace.

His first priority was to get a van to carry his stock. Mum and Dad had both agreed that we would have to sell the little red Mini Clubman that had conveyed our family for as long as I could remember. Dad was less keen to trade in the comfort of a family car for a functional vehicle with only two seats but Mum insisted that he would need all of his redundancy money to buy stock. I felt a dreadful sense of betrayal, abandoning a faithful servant with such apparent capriciousness. It was also the first time that the full impact of Dad's redundancy was brought home to me. It was no longer an abstract idea. It was a reality that would have proper consequences for all of our lives.

I agreed to go with him to the car auction at Provanmill. Dad asked Sophia to come along, but she refused to sit in the same car as me. She was still in a bad mood over the way I had treated Lyndsey, which, she insisted, was a brazen attempt to wreck her friendship with Cumbo. Apparently Cumbo's mum had given him a hard time over it and had forbidden him from seeing Sophia again.

She credited me with a cunning and a foresight I didn't possess. I told her the reason Lyndsey and I had failed to hit it off was because she was a girl and I hated girls, a sentiment which Sophia was doing more, not less, to reinforce.

The car auction was a national institution – an expansive emporium where the acrid smell of scorched rubber rode shotgun to the muffled thunk of misfiring carburettors and the rustle of dodgy tenners. The narrow aisles separating the hundreds of near-redundant, grime-blackened hulls were populated by patrons who looked like they were used to institutions of a different kind.

Overweight women dressed in beer-stained overcoats and rain-mates carried handbags stuffed with rolls of grubby banknotes. They kicked balding tyres as their spindly, nicotine-stained men ran their hands along rusting undercarriages.

I'd never been to the car auction before, though playground tales of its dubious magnificence were legend. This was second-hand car dealership in the raw, where a top-of-the-range model was one that started and brakes were optional extras. Rows of rusting Zephyrs, Anglias and Cortinas stretched as far as the eye could see, all bearing the scars of highway battle. Smashed quarter lights, slashed tyres and twisted radiator grilles gave them the resigned, infirm appearance of patients in an army field hospital.

Dad set about trying to get a good price for our car. He had spent the whole of the previous day lovingly shampooing, waxing and valeting it so that it was in pristine condition. That clearly counted for nothing in his negotiations with a taciturn dealer who looked as though he would have been equally at ease snatching children from their parents.

– I'll give you two hundred, said the overall-clad operative.

Dad laughed derisively.

– You're joking.

The man maintained a poker-straight face, leaving the unmistakeable impression that comedy was not in his repertoire.

– Come on, it's worth more than that, Dad coaxed. It's a fine-looking car, in beautiful condition.

– OK, I'll buy it flowers and take it to the pictures. The price is still two hundred.

– Give me a break, Dad pleaded. It's only eight years old and it's got very low mileage. It must be worth at least four hundred.

– Look, pal, this isn't a fucking debate, the man said. The price is two hundred. Take it or leave it.

It didn't take a genius to work out that we weren't going to get much of a van for two hundred quid. Dad looked shattered as we moved between the aisles inspecting what we thought might fall within our price-range. It wasn't encouraging. Of the dozens of vehicles on display, Dad estimated we were limited to a choice of three – a dilapidated white Simca 1000, a clapped-out grey Ford Transit MkI and a ramshackle black Austin Morris J4.

The rules of the auction, typed on a sheet of foolscap and pinned to the wall of the cashier's office, stated that you could: inspect the outside of the vehicles; lift the bonnets to examine the visible internal engine parts; and turn the ignition; but you couldn't take them for a test drive.

The vehicles were driven into the auction area before going under the hammer, as proof that they were functional, but the only other concession to consumer protection was a twenty-four-hour money-back guarantee if the customer could prove there was some fundamental flaw which made the vehicle unroadworthy.

Dad bought us a cup of tea and a Tunnock's caramel wafer from the mobile cafeteria while we waited for the sale to begin. He stood silently, sipping from the polystyrene cup, lost in thought. His exchange with the grumpy dealer had exposed his powerlessness.

Drops of rain began to spit onto the large plastic canopy covering the main sale area which, as the start time approached, gradually filled up, and with a couple of minutes to go, the first of the vehicles, a filthy 1965 Rover 2000 P6 with a smashed head-light and a mangled fender, was driven in. Suffocating plumes of black smoke belched from its exhaust.

On a raised platform, a man clutching a wooden gavel intro-duced it as the first lot.

– Who's going to open the bids? he asked.

No-one spoke. The silence was broken only by the pitter-patter of raindrops on the canopy.

– Do I hear two hundred?

More silence.

– One eighty?

Still no-one spoke.

– Come on now, folks, this isn't a charity. Who's prepared to start the bidding at one sixty?

Someone in front of us raised a hand.

– That's more like it. I have one sixty, now who'll give me one eighty?

Another hand went up.

– One eighty.

And another.

– My word, sir, the last of the big spenders, two hundred. Finally we're getting somewhere. I have two hundred, who will offer me two twenty?

Dad's eyes darted frantically from the auctioneer to the crowd and back again with every bid. The more the price rose, the more nervous he appeared. He pulled out the fold of ten-pound notes the cashier had handed him in exchange for our Mini and, methodically, he thumbed through them. Silently, he mouthed one to twenty and then folded them and returned them to his trouser pocket. Ten minutes later, he pulled out the banknotes again and went through the same ritual.

I lost count of the number of cars that passed across the auction floor until, eventually, the first of the vans that we had earmarked as a potential purchase arrived.

– This is a 1965 Ford Transit Mark 1, with 90,000 miles on the clock, said the auctioneer. It is road taxed until the end of the month, and it has a full MoT certificate. Right, who's going to start the bidding?

– Two hundred, shouted a voice from the crowd.

Immediately a hand went up behind us.

– Two twenty, said the auctioneer.

The bidding ended at three hundred. Dad looked crestfallen. Next up was the Simca. While hardly in mint condition, it was the newest of the three vans we had our eye on and it had the lowest mileage – the best of a bad bunch. Dad intended to start the bidding low but one of the fat women at the front jumped in ahead of us with an offer of one sixty and, within seconds, the bidding had topped two hundred again.

Dad's face was ashen. He rocked back on his heels, his body language betraying a sense of dread that he would be forced to leave this place empty-handed, to catch the bus home and to admit to Mum that he had fallen at the first hurdle of self-employment. That he'd been stitched up by some plausible spiv and, forced to accept a paltry sum for our car which hadn't been enough to buy a van.

We waited an age until the last of the three vans we'd earmarked appeared – the 1960 Austin Morris J4, with no tax disc, no MoT certificate and 120,000 miles on the clock. The auctioneer was still reading out the vehicle's particulars when Dad shouted out.

– One hundred. I bid one hundred.

The auctioneer halted abruptly and pulled a face. Everyone laughed and turned around to look at Dad. Fortunately, he saw the funny side and laughed as well.

– I do believe we have an opening bid, said the auctioneer to more laughter. One hundred, do I hear any advance on one hundred?

A hand went up in front of us and then another in quick succession. My heart sank as I predicted the price would go through the two hundred pound limit before Dad had a chance to draw breath.

– One hundred and forty, I have one hundred and forty. Do I have any advance on one hundred and forty?

But then, no-one spoke or raised a hand. The bids stopped, the auctioneer paused, and, for a few tension-filled moments, there was silence.

– One sixty, Dad said.

– One sixty, one sixty, any advance on one sixty? Once, twice.

The auctioneer brought the gavel down on the lectern.

– Sold for one sixty.

Dad and I erupted, overcome with elation, to the bemusement of the other customers. We hugged and cheered and punched the air, like we were celebrating Dixie Deans scoring the winning goal in the European Cup final. I was excited and relieved but above all else, I felt victorious. It was a jubilant feeling, made all the sweeter because I was sharing it with Dad.

As we walked over to the cashier's office to hand over our money and collect the keys, we laughed and joked about what might have been if we hadn't pulled it off at the last minute. We'd even made a profit of forty pounds, which would help to pay for the MoT and the tax disc. Never before in the history of motoring had two people boarded such a ramshackle old rust bucket with such unconfined joy.

We drove to Shaheed's in our new van, still on a high, to buy the stock which Dad would need to sell at the markets. He decided that, since we'd been such a successful partnership at the car auction, I should join him on his first buying trip. He said we made a good team, which made me bristle with pride.

Shaheed's was one of a dozen or so warehouses which lined the dockyards at Tradeston, on the site of redundant shipyards. The closest shipyard was now a couple of miles away at Govan. Where once this area clattered and hummed with the sound of heavy industry and fizzed with phosphorescent blowtorches, now it pulsed with the rhythmic beat of cheap watches, and the crackle and whine of plastic transistor radios imported from Hong Kong and Taiwan.

Mum and Dad had already visited several of the warehouses to decide how they should spend Dad's five hundred pound redundancy payment. They agreed they shouldn't buy expensive items, like large, brand-name radio cassettes, which might turn out to be costly white elephants. They would stick to low-cost, high-volume products – cheap lighters, watches and radios, telescopic umbrellas, screwdriver sets, playing cards, nail clippers, mug trees, dish cloths and blank cassettes – so that, even if they didn't sell, they wouldn't blow a big hole in the overall budget.

Shaheed's was like *Dr Who*'s Tardis. On the outside it was a low-slung, unimpressive whitewashed building, but inside it was a labyrinth of avenues and alleyways crowded with brown cardboard boxes of electrical and electronic booty from exotic locations.

In Shaheed's, lofty corporate considerations like copyright and brand identity were trifling annoyances which only got in the way of the main business of selling large quantities of cheaply made imports to the credulous and the unsuspecting.

It was here that I learned, more than I ever did at school, the value of punctuation and phrasing. How the addition of a single word could hold such semantic power and nullify the pernicious threat of trading standards officialdom. They didn't sell gold jewellery, they sold gold 'look' jewellery. They didn't have Swiss watches or French perfume, they had Swiss 'type' watches and French 'style' perfume. I learned how inserting or substituting even a single letter represented an ingenious and lucrative marketing ploy, facilitating the sale of Bronson lighters, Tymex watches and Sonny hi-fis.

I learned how cassettes entitled 'The Songs of the Beatles' didn't necessarily mean they were sung by the Beatles, how sunglasses 'as worn by Paul Newman' didn't mean *the* Paul Newman and how 'long life' batteries only meant they were long in the life of a butterfly. I learned that rainproof didn't mean waterproof, that unbreakable meant 'as long as you didn't drop it' and that a warranty didn't mean anything at all. I also learned that, if all else failed, if the chips were down and the wolf was at the door, the stunning ubiquity of the phrase 'as seen on TV' would always pull you through.

We piled all our purchases onto a trolley, which we then wheeled into the car-park to load up the van. The final bill came to four hundred and ninety-nine pounds and sixty pence which sounded like a fortune – enough for ten Raleigh Choppers or a trip round the world – but when I surveyed the small pile of boxes, which represented our family's future, suddenly it didn't seem all that much.

With the eight bob change, Dad bought us each a can of Fanta and we sang 'If I were a Rich Man' from *Fiddler on the Roof* all the way home. Over dinner that night – Dad had made Spaghetti Bolognese, which was everyone's favourite – he talked excitedly about net gains and profit margins.

– I really feel like I'm doing something positive with my life, Christine, rather than just ticking over, day after day. Do you know what I mean?

Mum smiled.

– I mean, being made redundant might be the best thing that's ever happened to me. To us.

Mum was helping everyone to seconds of spaghetti.

– Don't get ahead of yourself, Robert. You've only bought the gear. You haven't sold any of it yet. Let's reserve judgement until we see how much of it shifts.

– Oh, don't listen to your Mum, kids, Dad said laughing. She's such a doom and gloom monger.

There was a market in Saltcoats the following day, and Dad planned to be up early and down there, in plenty of time, bidding for a pitch. Despite some initial opposition from Mum, he said I could go with him because I had already proved such an able deputy.

As I lay in bed, I felt happier and more satisfied than I had in a long time. Tony was sitting at his desk with the light switched on, which kept me awake, but it didn't bother me because he was studying for his prelims which meant Mum was in a good mood. Dad had a job and a renewed sense of purpose, which kept him off Mum's back. He'd even promised that, if things went well at the markets, he might give Sophia the money to buy a ticket for the Bay City Rollers concert, which had put a smile back on her face.

When I reviewed the events of the past few months, I had to admit that life had taken a turn for the better. I'd been to a common wedding, I'd discovered that I was, at the very least, a half Catholic, I'd attended my first Celtic match, and I'd gained a reputation for valour following my near-death experience on the scrumping raid on Glencairn Drive.

I couldn't pretend that it had all been an unqualified success. I'd watched my brother shagging in a bush, which I was still trying to come to terms with, but it was the feelings it had aroused in me which were more troubling – the nagging conviction that I might have enjoyed it and was, therefore, a moral degenerate.

There was something else in the debit ledger. For some reason, I'd started thinking about Johnny Nae Da. Why he had crept into my head, I couldn't explain. Perhaps I felt guilty at the way we had treated him over the whole edgy man business. Perhaps it was because I was seeing more of Dad which made me more acutely aware that that was a relationship which Johnny Nae Da didn't have.

I found myself thinking about things he wouldn't be able to do. He had no brothers and sisters, at least none that he knew, and his mother was poorly, so who would take him swimming, or to the pictures, or to a football match? He would never be able to bid for a van at the car auction or to buy two dozen Taiwanese self-winding watches at cost from Shaheed's.

I didn't remember falling asleep but I was woken by the sound of shouting. It was daylight but only just, judging by the thin shards of light filtering through the curtains. I looked out of the window onto the driveway where Dad was standing in his pyjamas, next to the van. The back doors were wide open, and there was glass every-where. A few boxes of lighters and playing cards lay strewn on the pavement but the van was empty. Everything was gone.

12

It began as a rumour, which slowly gathered momentum, on street corners and in huddled playground conversations, before giving way to open conjecture and finally to prayer. Could it be true? Had some divinity delivered salvation upon a stricken people? Was a sequel to *The Godfather*, the greatest sequence of acted scenes ever committed to celluloid, about to hit our cinema screens?

If there was any substance to the speculation – and, as anyone with a grounded disposition counselled, there had been no official confirmation – then we were blessed. A sequel would reverse the misery of ignorance and worthlessness inflicted on those, like me, who had been too young to see the original.

The arrival of *The Godfather* at the Rialto two years earlier had changed the world. Suddenly it was cinematic year zero and all previous bets were off. That Bubbles Fraser had seen *The Great Escape* four times meant nothing. That Rab Quigley claimed to have seen *Emanuelle*, after his brother sneaked him into the dirty picture house on Jamaica Street, was a mere footnote in history.

The Godfather was now the only show in town. Its references became ours, its terminology the lingua franca of our generation. It divided the world into two groups – those who had seen it and those who hadn't. I was a member of a third, unacknowledged group – those who hadn't seen it but pretended they had, because to admit to being a *Godfather* virgin was to sign your own social death warrant.

Thereafter, I was afflicted by a form of cultural blindness, forced to parrot words and phrases without having the first clue about what they meant. My friends were no longer my friends, they were members of my family, and I made people offers they couldn't refuse, but inevitably I stumbled upon my own ignorance. I was unaware that Don Corleone was a title – I thought it was short for Donald. I used the phrase 'Going to the mattresses' when I was tired, and I told people they would be 'swimming with the fishes' when they were going on holiday to the seaside.

They were empty expressions lacking meaning and context. I had a vague sense of the film's dark themes and I was able to assemble occasional, disjointed fragments of plot in my head from the exhaustive discussions I overheard in the playground, like unwritten, native wisdom being passed orally from parent to child.

But I knew my life was an accident waiting to happen. I woke every morning, fearful that my fraudulent existence would be revealed like a Mafia informer on the witness protection programme. I lived in dread that some faux pas would expose me and that diversionary tactics like rapidly changing the subject or suddenly feigning illness would be hopeless.

My paranoia was heightened by the spectacular fall from grace of Graeme Healey who claimed to have seen the film and, thereafter, became a self-appointed sage, passing judgement on every issue of *Godfather* orthodoxy. If you wanted to know how much Luca Brasi weighed, you went to Healey. If you wanted to know what kind of pasta Sollozzo the Turk was eating when he was gunned down by Michael, you asked Healey. If you wanted to know how many bullet holes were fired into the car in which Sonny was killed, Healey was your man.

That Healey had seen the X-rated film was never questioned, lest attention might rest on the questioner. How an eight-year-old boy had managed to evade Frank, the notoriously officious commissionaire at the Rialto, the box office staff and the usherette, was summarily glossed over.

It was later discovered that Healey hadn't seen the film at all, and that the information was being fed to him by his elder brother. The school was rocked by the shocking revelation. People failed to comprehend how fraud could be perpetrated on such a scale. It was like the American game show scandal of the 1960s, with Healey the Herb Stemple of Maxwell Park Primary. He went from being a Don to a Fredook. Humiliated and ostracised, he cut a pathetic figure in the playground, begging face time with the stamp-collecting dropouts and Mark Crawford, the disgraced Woolworth Lothario.

For me a new film meant a clean slate, because I knew that the original would quickly be forgotten. Now all that mattered was ensuring that I saw the sequel. The clamour for reliable information became unbearable. Newspapers were scanned, television and radio programmes monitored and gossip unpicked to the nth degree for the first hint of confirmation.

Then it came. The 'What's On' section of the *Evening Citizen* revealed that, from Monday, the Rialto would be showing Francis Ford Coppola's *The Godfather: Part II*, starring Al Pacino, Robert Duvall, Diane Keaton and Robert de Niro.

An excited buzz went round the school. Getting in to see the film became our sole preoccupation, and anyone who strayed from the subject was considered suspect and subversive. We had no illusions it would be easy – it too was X-rated and security at the cinema would be tight – but Chabs had an idea.

He had spoken with Jukebox Durie, whose big brother worked at the Rialto as an assistant projectionist. He had sneaked Jukebox and his pals in through the fire exit on a number of previous occasions, before almost being sacked when Jim Buthley burst into tears in the middle of *The Exorcist* and had to be removed by the usherette, screaming for his mummy.

Chabs put it to Jukebox that, if he managed to get us in to see *The Godfather: Part II*, we should pool our pocket money for two weeks and give him the lot. With me, Bifter, Chabs, Cuddihy, Wally and Jukebox, that would come to thirty bob – a king's ransom. Jukebox was as keen to see the film as the rest of us so it didn't take long for him to agree to put the proposition to his brother. He went home for his lunch, and, so he said, he would drop by the Rialto on the way back that afternoon and raise the matter with his brother – he would make him an offer he couldn't refuse.

For the rest of us, sitting in the school dinner hall suspiciously forking our Belmont Pie and mash, the tension was unbearable. Chabs wondered aloud if the sequel would be as good as the original. I hated these conversations, where evidence of a single gap in your *Godfather* knowledge might suddenly expose you. Eyes darted from person to person. Breathing became laboured. I felt a build-up of blood behind my cheeks and an irresistible urge to fill the silent void.

– I can't see how it could be. The first one was such a master-piece, I ventured, scanning faces for any sign of suspicion, for an indication that some involuntary inflection in my voice had given the game away.

It appeared not. In fact everyone seemed to be taking an unusu-ally intense interest in their food.

– Where do you suppose the story will pick up? Bifter asked, raising the stakes yet higher.

Panic and mistrust crowded in. Was he prompting a genuine and open debate, or was he as unsighted as me, using a ploy to turn the tables on those he suspected of having an advantage over him? Suddenly Cuddihy had an urgent need to tie his shoelace, and Chabs developed a coughing fit which, again, left me as the focus of Bifter's attention.

– Who knows? I said. It probably picks up where the first one ended.

He scrutinised my features expectantly, like a poker player eyeing an opponent for the merest hint of bluff.

– Yeah, it's got to be the end, he said with a vague mystery in his voice. Couldn't be anything else.

By the end of the lunch break we still hadn't seen Jukebox and so we would have to wait until home time for further news. Afternoon lessons dragged on interminably but I wasn't paying attention. I couldn't take my mind off the film. I had to see it. I simply had to. I was gazing through the window, across the river to the steeple of the university when I suddenly became aware of a piercing attention trained on me.

– Steven Duff. I asked you a question! Wutherspoon shouted.

I stared back at her blankly. Forty sets of eyes swivelled in on me, and the room descended into a hanging, portentous silence. I had no idea what she had asked. I didn't even know what subject she was teaching. At the start of the afternoon it had been Roman history but there was every possibility we had moved onto something else. I would have to wing it.

– Julius Caesar, I said, playing the percentages. The answer to most questions in Roman history was Julius Caesar.

The instant the words left my lips I realised my spectacular gaffe. A roar of mocking, humiliating laughter engulfed me. A smirk shot across Wutherspoon's face before it resumed its standard Presbyterian scowl. I knew I was in big trouble.

– No, I'm afraid the square root of eighty-one is not Julius Caesar, she said. Just to update you, we finished our history lesson half an hour ago. We are now on Arithmetic.

– Nine, I said, trying to rescue the situation.

– Too late, boy. See me at the end of the lesson.

When the bell rang I remained at my desk until everyone had left the room. Wutherspoon spent an age collecting books, cleaning the blackboard and writing things in her ledger before she even acknowledged that I was there. Then she summoned me to the front of her desk and delivered a lengthy lecture on what a waste of space I was.

I wasn't even listening. I was willing her to get to the point. What was my punishment to be? Was it the strap or detention? When she ordered me to hold my hand out, I almost leapt for joy. Even six big ones from the rat's tail end was preferable to spending another hour not knowing if Jukebox's brother was going to sneak us into the cinema.

When the last whack of the strap came down on my throbbing

palm, I bolted from the classroom with obscene haste and leapt down the stone steps three at a time. The rest of the gang were gathered around Jukebox in the playground, and from their smiling faces I immediately knew that the answer was yes. His brother had agreed to the deal. He wanted the cash up front and, if we were caught, he would kill us, but we didn't care about the caveats. That was unimportant detail. All that mattered was that we were going to the pictures. We were going to see *The Godfather: Part II*.

We decided the best opportunity would be the matinee showing the following Saturday. It was unlikely the cinema would be filled to capacity then and it would allow us to sit near the front where we were less likely to be detected by the eagle-eyed usherette.

I had another reason for favouring that time – it would get me out of the house for a couple of hours, away from Mum and Dad. It had been a fortnight since the van was broken into, with its contents plundered, and a funereal pall continued to hang over the house.

If things were not bad enough, the van appeared to have given up the ghost. Dad asked Benny, one of his former workmates in the restaurant who was handy with cars, to come round and have a look at it. It didn't take him long to diagnose the problem – a bad starter solenoid. We'd need a new one if we wanted the van to start. That wasn't expensive, no more than a few quid. Dad and I exchanged optimistic glances. But Benny hadn't finished. If we wanted the van to move, we'd need a new gearbox and a new clutch. And if we wanted it to stop, we'd need a new set of brake shoes, brake pads and brake cables.

The confident enthusiasm of the car auction and Shaheed had vanished. All the money we possessed had been invested in a vehicle which had turned out to be a pig in a poke and a dozen or so boxes of cheap trinkets which were now being hocked around the pubs and bingo halls of Govan.

If Mum had launched into an incandescent rage, if she had accused Dad of rank stupidity and incompetence, if she had fired mortar rounds of crockery and plant pots at him, then he might have been able to recover, to acknowledge his shortcomings and to move on.

Even brooding silence would have been preferable to what he had to contend with – understanding. Equable, cheerful, patronising understanding. Mum even said Granny and Granddad had offered to lend him the money to fix the van and replace his stolen stock.

– I'm not borrowing from your parents, Dad said with quiet, determined anger.

– For heaven's sake, Robert, why ever not?

– Because I know what they're thinking.

– They're not thinking anything. They're offering to help us out of a difficult spot.

– They're thinking, Hey, look who screwed up again.

– They're not thinking anything of the sort.

– They're thinking, Losing his job isn't enough. He has to blow his redundancy money as well. They're thinking, What kind of moron leaves five hundred quid's worth of gear out overnight in a van with no alarm?

– They're trying to help us get back on our feet, Mum insisted.

– They're thinking, But then again, the alarm would probably be worth more than the van because it's a clapped-out squib. They're thinking, Whoever sold him that dodgy old rust bucket must have really seen him coming.

– Stop it, Robert.

– They're thinking, We thought he was a loser before, but this really puts the seal on it. What kind of man can't even provide for his own family?

– I give up.

– I'm not taking money from your family, Christine. I got us into this mess and I'll get us out. Tell your parents thanks very much for the offer, but we don't need their help.

We gathered outside the Rialto at half past one, an hour before the film was due to start. Jukebox's brother insisted on vetting us beforehand. He wanted to be sure we were dependable, so there would be no repeat of the Jim Buthley incident.

It was a cold November afternoon. There had been a heavy snowfall overnight, and it was now starting to thaw, leaving the pavements covered with a choppy coating of brown slush. Jukebox, Bifter, Cuddihy, Chabs and I were dressed in thick jumpers, boots and duffle coats, protected against the driving sleet and the biting, chilly wind.

Wally arrived late, wearing an anorak he had outgrown over a T-shirt, and a pair of torn, oil-stained jeans and canvas trainers, which were soaked through and squelched with every step. His teeth chattered, and his lips were blue. From the pungent smell preceding him, I guessed his clothes hadn't been washed in weeks.

A queue had formed outside the main entrance to the cinema. Frank, the ageing commissionaire, dressed in a crisp, burgundy uniform with gold braid and tasselled epaulettes, kept vigilant watch, to guard against any queue-related misdemeanours.

The Rialto, with its vanishing grandeur, was a relic from its 1930s heyday, a velour-upholstered yesterworld of Bakelite and brass fittings. A dirty, threadbare carpet ran up the centre of the marble staircase into the main foyer, which was dominated by an elaborate, cut-glass chandelier and a large, yellowing portrait of the Queen. A mahogany sign, handpainted in gold leaf and with the original seat prices in old money, directed customers to the main auditorium.

The scene was as familiar to me as breathing. Mrs Boyce, wearing her trademark horn-rimmed glasses, sat perched behind the metal grille of the box office, her clipper machine punching out the small, white tickets, which were torn in half by the usherette; the refreshments kiosk, its mirrored shelves stacked with cartons of Kia-Ora orange juice and boxes of Paynes Chocolate Brazils and Meltis Newberry Fruits; the dusty, dimly lit corridors with paint flaking from their high ceilings; the dark uncertainty of those first steps into the auditorium with its overpowering smell of mothballs; the Brownian swirl of cigarette smoke and dust looping around the projector beam; and the sudden burst of sound as the curtains parted and the Pearl & Dean soundtrack boomed over the heads of the audience.

I had been here a thousand times – going to the pictures on Dad's day off had been the one regular thing we did as a family – and its power never diminished; its glamour never faded. It was here that my worldview was shaped – where I laughed at *The Jungle Book*, cried at *Bambi* and feared the Child Catcher in *Chitty Chitty Bang Bang*. It was here that Charlton Heston instilled in me a deep religious conviction, which was to stay with me until I was twelve; where I learned the importance of personal morality from Gregory Peck; and where Paul Newman taught me the value of a deep screwback with right-hand side.

We gathered at the fire exit at the side of the cinema, as arranged. At half past one, the door swung open and Jukebox's brother appeared, dressed in overalls and smoking a cigarette. He paced back and forth, casting a critical eye on each of us like a slave owner deciding his next purchase.

– Who's the wee smelly one? he asked.

– That's Wally. He goes to the Conception, Jukebox explained.

Wally looked hurt, that such a pejorative description alone had been enough to identify him.

– He's not getting in, Jukebox's brother said with cold decisiveness.

Wally erupted.

– What, 'cos I'm a Catholic?

– No, because you're honking. The customers will complain and you'll all get chucked out.

I decided I had to take a stand. Wally was my friend. It was only through me that the others knew him at all. The thought of missing the greatest film experience of my life was too painful to imagine, but I felt responsible for him, and I couldn't watch him being discriminated against in this way.

– If he doesn't get in, I'm not going, I said.

I expected the others to close ranks – Jukebox's brother would still get twenty bob even without Wally and me, but, to my surprise, they backed me up.

– I'm not going in either, said Cuddihy.

– Or me, said Bifter.

– Or me, said Chabs.

Jukebox was in a difficult position, his loyalties torn, so he stayed silent.

– Oh, for fuck's sake, said his brother. Right he can get in but you'd better not get caught. I'm not losing my fucking job over this.

We filed past him, handing over five bob each as we went. He stood counting the cash before he led us up a gloomy stone staircase and along a corridor until we reached the door leading directly into the main auditorium.

He pulled the door open a fraction. The overhead lights were still on, and the usherette was showing people to their seats. He told us he would have to return to the projection room before he was missed and that we should wait until the adverts were over and the film was beginning before we crept in.

He said the first three rows were normally empty during the matinee and so we should sit at the front, on the floor, and keep our heads down. He was like a general commanding his troops ahead of battle.

– And, remember, if the lassie with the torch catches you, you're on your own. It's every man for himself. If any of you grasses me up, I'll stick ma boot so far up yer arse ye'll think Doc Marten has started making hats.

We nodded our assent. He reached up and, with his sweater cuff over his hand, removed a lightbulb from the socket overhead, plunging us into darkness. He explained it was to prevent shafts of light streaming into the darkened auditorium when we opened the door. He would replace the bulb after the film had ended. It meant that, if there was a fire and people tried to escape, they would find the fire exit in pitch darkness, but that didn't seem to concern him.

After he left, we stood behind the door, with no-one daring to speak or even move. The air was thick with nervous tension. I felt like Anne Frank, hiding out in her attic from the Nazis. Eventually, we heard the mournful strains of the film soundtrack and Chabs, who was nearest the door, spoke first.

– Right, time to go boys, he whispered, his voice dry and husky.

Slowly he pinched open the door, leaving just enough of a gap for us to slip through. One by one we crept into the darkness. I was the last through, and just as I entered, the entire auditorium lit up like a Christmas tree, with the glare from the screen. I froze with my back to the wall, afraid to breathe. I was sure someone would turn their head from the screen to face me and raise the alarm. But, despite the brightness, the audience remained oblivious to my presence, their attention rapt by the scene of the party on Lake Tahoe, held to celebrate Anthony Corleone's first communion.

I crawled, commando-style, to the front row and crouched beside Wally. I stared up at the screen, and it was as if time stood still. The following three hours and twenty minutes were the shortest of my life. At the end, I felt a sickening sense of loss that I would never see it for the first time again.

As the credits rolled, I drew breath and looked around to gauge the reaction of the others. Chabs, Bifter, Cuddihy and Jukebox were still glued to the screen, fearing they might miss even the tiniest part of the experience. Wally was lying flat out on the carpet, fast asleep.

We walked home silently, struggling to assimilate what we had seen and to find the words to articulate our impressions. When we began to talk, there was none of the usual excitable jabber about action scenes and fight sequences, which inevitably followed a James Bond film or a John Wayne war movie. The discussion was about why things had happened the way they did and what it meant.

Until the final scene, I was convinced I had discovered a new screen hero. Michael Corleone may have been a murderous crime lord, but he possessed the cool, understated authority of a Captain Hilts or a Rick Blaine, only with an added touch of menace. Then he spoiled it by ordering the death of his brother.

– Why did he have to kill Fredo? I wondered aloud.

Chabs agreed.

– I know what you mean. Michael was always going on about how important the family was to him, and then he goes and gets someone to kill his brother.

Cuddihy pointed out that the family didn't really mean *his* family.

– That's just a name they used for the business – making money. That was the most important thing for him. Making money was more important than any of his relatives.

– Aye, but Fredo was just a daft, wee diddy, said Bifter.

– He didn't know the Rosato brothers were going to try and kill Michael when he agreed to help them. He just thought they were going to put the frighteners on him. He was just trying to get a piece of the action because he felt left out.

Fredo was the least glamorous of all the *Godfather* characters; he was no hero and yet he was the one who had touched us most profoundly. I was struck by the thoughtfulness of our discussion and the maturity of the conclusions we reached. As we wandered the dark, snow-covered streets, I couldn't help thinking it was a sign we were growing up.

As we approached the bottom end of Gower Street we stopped in our tracks. On the other side of the Paisley Road was Daft Davie, coming out of the Crit. We all spotted him simultaneously.

– HOI, DAFT DAVIE, YA MAD BASTARD! HOW'S IT GOING? Chabs shouted at the top of his voice.

Bifter and Cuddihy did monkey impressions, tickling their armpits and beating their chests.

– GO ON, DAVIE, SAY SOMETHING DAFT, YA MENTAL BIG MONG! Cuddihy shouted.

Daft Davie looked up from his chips with a wildness in his eyes and sprinted across the busy road without caution or heed to the traffic. As he mounted the central reservation, several cars skidded to a halt on the slippery surface and horns blared.

We bolted like rats from a burning building, some heading east along the Paisley Road, some retreating in the direction we had come from. I ran up Gower Street, heading towards the railway bridge with my head tucked down into my chest, pushing forward against the driving sleet. Wally was behind me but he was struggling to keep pace as his rubber-soled shoes slid on the slushy surface. As we crossed the junction of Clifford Street, he lost his footing and fell, sprawling across the road. I knew I couldn't leave him stranded and, fighting every survival instinct in my body, I stopped to help.

I struggled to lift him with Daft Davie just a few yards away, bearing down on us with murderous intent branded into his features. He had thrown away his chips, so I knew he meant business. I hauled Wally to his feet, and we charged off again with the sound of our pursuer's laboured, nasal gasping in our ears. With terror driving us on, we managed to find reserves of strength to keep just ahead of him.

We approached the brow of the hill and, as we passed the door of Ali Sud's corner shop, some customers stepped out onto the pavement, which slowed Daft Davie up and gave us fractionally more breathing space. We reached the junction with Maxwell Drive at lung-bursting pace, and I had to decide which way to run. I didn't want him to know where I lived but the instinct to reach the safety of my own home was irresistible. As we began the final ascent up the hill I felt my legs tire as Daft Davie's more powerful frame began to tell.

I reached the front gate first, with Wally immediately behind me. We scrambled down the path and onto the front step. I grappled with the door handle and, to my immense joy, it turned and the door opened before us. We fell into the hallway and, as I looked behind me, I saw Daft Davie clearing the hedge in a single leap and lunging towards the door.

The next thing I knew, I was in the living room cowering behind Dad, whimpering pathetically, with tears streaming down my frozen cheeks, as I begged for mercy. Daft Davie stood in the centre of the room, veins pulsing on his bright red forehead, ranting incoherently. Mum and Tony, who'd been sitting on the sofa, sprang to their feet. Dad looked nervous as he held out a hand to restrain Daft Davie.

– OK, big lad, hold it right there. Now, calm down, just calm down.

Daft Davie gesticulated wildly and yelled at the top of his voice, but it was impossible to make out what he was saying. He lunged forward. Dad wasn't enough of a force to hold him off and he crumpled under his weight.

I stood facing Daft Davie. This was the closest I'd ever come to him and it was only then that I realised how old he was. Despite his height, from a distance he had the face of a child, but up close his skin was flaccid and his hair faded with age.

I was aware of my family standing open-mouthed in various stages of alarm. Wally, who was to my right, was breathing heavily after our exhausting run, but he wasn't sobbing uncontrollably, like me. If anything, there was a mischievous glint in his eye, as though he was enjoying the theatre.

Daft Davie reached out and, with one of his large hands, tapped me on the shoulder, so gently I barely felt it.

– Tig, he said, his face breaking into a broad grin. You're it.

13

Out of adversity comes opportunity, Granny used to say, which, according to Dad, was a posh way of saying every cloud has a silver lining. The silver lining in the cloud of being terrified half to death by Daft Davie was that Mum appeared to change her position on allowing Wally into the house. I didn't even have to ask. She took one look at him and ordered him into a warm bath.

– Does that boy's mother know he's out dressed like that in this weather? she asked when he was out of earshot.

– Dunno, I shrugged.

– He'll be lucky if he hasn't caught pneumonia.

Mum gave him some of my old clothes to wear while his own were being washed and dried. They hung on his gaunt frame like rags on a scarecrow, and he squirmed with discomfort. When she asked if he wanted to stay for tea, he looked terrified at the prospect but nodded his consent. Anything was better than returning to his own home.

Dad, who was doing the cooking, asked him if there was anything he didn't like. Wally pondered the question as though he'd just been asked to prove the third law of thermodynamics.

– I'm not too fond of sweetcorn, he said quietly, almost apologetically.

– Anything else?

– Raisins.

– OK, I'll make sure you don't get any raisins or sweetcorn.

I'd never seen Wally so discomfited. Gone was his usual brashness, now replaced with a hunted distrust, like a recently captured wild animal in a zoo. He was especially ill at ease as we gathered around the dinner table, something he said he'd never done at home. Mum chided us over our treatment of Daft Davie as Dad delivered up plates of piping hot, home-made minestrone soup.

– Why do you boys have to bully that poor lad? He's perfectly harmless. His only crime is to have been born slightly different from you, and you persecute him mercilessly.

– Aye, all right, Mum, we know, I said, still mortified at my feeble capitulation in the face of Daft Davie's ultimately benign threat.

– You obviously *don't* know, Steven. Well, I'm glad that he put the fear of God in you. Perhaps next time you'll think twice about taunting him.

– Right, OK, Mum, we get the message.

Dad, Tony and Sophia ate in silence. Tony hadn't said a word since he helped Dad escort Daft Davie from the house. Either he was thinking up some particularly biting put-down or he had something else on his mind. We had almost finished our soup when Mum noticed Wally's plate hadn't been touched.

– Is there something wrong, Paul? she asked.

– I'm not too keen on vegetables, he said, with an embarrassed, half-smile.

Mum didn't make a fuss. She collected his plate and took it into the kitchen along with the others. For the main course Dad had made a Mediterranean lamb casserole which he served with sauté potatoes and roasted vegetables. As we ate, Sophia announced that she had some very exciting news. We sat captivated, open-mouthed in anticipation. It was, she reminded us, the Bay City Rollers concert the following day. How could we forget? It was all she had talked about for months. Well, Celeste had won two tickets on a Radio Clyde phone-in competition and she had agreed to give one of them to Sophia.

– Isn't that just the most brilliant thing you've ever heard? she beamed. Celeste's dad has agreed to drive us there and back so it means I don't even need bus fares. Isn't that great news?

I expected an argument from Dad concerning the suspect calibre of people who went to pop concerts, and the social and moral dangers posed by men with long hair. But instead he just shrugged.

– That's great, love. Make sure you stay safe.

It occurred to me that he too had been quiet. There was an atmosphere between him and Tony with neither of them addressing, or even looking at the other. Mum didn't appear to have much to say either, and, following Sophia's revelation, the room descended into a tense silence, broken only by the clink of cutlery on crockery.

Wally picked at the food on his plate, rearranging the location of the main items but, conspicuously, putting none of it into his mouth. I saw Mum glancing at his plate several times. I felt doubly responsible – for his peculiar behaviour but also because I had subjected him to this oppressive atmosphere.

– If it's the vegetables in the casserole that are putting you off, Paul, I can always take them out, Mum said to him.

– Nah, see, what it is like . . . I'm not that keen on meat and gravy, he replied.

Mum asked him if there was anything else she could get him, like beans on toast or an omelette.

– Nah, I'm all right, honest, he said.

– What about some bread and butter?

– Aye, I'll take some bread but no butter. I'm not that keen on butter.

Sophia laughed out loud.

– Where do you pick up your strange wee mates from? she asked.

– That's enough, Sophia, Mum said sternly. Paul is our guest, and I'll thank you not to be so rude.

Sophia twirled her index finger round her temple to indicate that he was mental, and Tony smiled for the first time that evening.

After dinner, we sat down to watch *The Generation Game* and Wally fell asleep on the couch. He woke up just as *Kojak* was starting, and Mum asked him if he wanted to stay overnight. He didn't take much persuading.

– Shouldn't you call your parents and let them know? Mum asked.

– Och, no, they'll be fine, Wally insisted. They'll be out anyway. They won't even notice I'm gone.

Later, I overheard Mum and Dad arguing in the kitchen.

– This isn't the time to clutter the house with waifs and strays, Dad said. We've got things we need to talk about.

– What would you have me do, Robert? Put the boy out on the street? Mum replied.

Wally slept in Tony's bed, and Tony bunked downstairs on the couch. I thought he would kick up about being thrown out of his bed, but he didn't utter a word of complaint.

The following morning there was the same strained mood at the breakfast table. Sophia broke the silence by announcing that she wouldn't be going to Sunday school. She was going round to Celeste's house instead because they wanted to spend the day getting ready for the concert.

She was already fully dressed in her Rollermaniac uniform, which Mum had run up on her old Singer sewing machine. Modelled on Eric Faulkner, the lead guitarist and Sophia's favourite Roller, it was made from an old white school shirt, onto which Mum had sewn tartan epaulettes and breast pockets. For the trousers, she had used a pair of Dad's old chef's whites, taking them in at the waist and adding tartan piping to widen the legs. The look was finished off with a pair of baseball boots and a tartan scarf tied around each wrist. I had to admit that she looked pretty groovy.

She said she and Celeste would be spending the day doing their make-up and perfecting their feather cuts. I thought Mum would throw a wobbly, lecturing her about commitment and loyalty to Reverend MacIver, but she said not a word.

I had no excuse not to go to church, but I said I might go to Wally's place afterwards to hang out and might not be home for lunch. Dad just nodded his approval, and Mum said there was no need to hurry home. If I didn't know any better I'd have said my parents wanted us out of the house.

As I kissed them goodbye I was already hatching a plan. I had no intention of going to Sunday school. Instead I would accompany Wally to St Bernadette's, the Catholic chapel. Not that Wally was planning to go to mass until I suggested it – he hadn't been in weeks – but when I massaged his ego, telling him he could show me the ropes, he agreed. This was it. I was about to make my debut as a fully fledged Catholic.

The first thing I noticed about St Bernadette's was how casually everyone dressed. With the odd, elderly exception, the congregation arrived in their normal weekday clothes – jeans and sand shoes, unshaven and unmade-up. There was little concession to pomp. They were not here to parade themselves in their Sunday best, like they did at the Kirk; they were here to praise God.

They trudged into the chapel sleepy and grudging, like an early shift in a factory, crossing themselves as they passed a small statue of Christ with his hands outstretched, their heads bowed and their faces starched with grim solemnity, lest they be accused of finding anything remotely funny about stigmata.

I followed their example and quickly scanned the faces around me to see if I'd been rumbled as a rank novice, but it appeared I'd got away with it. We took our seats on the hard wooden pews and waited for the service to begin. I braced myself for the spectacular floorshow, the fire and brimstone, the deafening claps of thunder, the blinding flashes of light, the lashing of tortured souls. Perhaps even Satan himself would make an appearance.

After a few moments Father Byrne shuffled into view from behind a curtain, accompanied by a pair of altar boys who helped him to arrange a collection of silver-plated paraphernalia. Then he spoke. I made the pretence of trying to follow what he was saying but after a while I gave up, engulfed in a wave of unfathomable, sanctimonious adult-speak. Periodically he stopped to allow the congregation to mumble their rejoinder but that too was lost on me after a few words. Barely ten minutes had passed and I was paralysed with boredom.

Father Byrne was stern and humourless, with a solid, diminutive frame, tightly enshrined in a no-nonsense black cassock. He had a hard, heavily contoured face and a fleshy mouth which delivered his priestly monologue in a nasal Irish bray. He was no Bing Crosby in *The Bells of St Mary's* but he was hardly the forbidding enforcer of the faith I had been led to expect. Viewed from a certain angle, he bore a passing resemblance to the bald, breast-obsessed midget in *The Benny Hill Show*.

The service dragged on, its painful monotony alleviated only by the brief sight of a nun playing a tambourine, and even the holy communion was a let-down. The blood of Christ turned out not to be blood at all, but red wine, and the body of Christ wasn't – as I had been told – still-warm flesh recovered earlier that morning from the city mortuary. It was a thin slice of rice paper, placed on the tongues of all who approached Father Byrne at the altar.

I waited in line behind Wally and, as I neared the priest, he eyed me suspiciously. I opened my mouth and his hand reached out, the wafer hovering over my extended tongue, but then he withdrew it.

– Are you a pupil at the Conception? he asked.

– Er, no, I said limply.

– You're not a member of this parish, are you?

The queue had stalled and, out of the corner of my eye, I glimpsed several craning necks.

– Eh, no, not exactly.

– Have you been confirmed?

I froze, panicked. I didn't have a clue what he was talking about. I reasoned that 'being confirmed' must be some requisite to getting the bit of wafer and I thought about lying. But then I remembered where I was. I had a split second to decide and, foolishly, I opted to hedge.

– I might have been. I can't remember.

The priest retracted the wafer.

– Look, son, if you haven't been confirmed you can't take

communion. This is a sacred religious commitment. It's not a game. Now, move along, you're holding everyone up.

As I returned to my seat I felt the eyes of everyone in the chapel searing into my back and I spent the remainder of the service staring at the floor. I felt conspicuous and out of place and I couldn't wait to get out.

At the end of the service I hurried up the aisle and out of the large double entrance, willing Wally to catch up. But as we neared the gates of the chapel I spotted Kane approaching us with two of his pals. I froze. My only blessing was that we were in the grounds of a church. Surely he wouldn't get violent here?

Kane and his mates were only a year older than us, but they were taller and heavier. They were dressed scruffily, and I could see them eyeing me up and down, in my Sunday best suit trousers and shirt.

– Hey, Rafferty, what's yer wee Proddy mate doing here? Kane asked Wally, laughing.

His two pals cackled maliciously. Wally joined in the laughter, but I couldn't blame him for his complicity. I'd have done the same in his position.

– He's here to see what a proper church looks like, Wally said.

Suddenly Kane stopped laughing. His face turned deadly serious.

– Well, I'll show him what a proper kick in the baws looks like unless he gets ma old man's ladder back.

– Aye, don't worry, Kevin. I've told you, we'll get it back. There's no problem, Wally stuttered.

Kane put his arm around Wally's shoulder and, gripping him proprietorially, swung him around so that they were facing away from the rest of us. But he spoke loud enough so that he was sure I could hear him.

– You're all right, wee man. I'm OK with you. But I don't trust wee Protestant poofs like yer mate there. My old man's doing his dinger about his ladder. Without it he can only dae ground floors. He canny dae the Ibrox flats and he's gaun spastic at all the cash he's losing. The old dear next door has been nipping his ear, telling him it was my mates that nicked it. He can't prove anything yet but he's not letting it drop and it's only a matter of time before his tackety boots pay my baws a visit. And if I end up with bruised plums, ye can rest assured I'll be passing on the favour.

– I've told ye, Kevin, we'll get it back, Wally insisted.

– It's just a question of time. We need to choose the right moment.

– Well, the right moment better be soon, otherwise yer wee mate there won't be pissing straight for a while.

Kane turned around and, flanked by his two henchmen, began to walk away. As he passed, he slowed down, almost imperceptibly, and winked at me.

As we walked home, I pondered my first experience of Catholicism. I was forced to conclude that it hadn't been an unqualified success. I had been bored, publicly humiliated and threatened with physical violence – perhaps a typical Sunday for some Catholics but not my idea of fun. It occurred that what had attracted me in the first place wasn't the faith at all – listening to Father Byrne droning on was even more stultifying than one of Reverend MacIver's sermons – but the chance to rebel against it.

There was nothing to rail against at the Kirk because there was no compulsion to attend and no threat of punishment if I didn't, except for the mild disapproval of my parents. Reverend MacIver didn't turn up at your house and warn that you were going to burn in hell because you hadn't been to Sunday school. The stakes were higher at the chapel, and so, naturally, there was more excitement in cocking a snook. If you missed one week of mass, you were knocking on the door of purgatory. If you missed more than one week, the flames of hell were sizzling at your ankles.

What I found most impressive about Wally and the other Papes was the blitheness with which they shunned the chapel, dismissing the prospect of eternal damnation like it was a slap on the wrist. I knew then that I didn't want to be a practising

Catholic at all, I wanted to be like them, a lapsed Catholic, a renegade Catholic, who flicked the Vs at temporal punishment, mooned at hellfire and broke wind in the face of Satan. If there was any fun to be had in religion at all, that's where it lay.

It was obvious that Wally, normally a model of devil-may-care calm, had been rattled by Kane. He suggested that we immediately round up Cuddihy, Bifter and Chabs, and make our way over to Glencairn Drive to try to recover the lost ladder. We would need to go team-handed because it would take all of our combined strength to carry it back to Kane's flat in Govan.

I was faced with a dilemma. On the one hand I didn't fancy the prospect of Kane playing keepie-uppie with my testicles but I couldn't risk us returning, en masse, to the scene of my greatest deception. As far as the others were concerned, I had shown superhuman courage in cheating certain death at the hands of a rabid Alsatian and a child-snatching despot and, frankly, that's how I wanted it to remain. If word ever got out that, in fact, the closest I had come to death was drowning in a pool of St Bernard drool, then I was finished.

I managed to convince Wally that we should make a discreet reconnaissance trip to the house beforehand, to make sure that the ladder was still there before rounding up the others. If a team of us went round now in broad daylight, I cautioned, we were more likely to attract attention. Fortunately, he agreed.

I suggested we should cycle there, but Wally said his bike had been stolen. I was shocked at the casual way in which he chose to drop such a bombshell.

– You're kidding. When did that happen?

– Oh, I can't remember. A couple of weeks ago.

– How? Where?

– Och, someone grabbed it from the backyard, he said almost carelessly

– Did you not have it chained up? I asked.

– Nah, I forgot.

There was a kind of poetic symmetry about such a turn of events, but I still couldn't help feeling sorry for Wally. He had wanted a bike for so long and, even if he had stolen it in the first place, it just didn't seem fair that he should have had the pleasure of it for such a short time.

We walked the mile or so to Glencairn Drive in silence. I could only imagine Wally was contemplating the painful fate that would befall us if we failed to return the ladder. I was hoping against hope that we wouldn't come face to face with the owner of the house, lest she reveal the mundane truth about the events of the night when it was lost.

I felt like Billy Liar, with the massed ranks of the Ambrosia marching band playing behind me, trapped by the suffocating tentacles of my own dishonesty. I knew that my only option, if cornered, was to fabricate an even more elaborate story to prevent Wally from knowing the truth and spreading it around. If only I had Tony here now to help me construct a suitably contrived scenario.

I could always claim that I was working undercover for MI5 with Aunty Betty and that the house on Glencairn was occupied by a Soviet sleeper cell. I had orchestrated the apple raid to allow Betty to slip unnoticed into the house to recover stolen blueprints for a new generation of inter-continental nuclear warheads, and I had been forced to make up the story about escaping the clutches of a sinister child slave labourer as a necessary cover story. But would anyone believe me?

When we arrived at Glencairn Drive, we walked round into Colquhoun Lane on the remote chance that the owner of the house might have left the ladder there. She hadn't. We walked round to the front of the house. The gate was wide open and there was no car in the driveway so we sneaked inside and crept along the path. We approached the rear of the house, and I scanned the familiar scene – the lawn, the greenhouse, the orchard – but there was no sign of the ladder.

Suddenly, I became aware of a presence behind me. I turned around to find the lady of the house, the one who had worn the cowboy hat weeks before, who had placed a gentle, custodial arm around my shoulders and told to help myself to her apples. I froze with fear. Not of what she might do, but what she might say in the presence of Wally.

I smiled. I couldn't help it. Smiling was a default reaction to someone who had exhibited such pleasant charm the last time we met. I watched the confusion on Wally's face at my behaviour. I could see him thinking that mine was an odd and ill-advised response to the threat of abduction and torture. He turned on his heels and fled.

– Quick, run! he shouted as he bolted down the driveway.

I was rooted to the spot. It seemed so silly, so rude to depart the scene when I knew there was no real danger, but there was something else holding me back. In the clear light of day, I saw the full extent of the woman's beauty and I felt a warm, exhilarating rush. She had high, angular cheekbones, dusky velvet skin, which I felt an irresistible desire to reach out and touch, and lustrous locks of blonde hair which ran halfway down the length of her tall, slim frame. I had never seen anyone look so perfect.

As her face expanded into a broad smile, I drank in her features. I felt as if I could stand watching her for the rest of my life and never become bored. She was ephemeral, like a ghostly, cloud-framed fantasy which appeared to move in slow motion, and it seemed appropriate that her every gesture should be accompanied by an elaborate classical orchestration.

– What peculiar friends you have, she said as Wally disappeared onto the road and out of sight. Am I so frightful that they feel the need to scram whenever I appear?

Her voice was posh, not harsh and braying like some snobby people could sound, but soft and inviting. Listening to her speak was like having your ears gently kissed by honey-coated lips.

– I suppose you're here about the ladder? She asked.

I stood transfixed as her moist, ruby lips enunciated the words. I was aware of their melodious sound but I was beyond the point of processing their meaning, far less responding. I imagined her leading me by the hand into the clearing in the Cunyon, on a hot, cloudless day, and laying me down on the sun-bleached grass, the warm solar rays washing over our skin as the gentle sound of midsummer birdsong was heard in the distance.

I pictured her sitting beside me, toying with the slender gold chain that hung around her perfectly formed neck.

– There's no point looking there because you won't find anything, she said curtly.

I snapped back into consciousness.

– What?

– In the garden. You won't find the ladder there. My husband moved it.

– Oh, right, I said, my heart pounding.

Out of the corner of my eye, I could see the partially concealed figure of Wally, behind the privet hedge, watching our every move. I couldn't be sure, but I reckoned he was close enough to hear our conversation as well.

– I thought about leaving it out in the lane because I figured that you'd be back for it, but it would have been an open invitation to burglars. We kept it for a couple of weeks but then my husband got the cleansing department to come and take it away. I'm terribly sorry, but we had no use for it and it was cluttering up the garden.

My heart sank, but I couldn't bring myself to feel anger and instead I thanked her, for what I didn't know. She told me they had made cider with most of the apples, but there was still a barrel full of windfall in the orchard; she invited me to help myself.

I politely declined. If Wally hadn't already twigged that she wasn't the child-eating tyrant I had depicted, then emerging unscathed from our confrontation with an armful of free fruit would almost certainly set his antennae twitching.

I made my excuses and jogged down the driveway, to give the pretence that I was running to escape, and met up with Wally out on the road. I told him how the woman had got rid of the ladder and that there was no way of getting it back. I tried to play up the danger aspect, telling him how I had made a hasty exit before she set her dog on me. I said the only reason she hadn't tried to kidnap me this time was because it was daylight and any of her neighbours might have witnessed it.

But I could tell Wally wasn't convinced. Even if he had been unable to hear our conversation, her body language would have been enough to convince him that she posed no threat. He didn't say anything as we walked home, which only reinforced my conviction that he had rumbled me. The longer the silence lasted the more paranoid I became that he planned to out me as a fraud. We arrived at the junction of Gower Street and Maxwell Drive as the light was fading. Wally was heading home in the opposite direction but I couldn't let him leave without trying to find out what he knew.

– We'll just need to tell Kane that the ladder's lost, I said.

– Aye, Wally replied enigmatically.

– Nothing else we can do.

– Nope.

I realised I wasn't getting anywhere and steeled myself for a more direct approach.

– You won't say anything, will you? I implored.

He frowned.

– About what?

– About what you saw. Back there.

He shrugged.

– I didn't see anything, mate. I was off my mark, burning rubber down the street at the first sight of the witch.

I studied his face for a hint of irony, but his expression remained firm. Then he said something odd.

– *You* won't say anything, will you?

– About what? I asked, genuinely confused.

– About the bike.
– The *bike*? I repeated incredulously.
– Aye, the bike.
– No, I won't say anything.

I decided not to push the matter, largely because I didn't want him questioning me any further, and we parted company. As I walked up the hill, towards my house, a thought occurred to me. I decided to take a short detour to Fleurs Avenue.

Wally's story about his bike being stolen didn't ring true. It was his most prized possession, and I knew there was no way he would ever have left it out, unsecured, in his backyard, which everyone knew was a thieves' paradise.

I stopped at the house where Wally had stolen the bike. Despite his protestations, I knew he must have been ashamed at thieving it from an old lady. So ashamed, in fact, that he couldn't bring himself to admit his action to the other guys. But I knew there was something he would regard as more embarrassing – being shamed into returning it. He would go to any length to prevent that ever getting out, even entering into an unspoken pact – a quid pro quo – with his best friend. If I had interpreted his message correctly, what he was saying was that he wouldn't blow the whistle on my grand deception about the apple raid on Glencairn if I didn't blow the whistle on his . . . well, I decided to test my hypothesis.

The street was deserted, and the old lady's house looked empty from the outside. When I was sure the coast was clear I crept up the path and into the back garden. And there it was – chained to a water pipe – the red Raleigh Colt.

14

I arrived home to find Mum, Dad and Tony sitting in the living room in silence. They all looked exhausted. The television was switched off and, despite it being tea-time, there was no sign of any activity in the kitchen. I asked Dad what we were having for tea, but he ignored me. I asked Mum and she sighed loudly. I thought she was either going to lose her temper or burst into tears, but instead she just smiled and clutched my hand.

– We haven't had a chance to make anything, love, she said quietly, almost in a whisper. I'll do it now. What do you fancy?

My mind was a blank. Culinary choice on a Sunday was an alien concept. Sunday dinner was and always had been roast chicken with all the trimmings. Anything else didn't compute.

– Why don't you nip down to the shop before it closes and get a couple of tins of spaghetti? she suggested.

Something was definitely amiss. Tinned spaghetti was seriously common as far as Mum was concerned. On her demonological scale of commonness, tinned spaghetti ranked somewhere between snorkel parkas and *Carry On* films. The only time I'd tasted it before was once when I was round at Wally's, and he was eating it cold, straight out of the tin. Whenever we were in the supermarket I pleaded with Mum to buy some, but she always refused. Now she was proposing it for dinner, without having to be prompted. Not only that but she said we could have Angel Delight and tinned mandarins for pudding as a special treat. Something was very wrong, but I couldn't believe my luck.

Our meal was a predictably quiet affair, but I didn't care because I was eating tinned spaghetti on toast. Tony picked at his plate and then refused the offer of Angel Delight and tinned mandarins, so

I had his portion as well as my own. Afterwards Mum said she thought I should have an early night. I didn't need to have a bath as long as I promised to wash my neck before school in the morning.

What was happening – tinned spaghetti, Angel Delight, no bath on bath night? I gave the impression that going to bed early was a major concession, but secretly I wasn't too bothered. The only things on telly were *Poldark* and *Sunday Night at the London Palladium*, which were both rubbish, and it meant I could finally get round to recategorising my football card collection.

As I brushed my teeth in the bathroom, I heard raised voices downstairs. I crept onto the landing and sat on the top step, in the dark. The living room door was closed, but I still had no difficulty hearing every word. Mum said she was tired and didn't want to argue any more, but Dad insisted there were things that needed to be sorted out.

It sounded like Tony was getting into trouble for something. I couldn't tell what, but it appeared to be serious – much more serious than him making up stories or not studying hard enough for his exams – though, as with all my parents' discussions, it never quite got to the point.

– The boy has responsibilities now, Dad said as though Tony wasn't there.

– He has a responsibility to make the most of his life, Mum replied.

– Well, he hasn't been very responsible so far. Maybe this is the best thing that could happen to him. Maybe this will make him realise that he can't spend his whole life having a good time and treating everything as a joke.

– Oh, for God's sake, Robert, he's sixteen, Mum shouted.

A few moments into the debate and already I had lost the thread. It was that old, familiar pattern – the words that didn't mean anything, the disjointed sentences, the senseless leaps of logic. It was the shipping forecast all over again.

– So what are you saying, that he shouldn't have to answer for his actions because he's only sixteen? Dad asked.

– No, I'm not. All I'm saying is that he's a young boy, and we shouldn't expect so much from him. I don't think we should be forcing decisions on him that he might regret for the rest of his life. We're his parents, and he needs our understanding, not our judgement and condemnation, Mum replied.

For all the sense she was making to me, she may as well have said *Forties, Cromarty, Forth, Tyne, Dogger, southeasterly four or five, but variable. Mainly fair. Moderate or good with fog banks.*

– Well, I don't remember having the luxury of parental understanding when I was his age, Dad replied. I remember having to work every hour of the day and night to pay for a new baby and the rent on a pokey flat where you couldn't swing a *Humber, Thames, Dover, easterly four or five. Mainly fair. Moderate or good, with fog patches in North Humber.*

– Precisely, Robert. And is that what you want for your children? For them to have to endure the same abject misery as you did? All for the sake of a *Wight, Portland, Plymouth, easterly five or six, veering southerly four in Plymouth. Showers later. Moderate or good, occasionally poor later.*

– Oh, right, so that's what you think of sixteen years of marriage – abject misery? Well, I wish you had told me that when I was still *low south Portland 992 moving quickly east; low Malin 998 losing its identity; new low expected Finisterre 990 by 0600 tomorrow.*

And so it went on. After a while, I gave up and went into my bedroom. It was a pointless discussion going nowhere, and I had more important things to occupy my mind, like how I was going to arrange my football cards.

A person's system of football card classification said much about them as an individual. The size of your collection dictated how elaborate your system could be, and how often you could change it. The bigger the collection, the greater the options and, by extension, the greater the credibility you commanded.

Those with only a few cards were inevitably restricted to an alphabetical system by surname. If you had at least one player from every club then you could adopt a more advanced system based on team and division which, in my opinion, was the best, both for ease of reference and for aesthetic reasons. It was more pleasing to have your cards effectively colour-coded, rather than having a different-coloured strip emerge after every turn.

By any standards I had a large collection, running into hundreds and going back several seasons, which meant I was able to deploy any number of different systems, often based on two or more degrees of separation. I was, for example, able to separate bearded from non-bearded players and then to sub-divide them according to position, age or even county of birth. I had done the same by dividing those wearing short and long sleeves and those in a standing or crouched pose from those in action shots.

Football cards were sold in packets of five, along with a strip of hard, unappetising bubble gum. Each bore a picture of the footballer with his name and team on the front and, on the back, some biographical detail like his age, where he was born, along with his position, how many league appearances he had made, the number of goals he had scored, etc.

The idea was that you bought the cards until you had collected the entire set. They were packed randomly, which meant you often found yourself with two or three copies of the same card – known as a doubler or a trebler. These could be swapped with friends for cards that you didn't have, but the distributor made a point of issuing only a small number of selected cards to make completing the set more difficult and, therefore, to encourage you to buy more. The bigger your collection, the more likely you were to have those rarities, which were the high denominations of playground currency – a Denis McQuade (Partick Thistle, without beard), a Henry Hall (St Johnstone, not Dundee United, with hair) or a Peter Marinello (Hibs, not Motherwell, action shot with sideburns).

The jewel in the crown of my collection was a Dixie Deans, before he signed for Celtic, without facial hair and crouched on one knee. Though I had never revealed the provenance of my prized possession to anyone, it had, in fact, come to me via Johnny Nae Da.

He bought the cards, not because he was interested in football or because he was a collector, but because he liked the gum. I learned this by chance one day when we were both opening packs outside Carter's, the newsagent, and immediately I spotted an opportunity to significantly increase the size of my collection. I struck a deal with him whereby he gave me all of his cards in return for my pieces of gum.

It was a peculiarly one-sided arrangement, but not one which I was likely to question, given that its terms were so favourable to me. I could easily have pointed out to him that, for the price of a packet of football cards he could have bought three Bazooka Joes and in doing so acquired a far superior quality of bubble gum.

Johnny Nae Da barely looked at the cards, and, even if he had, he wouldn't have known a Harry Hood (standing pose, with hair) from a Joe Mason (Kilmarnock, not Rangers, clean shaven, action shot). The fact that in gifting me a Dixie Deans (Motherwell, not Celtic, no moustache, crouched on one knee) he had given up the football card equivalent of a Canaletto original or a Shakespeare first edition was something to which he was oblivious, and I was not about to bring it to his attention.

There was, as far as I was aware, only one previously recorded acquisition of a Dixie Deans (Motherwell, not Celtic, no moustache, crouched on one knee) in the entire history of the South Side. A friend of a friend of the son of Jebsy MacBride's dad's boss had found one in a packet of cards purchased from a mini-market in Govanhill. He was constantly badgered with lucrative offers, eventually parting with it after being made an unrefusable bid of a flick knife (smuggled through customs after a holiday in Benidorm), the entire Locomotive Leipzig Subuteo team (away strip) and a half-finished raspberry jubilee.

Since taking possession of the cherished card a couple of months ago, I had acquired a form of minor celebrity and had come to the attention of some fairly important people. Primary

Seven boys from the Conception would come down to our school gates just to ask if I was the kid with the Dixie Deans card. They would inevitably ask if there was anything that would tempt me to swap it, but when I said no, they just smiled knowingly and said they understood.

The closest I had come to parting with it was when an anonymous bidder, using Kenny McRae as an intermediary, offered me a Space Hopper, a bicycle repair kit and a pair of goalkeeping gloves signed by David Harvie, the Leeds United and Scotland goalkeeper. But I held firm – Dixie deserved more, and, besides, I was enjoying the attention too much.

Now I was toying with a new classification system which, to my knowledge, no-one had yet employed and which would be my most ambitious to date. It involved working across three degrees of separation, dividing players into teams, sub-dividing them according to the number of appearances they had made, and then arranging the teams in a league table based on the total number of appearances.

It was a contentious and challenging method, which I knew would generate controversy because it placed older players ahead of technically superior team-mates and rewarded clubs for consistency of selection rather than discernment or tactical bravery. But it was one I was prepared to defend.

I began by selecting players from Aberdeen FC, alphabetically the first club. First up was Davie Robb, or 'Brush' to the Pittodrie faithful, a prolific goal scorer who, in addition to making 192 league appearances for the Dons, scoring 67 goals, also played for Scotland five times, all in 1971, including a Wembley appearance against England.

I zipped through Alloa Athletic, Arbroath, Ayr United and Berwick Rangers, because I didn't have many players from these clubs, before coming to Celtic. By the time I was onto Dundee United the noise level from downstairs was so high that it was affecting my concentration. Dad's booming voice shot through me like a blast of cold air. The Craigs, through the wall, would have heard everything and I shuddered with embarrassment. The subject of the conversation appeared to have moved onto my cousin Billy, whose wedding we had been to in the summer. What any of that had to do with Tony was a mystery to me.

– Is that what you want for your son? To see him standing at the front of a church next to some girl he barely knows, terrified to death, with the world on his shoulders, all because it's what's expected of him? Mum asked.

Why would Tony possibly want to get married, I wondered. He didn't even have a steady girlfriend, as far as I was aware.

– Well, I'd rather he did what was expected of him than see his honour destroyed. He'd never be able to hold his head up high in this neighbourhood again if he walked away from this, Dad replied.

Mum flew into a rage.

– Christ, is that what's bothering you? Tony being able to hold his head up high? We're not living in the nineteenth century, Robert. I won't let you ruin our son's life with some working-class bullshit notion about what's right and wrong. This is the 1970s. There are ways of dealing with problems like this that don't involve shackling together two young people who have nothing in common other than that they made a silly mistake when they were sixteen.

At that point Tony spoke for the first time, and it was only then that I realised he was crying.

– Don't I get a say in this? he said.

– No, you don't, Dad barked back.

– Can I just say that I don't treat everything as a joke, Tony sobbed. I do take my responsibilities seriously and . . .

But Mum interrupted.

– I think it's best if you don't say anything right now, Tony. Your Dad and I will decide what's best for you.

– But it's my life, Tony shouted, his voice cracking through the tears.

There was a momentary silence, and then Mum and Dad just continued their conversation as though Tony wasn't there.

– Yeah, of course I know there are ways of dealing with things like this, Dad said. Of course that would be the answer, but the girl's parents are Catholic. Do you think they would ever agree to something like that? Of course not. No, there's no alternative. The boy has made his bed and he has to lie on it.

The words made no sense to me, but their tone alone was enough to make me want to curl up in a corner of the room and bury my head. I put my hands over my ears and tried to concentrate on the rows of cards laid out on the floor in front of me. I had finished with Dundee United and had moved onto Dunfermline Athletic. I tried not to allow the loud voices to distract me. I had an important job to do and I had to finish it.

I had an Alec Edwards (action shot, away strip with sideburns) and a Willie Callaghan (crouched on one knee, clean shaven). The voices grew louder. Mum and Dad now appeared to be arguing over whether Tony should be getting a job rather than going to university, which threw Mum into a flat spin.

– This is the one opportunity he has to make something of his life and you want to take that away from him. What right do you have to deny your son the opportunity to better himself?

– He can better himself once he has provided for the people that now depend on him, just like his father had to do.

The tone of Mum's voice lowered suddenly. Gone was its incandescence as she tried to appeal to Dad's better nature.

– Robert, be reasonable. What chance will he have if he has to go through life without any qualifications?

– The same chance as me and all my brothers, Dad replied.

I hadn't heard Tony cry for years. Three years to be precise. Not since the holiday we spent with the Churches at their cottage on Deeside. Isabel Church was an old schoolfriend of Mum's and her husband, Donald, was a lawyer with a big firm in town. Dad was always going on about how much money they had. He said it with a kind of disdain, as though it was a major character flaw, which only riled Mum.

I was six, going on seven, but I remember every detail of the holiday as though it was yesterday. Dad hadn't wanted to go in the first place, and there had been a lot of discussion about it beforehand. Even on the drive up, with us all packed into the Mini Clubman and our suitcases crammed into the tiny boot, Dad was still complaining, saying what a bad idea he thought it was.

The first few days were tense and interminably boring. The Churches had a son, Ruaridh, who was the same age as Tony. He and Donald spent the days hillwalking, shooting rabbits and playing golf. Donald offered to take Dad and Tony along, but Dad refused. He had never done any of these things before and he didn't have any equipment. Donald offered to lend him a gun and a set of golf clubs, but Dad wouldn't hear of it. He said he wouldn't do anything unless he could pay his way. The result was that we spent the time pottering around the cottage, taking the occasional walk into the local village but doing little else.

The only activity Dad agreed to do was fishing, because he had brought along his own tackle and rod, purchased in the Woolworth January sale for five pounds. Fishing was the one sport Dad took part in. Two or three times a year we would pack a picnic and head off to the public reservoir at Barrhead to fish for carp using worms dug from the back garden as bait.

But when we went fishing with the Churches, it was a different experience altogether. The back of their Volvo estate was crammed with expensive equipment, including waders, nets and long fibreglass angling rods. After taking advice from the local ghillie on the best flies to use at that time of year, Donald and Ruaridh stood waist deep in the fast flowing Dee, casting with the flamboyant ease of master anglers. They landed two large rainbow trout which we ate, poached, with asparagus and buttered new potatoes that evening. In the event Dad was unable to use his rod and reel because permit restrictions on the river forbade the use of live bait.

The cottage had no television set and so, in the evenings, after we had eaten, we played a selection of card and board games at which the Churches proved infuriatingly proficient. After having been roundly beaten at switch, bridge, gin rummy, draughts and chess, Dad eventually recorded a significant moral victory when he and Tony overcame Donald and Ruaridh at Scrabble.

Dad milked this triumph for all it was worth and at every opportunity, cracking jokes about how he had failed his Eleven Plus yet still had a better vocabulary than a hot shot lawyer like Donald with all his Highers and degrees. Donald took the ribbing in good spirit, and the atmosphere between them lightened.

The following evening Dad and Donald disappeared off together to the local pub, eventually rolling home after midnight amid roars of laughter. In the morning, over breakfast, we were regaled with tales of derring-do, about how they had taken on the locals at pool and darts, and trounced them at both. Later that day, Dad even agreed to borrow a pair of Donald's hiking boots, and they set off, in buoyant spirit, to climb Ben MacDui.

The mood was still jovial when they returned in the early evening and we sat down to eat. The cottage, which was at the end of a track on the outskirts of Ballater, had previously been a boarding house, and the dining room remained as it had been when it catered to a large succession of paying guests. It was dominated by a long mahogany dining table and twelve heavy chairs. A hand-pulled dumb waiter in the corner of the room delivered food from the kitchen below.

With the soup and main courses over, we had a short rest before embarking on pudding. The tension of the first few days had lifted completely, and everyone was chatting and laughing enthusiastically. I remember Isabel asking what everyone wanted for dessert. She and Mum had spent most of the day in the kitchen preparing the meal, and there were several choices, including a raspberry junket, a sherry trifle and a chocolate mousse with fresh cream piped decoratively on top.

I had been eyeing up the puddings since mid-afternoon and had decided early on that I would have some of each. I made a quick mental calculation to establish whether, if everyone followed my example, there would be enough left over for seconds. I decided there probably would but figured I would have to finish my helping first so that I would be at the head of the queue.

There was a momentary silence as everyone pondered their pudding options. Then, out of the void and apropos of nothing, Ruaridh spoke.

–Tony said that he and Robert cheated at Scrabble, he announced, matter-of-factly.

The immediate aftermath is a blur. My next memory is of our family gathered in Mum and Dad's bedroom, Dad incandescent with rage and Tony in tears. Dad ordered Tony to retract what he had said and to tell Ruaridh, in the company of both families, that he had made the whole thing up. Tearfully, Tony refused. Dad then gave him until the following morning to reconsider. If, by then, he still refused to admit his lie, we would leave for home.

I barely slept, kept awake by a feeling of dread and the painful, nervous pumping of my heart. In the morning Dad gathered us all together again and asked Tony if he was prepared now to tell the truth. Tony tried to hold back his tears, but he couldn't and he broke down.

– But we did cheat, Dad, he sobbed. We looked at where all the letters were before the game started so that we could pick the ones we needed. That's the truth.

Dad flew into a violent rage and began throwing things into suitcases. The Mini was packed before breakfast, and we set off for home. The Churches tried to persuade Dad that we should stay. Donald said it was just silly kids' talk and that no-one took what Ruaridh said seriously, but Dad was insistent. He said he wouldn't be humiliated by his own son lying and blubbing like a baby. It was the last time we saw the Churches.

I packed away my football cards. I was only at Heart of Midlothian, but it had been a long weekend and I was tired. *The Godfather: Part II* now seemed an age ago. I looked at the clock.

It was ten thirty. Sophia still wasn't home from the Bay City Rollers concert. If she was much later she would get into trouble from Mum and Dad, and I wanted to be awake to witness that.

Right now, though, they appeared to be more concerned with deciding what should be done about Tony. I would quiz him about it in the morning. The sound of raised voices swept over me as my head hit the pillow.

– So, are you giving me an ultimatum, Christine? Dad asked.

– I'm not giving you anything. You're the one who's forcing decisions on people. You're the one who's telling Tony he has to give up his education.

– I'm the head of the household, and that's the decision I've made, because I judge it to be in his and everyone else's best interests.

– And I'm saying that I don't want any part of it, that I'm not prepared to live in this house any longer if you're determined to ruin our son's future.

The birds were singing when I woke. It was still dark, and Sophia was on the lower bunk, fast asleep. The clock said five thirty. I climbed out of bed and went for a pee. Everything seemed to be normal but I had a strange, intuitive sense that all was not as it should be.

I crept into my parents' room and found Dad in bed, alone. I thought Mum had perhaps slept on the sofa downstairs, but I checked and she wasn't there. She was gone. As I stood in the coldness of the living room, the words that Wee Jean had never got to sing at Billy's wedding flooded into my head. *Last night I heard my momma singing this song, Ooh wee chirpy chirpy cheep cheep; Woke up this morning and my momma was gone, Ooh wee chirpy chirpy cheep cheep, chirpy chirpy cheep cheep chirp.*

15

A funny thing happened in gym class. Wutherspoon had made us retrieve all the gym equipment from the store and set it up in the gym hall so that we could do circuit training. It was pure badness on her part because it was so bitterly cold, and she stood at the side, swaddled in her overcoat and fur hat, watching us shivering as we passed medicine balls over our heads and queued for the vaulting horse.

I was exhausted after a night of broken sleep and I was struggling to stay awake. But when I shimmied up one of the ropes and slid down it, with my body rubbing against its rough, thick twine, I felt the same sensation that I had experienced at the Cunyon, watching Tony and the faceless girl doing *that*.

It left me quite disorientated and, for a moment, I lost track of where I was. When I hit the floor, I staggered hither and thither with everyone laughing and Wutherspoon shrieking at me, like a strangled cat, to move onto the wall bars.

It had been the strangest of days. I lay in bed dozing until half past eight, when finally I got up, washed and clothed myself and grabbed a bowl of cornflakes. Everyone else was still asleep so I went into Dad's room and shook him awake.

– I'll have to leave now, I said. I'm going to be late for school.

Dad yawned, then he smiled and ruffled my hair.

– OK, off you go, son. We'll talk tonight.

– Where's Mum? I asked.

He sighed and looked lost, like he didn't know how to answer.

– She's gone away for a bit.

– Is she coming back?

He paused long enough to be unconvincing.

– Of course she is. She just needs some time on her own. It's nothing to worry about. Have you got money for your lunch?

– I eat lunch in the dinner school.

– OK, off you go then.

When I arrived at school I decided to give the Papes v. Prods football game a miss. After all the tribulations of the night before, I didn't feel up to competitive sport. Instead, I hung about the railings until the bell rang. Bobby Gilchrist had broken his arm, after falling off the monkey-puzzle frame at the swing park, and people were lining up to sign his stookie. Mark McGilvray had written 'Marc Bolan Rock God' so underneath I wrote 'Dixie Deans Football God'.

Word had got round that we had been to see *The Godfather: Part II* at the weekend and everyone, including the girls, wanted to know all about it. At any other time I would have revelled in being the centre of attention, but it just didn't seem that important any more and I affected an air of blasé detachment, as though watching X-rated films were part and parcel of my hectic social life.

Wutherspoon was in a cranky mood during morning lessons and I couldn't concentrate. Kevin Kane's ladder was preying on my mind. I couldn't see how that situation was going to resolve itself with my extremities remaining bruise free. The only saving grace was that, if he wanted to beat me up, he'd have to come looking for me. Then there was my football card collection, half of which I had yet to categorise, and, even if I did, I was worried how my controversial new method of classification would be received.

But what was most concerning me was Mum's sudden disappearance. I didn't know where or why she had gone or when she would return – if at all. I was worried, seriously worried, because I was due to sit my Grade Two survival badge at Calder Street baths the following Monday. It involved treading water for five minutes in my pyjamas and the only pair I had were the ones I got from Granny and Granddad for my seventh birthday with a Joe 90 motif on them.

Mum had promised to buy me a new pair of big boys' pyjamas, but I knew, without having to ask, that Dad would be less understanding, given our current financial circumstances. I felt a knot in my stomach as I pondered my options – either to withdraw from the test or to parade my Joe 90 jimjams before a forty-strong audience of my peers.

After school, Cuddihy and Chabs said they were going round to McEwan's the greengrocer. Monday was the day McEwan collected his supplies from the fruitmarket and, if you helped him unpack his van, sometimes he gave you a bag of apples. They asked me if I wanted to join them, but I wasn't in the mood and I said I was going to walk home alone.

As I passed the Post Office, Bifter, Jukebox and Kenny MacRae were standing outside, taking the piss out of the Prof., who was bobbing about like a swan in a flap, havering some shite to himself.

– They said he died from acute enteritis, but we all knew the real cause of death was being forced to do calisthenics in the baking sun while he was weak and sick, he muttered.

Although I was two or three yards away from the Prof., I caught a whiff of his stale, musky smell. The boys were doubled up with laughter, but I couldn't help feeling sorry for the mad old duffer.

I passed over the railway bridge and met Celeste coming from the opposite direction. My heart jumped at the sight of her. She said Sophia hadn't turned up for school that day and asked me if I knew why, but I said I didn't.

– Enjoy the concert last night? I asked, my voice creaking with embarrassment.

– What concert? she replied.

– The Bay City Rollers concert.

As I stood before her, memories of the rope incident in the gym flooded back into my head, like a river bursting its banks.

Her hair was tied in a ponytail. Her glossy pink lipstick glistened in the winter sun. Her breasts were pert and upright, and her nipples strained against the white cotton fabric of her school shirt.

– I wasn't at the Bay City Rollers concert, bozo. Sophia and me tried to get tickets but then she said, even if she did get one, she wanted to go with Cumbo, not me. Bitch.

Celeste was talking, but her words didn't register. I was running my eyes over every curve of her body and imagining how perfect it would be if I was able to replicate the rope feeling right now. All I needed was a rope. Where was a rope when you needed one?

– The last I heard, Cumbo had managed to get a couple of tickets off some tout who was charging over the odds. They must have got the money from somewhere. I don't know where. Do you know where they got it from?

I was shimmying up the rope and sliding down, my eyes trained on the forbidden depths of her cleavage, imagining her pulling off her hair-band, allowing her shiny, golden locks to cascade over her shoulders.

– I said, do you know where they got it from?

– Got what?

– Steve, are you even listening to what I'm saying? Christ, I don't know why I bother, she said, shaking her head and walking off.

The moment she left, I felt a crushing sense of guilt. A lot of bad things had happened recently, all of which seemed to stem from the incident at the Cunyon, and I knew I shouldn't be glorying in its grotesque memory. Those were the kind of thoughts I imagined would get you six months in purgatory.

When I arrived home, Tony and Sophia were in the living room, sprawled over the furniture, watching *Randall and Hopkirk (Deceased)*. The curtains were closed and empty tea-cups and cereal bowls littered the floor. Mum hadn't been gone a day and already her absence was noticeable by the state of the house. I poured myself a bowl of cornflakes and fashioned a space for myself at the end of the settee, edging Sophia's legs out of the way.

– How come you weren't at school today? I asked her.

– Piss off, she said, without taking her eyes off the telly.

We sat in silence for a few minutes until there was an advert break.

– Where's Dad? I asked.

– He ran off to join the Foreign Legion. Said he couldn't stand having a wee prick like you for a son any longer.

– You're dead funny, Sophia, I said. You won't think you're such a laugh when I tell Dad who you were at the Bay City Rollers concert with last night.

She sat bolt upright and a look of panic shot across her face. Then she regained her composure and eased herself back into a prone position.

– I was there with Celeste. Anyone who tells you different is a fucking liar.

– That's not what Celeste says. I just met her in the street, I revealed with a beaming smile.

– She's talking pish and you'd better not repeat it to Dad or I'll kick yer baws.

– Oh, aye, you and whose army, ya scabby hoor?

– Give it a rest, you two, Tony ordered. I'm trying to watch the telly.

After *Randall and Hopkirk (Deceased)* ended, I tried to get Tony to tell me about what had been going on between him and Mum and Dad the night before, but he wasn't giving anything away. He looked tired, and I knew not to push it.

He said Dad was working at Il Pescatore, the Italian restaurant at The Halfway, that night and he wouldn't be home until the early hours. A friend of Benny the mechanic had managed to get him a few shifts, cash-in-hand, because one of their waiters had called in sick. I was glad there would be some money coming into the house, but it meant I'd have to wait until the morning to ask Dad when Mum was coming home, which would mean another sleepless night worrying about the Joe 90 pyjamas.

He had left us money to buy our dinner at the chippie. Not only that, Tony and Sophia couldn't be bothered going, so I was dispatched on my own. Me, alone, with a crisp pound note, let loose in the chippie. I closed my eyes and took stock of this land-mark moment in my young life, pondering what munificent sacri-fice I could have made in a previous incarnation for such benevolence to be bestowed upon me now.

To Wally, Chabs, Cuddihy and Bifter, the Criterion Sea Fish Bar was a mundane and routine part of their everyday lives. The source of their evening meal more days than not, they neither liked nor disliked it – it was just there. To me it was an uncharted Eden, a lard-soaked citadel of illicit pleasures. Needless to say, Mum regarded it as common in the extreme and had banned us from even entering. It sat high on her list of proscribed venues, along with the café, the snooker hall and the slot-machine arcade.

But throughout my childhood, and well into my adolescence, everything about the Crit held my fascination, from its bubbling vat of beef dripping to its oversized, tumescent sausages and its live-for-the-moment, anti-nutritional hedonism, which decreed that cholesterol and calories were tasty things you ate with plenty of salt 'n' vinegar.

Food was Dad's singular, abiding interest. Because he worked in restaurants, he had always eaten good food. For him, food was a source of pleasure, education and personal enrichment. He read about it and considered its merits with the enthusiasm and intensity of a dedicated gourmand. He tried to include Mum but with little success. He did most of the day-to-day cooking at home and when Mum reluctantly understudied he was always on hand to offer advice and encouragement.

I lived in mortal fear of his gastronomic predilections becoming public. Our kitchen cupboards – permanently stocked with exotic and esoteric ingredients, fresh herbs and spices, foreign cured meats and cheeses and ethnic sauces – remained a dark and pulsating secret like Edgar Allan Poe's *Tell-Tale Heart*.

In contrast, those who patronised the Crit regarded food as a functional and suspect necessity. Anything that wasn't battered and deep fried was considered fanciful and effeminate. The very mention of filet mignon with sauce béarnaise would have been enough to spark a riot on the Govan Road. For them, sauce came in two varieties – red and brown – and the cosmic extreme of culinary experimentation was a Scotch pie in a roll.

For all that, I couldn't help myself; the Crit was my destiny. And from the moment Tony told me that the jars of pickled mussels on the shelf above the cash register were pygmies' brains in formaldehyde, I was hooked.

I preened as I stood in the queue awaiting my turn and, when Wally walked in, I almost exploded with pride. I pulled the pound note from my pocket and waved it across the counter, as though buying my tea there was a routine and laborious part of my everyday life. It was only when it came to making my order that I realised how out of my depth I was, and that a more contrite attitude was advisable until I learned the ropes.

The Crit employed a tightly defined system of ritual and terminology not easily penetrable to the outsider. You didn't ask for fish and chips, you asked for a 'fish supper'. A battered fish was just a fish whereas a fish with breadcrumbs was a 'special fish'; a deep fried pizza was a 'Tally pie' and a bag of chips a 'Glasgow salad'.

The balding, moustachioed owner, who went by the name of Fernando though whose Mediterranean credentials were, to say the least, dubious, oversaw the frying operation. He spoke in broken English with an unconvincing Italian accent. It was widely rumoured his real name was Maurice and he came from Drumoyne.

His grey-skinned, sepulchral assistant, Shirley, served and wrapped the orders with the dexterity of a Mississippi card shark. The flamboyance with which she wielded the salt and vinegar shakers belied an otherwise joyless and uninterested demeanour. The only time she removed the permanently fixed Embassy Regal King Size from her mouth was to demand money. Whenever she was handed a fiver she held it above the opened till and shouted *Five in Fernando!* across the shop floor.

After we had been served, Wally and I stood outside eating our chips, seeking the comfort of the hot air from the extractor duct as protection against the November night chill. Wally was in a bad mood because Suitcase and Briefcase had just announced that they were moving out of the house. They had new jobs at the John Brown shipyard in Clydebank, on the other side of the river, because there wasn't enough work for them at Govan. They had saved up the deposit for a flat in Clydebank they planned to share. Holdall was saving up for a flat deposit too, and Handbag was leaving school at Christmas, so Wally knew it was only a matter of time before they left home as well.

– Soon it'll just be me and that auld pair of drunken arseholes, he said, referring to his parents. I'm telling you, I couldn't stand it if that happened. I don't know what I'd do.

I told him that Mum was away for a few days and invited him to hang out back at my place for a bit. He didn't ask where Mum had gone – that was one of the things I liked about Wally. He just accepted things the way they were and he didn't particularly want to know why. On the way back, I asked him if he had seen Kane recently, but he said he hadn't been to school for ages, so I breathed a sigh of relief.

When we arrived at the house, Tony and Sophia were in a foul mood because I had taken so long. Sophia's Glasgow salad was cold and Tony's Tally Pie had gone soggy, but they ate them all the same. I'd had enough change left over to buy a bottle of Irn-Bru, a bar of Old Jamaica and twenty pink shrimps so we settled down to watch *Ironside*, which was a real treat because Mum never usually let me watch telly after nine o'clock.

I must have dozed off before the end of the programme. When

I came to, the telly was fizzing, and Sophia and Tony had gone to bed. I looked at the clock – it was half past eleven. Wally was lying curled up on the floor, snoring. I considered waking him to ask if he wanted to go home, but I already knew what the answer would be, so I threw a coat over him and went to bed.

I was woken in the morning by the sound of Dad and Sophia rowing. Sophia was still in bed, and Dad was trying to rouse her.

– You're not staying off school for another day, Dad shouted.

– What do you care? You'll probably make me leave before I sit my exams anyway, just like Tony.

– You never mind about Tony. What he does has got nothing to do with you, Dad said defensively.

– How do you work that one out? He's *my* brother and you've ruined his life.

Dad exploded with anger.

– I won't be talked to like that, young lady. While you live under my roof, you will do as I say, and I say you're going to school.

– No, I'm not, and there's nothing you can do to make me.

– You will show respect to me. I demand that you show me some respect.

Dad was shouting so loudly that his voice began to crack, like he was on the verge of tears. I closed my eyes and prayed for Sophia to stop goading him, but she carried on.

– What are you going to do if I don't? Throw me out of the house like you did to Mum?

– I did not throw her out of the house. You have no right to say that. Do you hear me. You have no right to say that.

I dressed quickly and slipped out of the room and downstairs where I found Wally, sitting on the sofa, enjoying the cabaret. I grabbed my coat and led him out the door. I desperately wanted time alone with Dad so that I could pin him down on where Mum was and when she might be coming home. But I was too embarrassed by all the shouting to hang around.

*

As things turned out, Wally remained our house guest for the rest of the week. Every day when I returned home from school, he was sitting on the electricity box in the Proffy waiting for me. It was just assumed that he would stay. He never asked permission, and I never refused. Sophia moaned a bit, but, since Dad was working late in the restaurant every night, he was not around to adjudicate.

By Friday, the house looked like a war zone. Four days of Crit dining had left its mark, with discarded chip wrappers littering every surface. The living room carpet was strewn with dirty tea-cups, cereal bowls and empty Irn-Bru bottles. Tony had ceased to be a clandestine smoker and was now indulging his habit openly, leaving overflowing ashtrays in every room.

Windows and curtains remained closed, leaving a fetid fug hanging in what little air was allowed to circulate. The kitchen had become impassable because of the build-up of abandoned dishes and half-eaten food; the bathroom was sodden and tide-marked.

Dad's Stakhanovite commitment to housework had waned since he began shifting at Il Pescatore, and the responsibility had switched to the rest of us. It had become a battle of wills. There was a collective, unspoken resolve that each of us was prepared to endure ever greater depths of squalor rather than be the first to wield a cloth or a mop in anger. Dad left a series of notes, each more intemperate than the last, complaining about the foul state of the house, but all of them were ignored.

On Friday afternoon, Wutherspoon sent us home early from school because the teachers were having an in-service day. Before we left she reminded us to bring our pyjamas with us on Monday morning. I had spent most of the week trying to forget the survival course, driving from my mind the constantly recurring image of me, dressed in my Joe 90s, surrounded by a baying, jeering mob. Now it all came rushing back and I shuddered.

I put my hand up and asked Wutherspoon if it was strictly

necessary for me to sit the pyjama part of the test. I told her that, if ever I were on a ship that looked like it might sink, I would make a point of never going to bed wearing pyjamas, so the matter was academic as far as I was concerned. She told me to wait behind and gave me four of the belt for impertinence.

When I arrived home that afternoon I was shocked to find the house was spotless. The surfaces had been vacuumed, dusted and polished, and a smell of fresh lemon disinfectant permeated the air. Tony and Sophia were not around – by then boredom had finally convinced Sophia to return to school and Tony had arranged an appointment at the labour exchange to try to find a job. It was early enough in the day for Dad still to be around, but when I wandered through the living room and into the kitchen, I found a woman standing at the sink, washing dishes.

At first, I thought she must be a cleaner Dad had employed, but when she turned around I realised it was Vivienne, the woman who ran the bar in the restaurant where Dad used to work.

– Hi, Vivienne, what are you doing here? I asked breezily.

She stood with her eyes darting from side to side. Her face was bright red and she smiled nervously. Suddenly Dad appeared behind me, looking flustered.

– What are you doing home at this time? he asked, but he didn't wait for an answer. Vivienne kindly agreed to help me out with the cleaning. I haven't had time because of the hours I've been working.

I didn't say anything, and Dad shuffled around me awkwardly, opening and closing cupboards and wiping surfaces that didn't need wiped. There was something cooking in the oven – it smelled like a steak and kidney pie and I felt a surge of satisfaction. I'd had enough of chips and was looking forward to some home cooked food. After a few moments Dad suggested we go upstairs for a 'chat'.

He told me to sit on the end of the freshly laundered lower bunk and he stood in the middle of the room. All the detritus that normally littered the floor – books, magazines, clothes and football boots – had been tidied away and the draught from the opened window had dissipated its musky smell.

Dad said he realised it had been a difficult time for me recently and he apologised for not being around during the week. He had been offered some work in the restaurant and he didn't feel he could turn it down because we needed the money. I told him I understood. He said he and Mum were going through a bit of a rough patch, but it was nothing to worry about. She would be home soon and everything would be back to normal.

I asked him where she had gone, but he said he didn't know. I asked him when she was coming back, and he said he didn't know that either.

– How do you know that things will be back to normal then? I asked. What if Mum never comes back?

– That's not going to happen, he insisted. Your mum wouldn't do that.

– But how do you know?

– Look, son, you're just going to have to trust me.

Then he sat down on the bed beside me and he said something which struck me as odd. He told me that there was no need for me to tell anyone that Vivienne had been here.

– She was just doing me a favour, but others might not see it like that.

– What others? I asked.

– Well, never mind. Let's just make it our little secret, OK?

He was smiling and he put his hand on top of my head and ruffled my hair playfully.

– Don't worry, everything will be fine.

I spent the weekend dreading the arrival of Monday morning. As expected, Dad had refused my plea for new pyjamas. I knew he would never let me stay off school, particularly after Sophia's absences. All day Sunday, I had a sick feeling in my stomach. I couldn't sleep and by Monday morning I was dizzy with nerves. My mood wasn't helped by a phone call from the headmaster of the secondary asking for a meeting with Dad later that day to talk about Sophia's behaviour. Dad was already in a bad mood because of her truancy and her hostile attitude, and this just sent him into a blind rage.

I inched my way down Gower Street with a growing sense of dread. I had decided to leave my Joe 90s at home and to pretend that I had forgotten them. I knew Wutherspoon would never believe that, not after what had happened on Friday. She'd know that I had done it on purpose and she wouldn't stop at four of the belt. But I felt it was the only recourse open to me. Dad had tried to convince me that there would be plenty of other people there with similar pyjamas, but I couldn't take the chance. I risked public humiliation on an unprecedented scale.

I turned the corner of Maxwell Drive and St Andrews Street like a condemned man approaching the gallows, but when I looked ahead, there, at the school gates, was Mum. She was carrying a Marks & Spencer bag which I knew could only contain one thing – a pair of big boy pyjamas. She had remembered. My heart lifted and tears welled up in my eyes.

Some of my classmates were hanging around the school gates, but I was too excited to care about what they thought. I ran towards Mum and threw my arms wide open, wrapping them around her neck as we embraced in a crushing hug. She swept me off my feet and, as she swung me around, I felt the cold, wetness of her tears against my cheek as she kissed me. She tried to say something but she had to give up because she was sobbing so hard.

– I thought I would have to miss the survival test, I said. I couldn't do it in my Joe 90s.

– You should have known I'd never let you down, she said, sobbing.

– Where have you been? I demanded. When are you coming home? You are coming home, aren't you? Dad said you were coming home, but then he didn't know where you were, so I said to him how do you know she's coming home?

Mum hugged me tight again.

– Look, don't worry. Things will be fine. I'm staying at Granny and Granddad's house for a few days until I sort myself out.

– What do you need to sort out? Why can't you just come home now? I asked.

Mum was silent for a few moments.

– Your dad and I are having a few problems that we need to sort out. It's just not possible for me to deal with them while I'm in the house so I'm taking a little holiday. But things will be sorted out very soon, and then we will be back together – you, me, Sophia and Tony.

– And Dad, I said quickly. What about Dad?

Mum smiled.

– Well, let's see what happens, shall we?

I passed the survival test with flying colours. The pyjamas that Mum had bought were a bit on the big side, but that worked in my favour because they were easier to take off when I was in the pool. As it turned out I would probably have got away with wearing the Joe 90s without attracting too much attention. Angus Dickie and Stephen Munro wore pyjamas featuring, respectively, Sylvester the Cat and Bill and Ben, the Flower Pot Men.

I arrived home just as Dad was leaving to attend the meeting with Sophia's headmaster, so he told me to come with him. He was in a doubly bad mood because he'd had to turn down a shift at the restaurant. Tony was sitting on the sofa looking nervous.

I was looking forward to settling down with a bowl of corn-flakes in front of the telly – *The Persuaders* was on at four o'clock – but Dad said he didn't want me hanging about the house. Tony was expecting a 'guest' and he needed privacy. He said they had important things to discuss and he didn't want me getting under their feet. It all sounded very mysterious. I didn't see why Tony couldn't take his 'guest' elsewhere and leave me in peace but I could tell from Dad's tone that he meant business.

Dad said he was in a hurry so I leapt upstairs three at a time, dumped my schoolbag and quickly changed out of my uniform, and ran back down, all inside a minute. As we were about to leave, the doorbell rang. Tony jumped off the settee like a scalded cat and raced to the front door. When he opened it, a girl was standing on the doorstep. She smiled at him weakly and, after an awkward pause, he invited her in. She brushed past Dad and me with her head bowed. Dad attempted to introduce himself, and she stopped for a split second, her face bright red, long enough to say Hi, almost inaudibly, before pressing on into the living room.

Despite the briefest of introductions, I had seen enough of her face to know that I recognised her. I didn't know her first name but I knew her surname. It was Kane. She was the elder sister of Kevin, the boy who was, at this moment, preparing to use my groin for penalty practice over the non-return of his father's ladder.

16

The secondary was a modern, red-brick structure of three sections which, end-to-end, formed a giant semi-circle. It was built on four storeys, which meant the classrooms on the top landing almost touched the sky. An outside passageway ran the length of all three blocks, on every floor, giving an external sense of connectedness – a feeling that, once you were inside, there was nowhere to hide.

It was the most imposing building I had ever seen, and, late on a Monday afternoon, when all the pupils had gone home for the day, it seemed especially menacing. Its grim utilitarianism reminded me of the old black-and-white prison films I'd seen on telly like *The Bird Man of Alcatraz* and *20,000 Years in Sing Sing*.

I'd never set foot in the secondary and yet I felt I knew every inch of its layout from Tony's elaborate accounts of the mayhem and torture that went on within its walls. Everything that was threatening and humiliating about the primary seemed multiplied tenfold at the secondary.

As an institution, it was overwhelming and alien in a way that made me cringe when I recalled the stomach twisting uncertainties I'd harboured when making the giant leap from nursery to primary. Other than its sheer scale, there was the mass of new teachers – one for every subject you studied, each with their own belt and reasons for administering it – and the Byzantine web of protocol that seemed to govern school life. Suddenly the certainties of Wutherspoon, with all her haggish malignance, didn't seem so bad after all. It was definitely a case of better the devil you know.

Tony was a self-appointed expert in pronouncing what was

and wasn't done at the secondary – what course of action would see you safely through the school gates at home time and what would see you strapped, half-naked, to a cistern with your tie while the fourth year used you for pissing target practice.

More rules seemed to govern behaviour in the toilet than in any other area of the school. Some cubicles were reserved for smoking – a habit you were expected to have taken up by the stroke of midnight on your twelfth birthday – some for playing cards and some for extortion and other kinds of felony. The one thing from which the cubicles appeared unconditionally exempt was their primary purpose. Anyone caught defecating in them was regarded as perverse and suspect, fatally compromising any hope of social acceptance.

The need to learn new subjects like French and science was a reality of the secondary too intimidating to contemplate. According to Tony you had to conduct entire conversations in French with the teacher in front of the class – including the girls – and if you made even one mistake, you were made to eat raw garlic until you were sick.

There was a crazy guy in Tony's class called Ulrick who was suspended because, when the teacher asked him to think of a question in French, he asked her, Did your parents plan to have you or were you a mistake? Ulrick turned out to be a bit of a serial bampot. He was later expelled for tying the gym teacher to the wall bars and throwing bean bags at him, and he ended up in the loony bin after setting fire to himself in Boot's.

Then there was the dreaded general health test at the end of second year, known simply as 'the medical', when you had to drop your pants in front of the school nurse and cough while she cupped your bawbag in the palm of her hand. Tony said that if you got a stiffy, she rapped it with a cold teaspoon which sat in an ice bucket at the side of her desk and your name went on a 'register of shame' which was read out before the entire school at the end-of-year prize-giving.

When he told me that story I didn't know what a stiffy was

– I'd never heard the term before – but following the incident on the gym rope, suddenly it all began to make sense. Not only did I know what a stiffy was, I strongly suspected I may even have had one. I was frozen with fear. If I could get a stiffy in the gym class, then there was every reason to suppose one might suddenly appear in the middle of my medical.

The humiliation would be too much too bear. It would be grinding, toe-curling degradation on an unimaginable scale. How would I ever be able to look my parents in the eye again? I resolved, from that moment on, to close my mind to any thought of the secondary. To me it was like contemplating death – I knew it was inevitable but it was so far ahead in the future that I wasn't going to ruin my life now worrying about it.

Dad had driven us to the secondary in the van for his meeting with the headmaster. He'd used the money he earned doing shifts at Il Pescatore to pay for some of the repairs that were necessary. It wasn't yet roadworthy, but at least it was back on the road. As we drew up outside the school gates, I saw Sophia waiting in the playground. Dad told me to stay in the van while he went in with her.

As a gesture of goodwill he had stopped at the Bungalow café on the way and bought me an Aztec bar. He said it would fill a gap until we had our tea, but I knew there was more to it than that. He could easily have bought me a Caramac or a Cadbury's fudge, both of which were cheaper. An Aztec, on the other hand, bore all the hallmarks of confectionery bribery.

He had been unusually accommodating over the last couple of days, and I couldn't help thinking it had something to do with Vivienne. He seemed determined to keep her visit to the house under wraps. There was something not quite right about it. Mum didn't like Vivienne – that much I knew from the number of times her name cropped up in arguments between them – but Vivienne had only been doing Dad a favour, offering to help with the cleaning and cooking. Surely Mum would be pleased if she thought there was someone else around, in her absence, to lend a hand? Having said that, Dad couldn't have been that worried about me divulging 'our little secret'. He was confident enough of my silence not to accede to my demand for a family bag of Revels.

He and Sophia made their way across the playground towards the large double entrance to the building. As they climbed the steps, a woman accompanied by a boy and a younger girl appeared behind them. It was Cumbo and Lyndsey. Dad held the door open for them. The woman, whom I took to be their mum, had a short conversation with Lyndsey, obviously telling her to wait in the playground.

I slumped down in my seat so that she wouldn't see me. I had a lot on my mind, and a confrontation with Lyndsey was the last thing I needed. My head was still racing after my brush with Kane's sister. What was she doing in my house, with Tony, I wondered? What possible business could she have with him? I could only imagine that their meeting must have had something to do with the lost ladder. How could it be about anything else? It was too much of a coincidence.

I raised my head slightly so that I was just able to spy on Lyndsey through the bottom corner of the window. Someone had drawn a hopscotch grid on the tarmac in chalk, and she was hopping and stamping, reciting a rhyme as she went. After a while she got bored and started to do handstands. I don't know why but I felt kind of sorry for her, playing all by herself in the large deserted playground. I also felt like a bit of a creep, hiding from her and spying on her, eating my Aztec bar all by myself.

I got out of the van and walked across the playground. She looked at me defiantly.

– What do you want? she asked.

– Fancy a bit of Aztec?

Her posture relaxed slightly, obviously disarmed by my olive branch.

– Don't know, what are they like?

– What? Have you never had an Aztec before? I said, affecting surprise.

Actually I wasn't that surprised. Aztecs were pricey and definitely in the top drawer of swedgers. I'd only ever had one before and that was at Christmas.

– It's nice. It's a bit like a Mars bar only it's made by Cadbury's.

– What, you mean a Sram rab? Lyndsey said.

– What's a Sram rab? I asked.

– It's a Mars bar in backwards language.

– What's backwards language?

– It's like egg language except you say everything backwards so that your enemies don't know what your talking about. Like egnaro eelibuj instead of orange jubilee and flah-azzip reppus instead of half-pizza supper.

– Gallus.

Lyndsey was always coming out with great stuff like that. Effortlessly, she seemed able to dispel all the negative preconceptions I had about girls. I knew she wasn't representative of the gender as a whole – I'd come across plenty of girls who'd done more than enough to reinforce my many prejudices – but, despite myself, I just couldn't help liking her. If only she was a boy, I was sure we'd have been good friends. I broke my Aztec bar down the middle and handed her half, and we sat on the bottom step munching in silence.

Despite my gesture of goodwill, I felt a dark cloud hanging over us. Relations were still strained and I knew the reason could only be the comments I'd made at Bella – the day we'd gone to Gino's for milkshakes and pancakes with golden syrup. She didn't say as much, but I sensed it as a barrier between us.

I really wanted to get back to how things were before, when we had swapped funny stories and she had tried to teach me how to do the splits. I knew I'd have to say something to clear the air, so I stood up to face her and steeled myself.

– Look, you remember that day at Bella, when I said all that stuff? I inquired gingerly.

– All what stuff? she asked.

I couldn't work out if she genuinely didn't remember or if she was just trying to make my apology as difficult as she could.

– All that stuff about, well, you know, about me hating you.

I could feel my face burn with embarrassment. I'd never spoken to anyone before with this level of intimacy, far less a girl, and I had to force every mortifying syllable through my mouth like I was pushing a giant boulder up a hill.

– No, I don't remember that. Why do you hate me then? What have I ever done to you?

– No, see that's just it, I don't hate you. I just . . .

– Well, why did you say it then? she barked, not allowing me to finish my sentence.

– Well . . . I just said it because my mates were there and they were trying to say that, eh . . . you were sort of . . . eh . . . my girlfriend . . . or something daft like that.

She looked at me with contempt. I wanted the ground to swallow me up.

– Your girlfriend? What made them think that?

My mouth was dry and my lips glued shut. I tried running my tongue between them but it was so devoid of moisture that it took a monumental effort to separate them. I also appeared to have lost control of my lower limbs. My legs jolted involuntarily and I had to hold them steady with my hands to dispel the impression that I was about to launch into an impromptu polka.

– I don't know, that's the thing. I mean I didn't do anything . . .

Again she interrupted me, preventing me from finishing my sentence.

– So, if you don't hate me, what are you trying to say? That you love me?

A bolt of mortal panic shot through my body, almost crippling me. Instantly my head emptied of all neural activity like a television set whose plug has been pulled from the mains. A white dot receded into the deepest reaches of my mind like a black hole closing in on itself, until there was nothing between my ears but a dense, expansive void. I was now, officially, incapable of advanced human functioning. My body, abandoned by the lack of any electrical impulses from the brain, was left to tremble and wilt. A thin dribble of saliva crept from the edge of my mouth and began to roll down my chin.

– Relax, you silly boy, I'm winding you up, Lyndsey said, her harsh expression dismantling and giving way to a broad, beaming smile.

– I know you didn't really mean what you said. My mum said your mates would have eaten you for breakfast if they thought you might actually be enjoying the company of a girl.

As she sat chuckling to herself, slowly I began to recover my composure and regain proper use of my limbs. I was surprised that she had been discussing me with her mother. My default reaction should have been of alarm and distaste but, unusually, I found the information had given me a warm glow of satisfaction.

– What do you think is going to happen to Gordon and Sophia? she asked.

I stood staring at her blankly, still incapable of coherent speech.

She looked at me, surprised.

– What, don't you know?

– Know what?

– They're in trouble with the police.

– The *police*?

My blood ran cold. I had always pictured being in trouble with the police as the last word in danger and excitement, like being in one of those old gangster movies with Jimmy Cagney and George Raft. I imagined the whining of sirens and the screeching of squad car brakes as hardened, cynical detectives called through loudhailers, telling me the house was surrounded and ordering me to give myself up, then kicking in the front door as I sneaked out through the kitchen window and disappeared into the night under a flashlit hail of bullets.

The reality was more prosaic. The word 'police' had barely

left my lips when an Austin Maxi panda car pulled up in the school car-park. Two middle-aged, overweight coppers emerged languidly, retrieved their hats from the back seat, slowly put them on and then strolled up the steps and through the front entrance to the school, as though it was the most tedious task they had ever undertaken.

– What do the police want with Sophia? I asked.

– I don't know. I just know that somebody – I think it was a parent – phoned the cops because of something Sophia and Gordon had done to their kid.

– Did it have anything to do with the Bay City Rollers concert?

– I don't know. No-one ever tells me anything.

– I know what you mean.

I didn't know what to think. Instinctively I felt concern for the shame that would be heaped upon my parents at Sophia being in trouble with the law. But I would be lying if I said there wasn't a small part of me that gloried in her discomfort and in the undoubted celebrity it would bring me at school – being able to boast that I had a sister with form.

Lyndsey and I sat in virtual silence, but it wasn't the same uncomfortable silence of our first encounter in Bella, when we had tentatively sized each other up. It was the silence of two people relaxed in one another's company, each with their own thoughts, as we waited for the first sign of life from the school. Lyndsey was wearing a girl's Timex, and I had to keep asking her for the time. After an hour there was still no sign of life and it was now dark.

Eventually the school doors opened and the policemen emerged, returning to their car with the same leisurely detachment as before. Then, a few moments later, Cumbo and his mum came out, followed closely by Dad and Sophia. Each pair marched purposefully in different directions. Lyndsey smiled at me and said a quick goodbye before racing off to catch up with her mother and brother.

– Thanks for the Aztec, she shouted as she ran.

I returned to the van. Sophia sat in the passenger seat, which meant I was relegated to the back, where I perched on the spare tyre, hoping against hope that there would be a long and detailed discussion about what had just happened. The early signs were not good. Dad and Sophia sat in stony silence, staring straight ahead. Dad had obviously decided it was not a matter appropriately discussed in my presence and that it should be dealt with later. Just my luck.

But as we drove through the rush-hour traffic, I could see his resolve waning. He glanced over at Sophia, then shook his head and sighed expansively. His anger level was rising rapidly, and I knew that it would only be a matter of time before he erupted in a crescendo of fury. He didn't disappoint. Good old Dad.

As we sat at the traffic lights, his hands gripped the steering wheel with growing intensity and his head rocked back and forth until he could stem the tide no longer.

– What the bloody hell do you think you were doing? he demanded.

Sophia said nothing, which worried me slightly. If she maintained her silence and it was a one-way conversation then it might be difficult to interpret. If I had to rely on Dad's intemperate and incoherent ramblings then it would be hard to establish a clear and precise chronological pattern of events. I braced myself for the inevitable shipping forecast but, in the event, I needn't have worried.

– Do you think that kind of behaviour is normal? Demanding money from children younger than you and getting your boyfriend to beat them up if they don't pay?

Bingo. I had the what. Now all I needed was the when, the who, the where and the why. Sophia said nothing, but she didn't have to speak – Dad was providing all the narrative detail that I needed. He was on a roll.

– Don't you realise the trouble you're in? This isn't some silly playground prank you've been involved in. It's criminal behaviour. It's called demanding money with menaces, and you're old enough to be prosecuted for it. You're old enough to go to court. The press will have a bloody field day if the procurator fiscal decides to press charges.

Still Sophia said nothing.

– What the hell are you doing hanging around with a moron like that anyway?

– He's not a moron, Sophia said quietly, but her defiance only made Dad angrier.

– He is a bloody moron. Who, other than a moron, would do something like that? he shouted, slamming his hands down on the steering wheel. Who the bloody hell do you think you are – Bonnie and Clyde?

I had been inching closer to ensure that I caught every nuance and inflection of their exchange, and my head was now level with the gap between the driver and passenger seat, but given Dad's outrage, I felt it politic to withdraw. Sophia recoiled too. Her head sank and she offered no resistance. We pulled into Gower Street and as we drew up outside the house, Dad's shoulders dropped and his tone quietened.

– If you wanted money for some stupid pop concert why didn't you just ask me?

Sophia lifted her head and looked him in the eye.

– I did ask you, Dad. I asked you a million times but you didn't listen. You never listen to anything I say.

Dad slumped forward and his forehead rested against the top of the steering wheel.

– What in the name of God is happening to this family? he whispered to himself. Where did everything go wrong?

We went into the house to find Tony standing in the middle of the living room, his head bowed, staring hard at the floor. Kane's sister was nowhere to be seen, and I braced myself for what he had to say about her, about me, about the ladder.

He had clearly been waiting for us to arrive and he struck a provocative pose. When he raised his head, I saw he was crying. We stood facing him, cast as statues. Sophia and I looked towards

Dad for guidance, but he was unable to react. It was a foreign situation which he was emotionally ill-equipped to deal with. The lack of any words from Tony compounded his sense of helplessness.

After a moment Dad took a step forward and held out a hand. It was the instinctive reaction of a father, reaching out to one of his children, but he was too overcome with embarrassment to be able to sustain it and, after a moment, he dropped his hand and retreated.

Sophia walked over and put a consoling hand on Tony's shoulder.

– What's the matter? she asked. Tell me what the matter is.

Tony tried to respond but he was too choked to speak.

– It's OK, she said softly.

The tension was electric. It was like a scene from *Cat on a Hot Tin Roof* with Paul Newman and Elizabeth Taylor. I felt my presence conspicuous, and I thought any minute now I would be asked to leave the room. I couldn't remember a day packed with such incident. Sooner or later Dad would surely realise that I'd breached my quota of adult revelation and banish me from the room.

– SHE GOT RID OF IT! Tony screamed.

The suddenness of his declaration and its sheer intensity made Sophia jump back and shriek with terror.

– OK, calm down, son, Dad implored.

– SHE FUCKING WELL GOT RID OF IT! he shouted, even louder.

– Look, I hear what you're saying, Tony. Let's talk about this.

– ARE YOU HAPPY NOW – YOU AND MUM? ARE YOU BOTH FUCKING HAPPY NOW? I BET MUM WILL BE ABSOLUTELY FUCKING DELIGHTED!

Dad said nothing and an unbearable silence filled the room. Tony walked over to Dad and eyeballed him, like he was squaring up for a fight. Their faces were no more than a couple of inches apart. It was the first time I had properly compared their physiques. Tony was taller and more muscular. I had always thought of Dad as being a big man, but he looked thin and stooped in comparison. His hair was greying around the edges and there were bags under his eyes. If it came down to a fist fight, I had no doubt that Tony could leave Dad for dead.

– TELL ME YOU'RE HAPPY! Tony shouted, straight into Dad's face. TELL ME YOU'RE FUCKING HAPPY, YOU BASTARD!

It was the most terrifying thing I'd ever seen and, at that moment, I saw no alternative but for the confrontation to end in violent death. My mind raced ahead to scenes of blood on the walls and broken bodies strewn across the floor. Perhaps I would be caught in the crossfire – an unfortunate, accidental casualty of domestic strife. Perhaps these would be my last moments on earth.

I tried to make a quick mental calculation of my life's worth. Had I done enough to warrant direct passage into heaven or was I destined for a period in purgatory? I had never properly regarded myself as hell fodder, but suddenly I was overcome with self-doubt. I considered all the bad acts I had done, the things I had stolen, the lies I had told. There was the time I shat in the fifteenth hole at Haggs Castle before replacing the flagpin and running away, just as a two-ball foursome appeared on the crest of the fairway. Then there was my hand in last summer's grass fire on the railway embankment, when two fire engines had to be called out to extinguish it.

What of my good deeds? I thought hard, but the only things that sprang to mind were my partial role in Wally returning the stolen bike to the old dear on Fleurs Avenue and the fact that I rarely made reference to Johnny Nae Da's singular testicle. It was hardly the testimonial of a saint.

I braced myself for the sight of flying fists but, instead, Dad reached out and grabbed Tony, who fell limply into his arms. Dad squeezed him tightly and the pair of them stood together, sobbing.

– It's all right, son, Dad said through the tears. Everything's going to be all right.

The relief was palpable for everyone in the room. Sophia was crying too and, before long, so was I as I collapsed into a chair. I was relieved that a violent altercation had been avoided, but I didn't share Dad's conviction that everything would be all right. Instinctively I knew that things were likely to get worse.

17

We spent the rest of the evening recovering in our own ways. Sophia lay on top of her bunk, reading a copy of *Blue Jeans* and listening to her singles, while I sat on the floor finishing sorting my football card collection. It was one of the few times that I remember the two of us choosing to occupy the same space. While we shared a bedroom, there was hardly a time we were in it at the same time, other than when we were asleep. Dad and Tony were downstairs with the telly switched off, talking quietly, so we decided to leave them alone.

Sophia climbed off her bunk to change a record, and I felt her eyes trained on the back of my head.

– Why do you sit there for hours putting them into little piles? she demanded irritably.

I ignored her.

– I mean, they're just stupid cards.

– They're not stupid, I countered forcibly.

She lay back on her bunk as the opening bars of 'My Coocachoo' by Alvin Stardust filled the room. I continued to concentrate on my categorisation. I had just finished with Raith Rovers and I was moving onto Rangers. I knew some people who categorised Celtic and Rangers under G for Glasgow Celtic and Glasgow Rangers but I didn't subscribe to such a method of alphabetisation. You then had to categorise Morton under G for Greenock Morton, Hibs under E for Edinburgh Hibernians and so forth, and it became too complicated.

– OK, explain what you're doing. I'm interested.

I continued to ignore her.

– No, seriously, I want to know. Tell me what you're doing.

I began to explain how my system worked, how it was based on three degrees of separation, dividing players into teams, sub-dividing them according to the number of appearances they had made, and then arranging the teams in a league table based on the total number of appearances, but she cut me short.

– OK, stop. I'm sorry I asked. I'm bored already, she said lifting the magazine in front of her face.

It was the last straw. Over the past few months I had endured ever greater levels of trauma and humiliation – the endless family rows, an absentee mother, parental neglect and a near violent altercation between my father and brother. Now Sophia's brazen sarcasm was more than I could bear, and I exploded with anger.

– Why don't you just get lost, you bitch, I screamed. Just fuck off. I don't slag off your stupid clothes and your poxy music . . .

My voice began to crack, and I felt tears welling up in my eyes.

– Actually, if you must know, my football cards are really important to me, but you wouldn't care about that. All you're interested in is your stupid self and your moron boyfriend.

The rawness of my monologue had the desired effect, and Sophia backed off, stunned. As I returned to my cards, Alvin Stardust's performance ended, and the sound of the record player arm lifting, returning to its cradle and clicking shut took on a booming significance against the pulsing silence of the room. After a few moments, Sophia spoke.

– OK, I'm sorry, she said, quietly and contritely.

– You're not sorry, so don't pretend! I bellowed back.

– I'm sorry. Really, I am.

I continued thumbing through my cards.

– Look, I know things have been tough for you, Steve, she continued. They've been tough for all of us. You and I don't always see eye-to-eye, but it's at times like these that we need to stick together, not to fight all the time.

I eyed her suspiciously, and she offered a warming smile to reassure me that her sentiments were genuine.

– I know you and Tony are closer, and you can tell him what's on your mind. But he's having a difficult time at the moment, so I want you to know that if things get on top of you, you can always talk to me. OK?

She climbed from her bed, walked over and knelt down so that she was level with me. She put her arms around me and squeezed me tight, kissing me on the back of the head. It felt odd, and I shuddered at such an open display of affection from my sister. It was bad enough when Mum or Dad did that sort of thing, but Sophia!

– OK? she demanded, breaking into a comforting laugh.

I smiled back.

– OK, I replied warily.

I appreciated the gesture. It made me feel better. I sat thinking deeply about what Sophia had said, about being able to talk to her about things that were happening. But when I rehearsed what I wanted to talk about – Tony shagging up the Cunyon, Kane's sister, the Goddess of Glencairn Drive – I knew those were conversations I could never have with my sister. I knew that, despite her apparent sincerity, I'd be providing her with ammunition that could be used against me to a reckless level, leaving myself as a hostage to fortune.

Nevertheless, I did consider that her olive branch might be used to my advantage in other ways. Such conversations could be used, strategically, to provide me with information. I waited for a suitable time, until she was back on her bunk, before testing the water.

– What about all that business with you and Cumbo, eh, sis? I said nonchalantly.

She remained silent.

– So, tell me, who did you demand money from and who did Cumbo beat up?

She continued to ignore my probing.

– What did the cops say to you down at the school? Did they read you your rights?

– Piss off, she said from behind her magazine.

I didn't know what time Dad and Tony went to bed, but the last time I looked at the clock, it was past midnight. When I got up in the morning, there were four empty beer cans on the living room coffee table.

Later that day Dad and I drove to Granny and Granddad's house. In the van, on the way there, I asked Dad if Mum was coming home. He didn't say yes or no. He just said they had things to discuss. When we arrived, they immediately disappeared into the main lounge, overlooking the Botanic Gardens, and closed the door behind them.

I hovered around in the hallway hoping to hear what they were saying, but they talked quietly and I couldn't make out a word. I was desperate to hear Dad's account of what had happened the night before because, although I had witnessed every second of it, I was still unclear what it had been about.

What had Tony meant when he said *She got rid of it*? He kept repeating it, each time more passionately than the last. Who was the 'she' he was referring to? Perhaps it was Kane's sister, but that didn't make sense. As far as I was aware Kane's sister didn't have anything that belonged to Tony which he would be upset about her getting rid of. More likely he was recounting something she had told him, and it was when I contemplated that possibility that my nerves began to jangle.

Perhaps the 'she' was the Goddess of Glencairn Drive and the 'it' was Kane's ladder. If that was the case, then things were more serious than I thought. I would never knowingly have under-estimated the gravity of the loss of a ladder, but if it was an issue capable of prompting tears and near violence then clearly I had missed a trick.

The worst of it all was not knowing. The secrecy with which the affair was being conducted only served to heighten my para-noia and the growing fear of how I might be made to atone for my part in the whole sorry mess. Whatever happened, I was determined that I was not going to take the rap for it single-handedly. What seemed to have been forgotten in all of this was that it had been a collective action. We had all been on the apple raid – me, Wally, Bifter, Cuddihy, Chabs and Johnny Nae Da, and, as far as I was concerned, we should all bear responsibility for the loss of the ladder. Granted, I was the last person to leave the garden, but I didn't see why, on account of that minor detail, I should be the only one to suffer.

Granny came into the hallway and told me it would be better if I left Mum and Dad in peace. She took me into the kitchen where I sat, at the table, with her and Granddad, making uncomfortable, stilted conversation. They asked me how I was getting on at school, and I said fine, then the discussion dried up. I had never really spoken properly to Granny or Granddad beyond superficial pleasantries, neither had Sophia for that matter. Granddad had taken a fleeting interest in Tony when Tony had taken an interest in politics, but even then their conversations were largely one-sided. They usually ended abruptly, with Granddad asking Tony if he had read all these books that Tony had never heard of and him saying no.

Granny and Granddad kept apologising for not having anything in the house that I could play with. Granny asked me if I wanted some paper and pens to draw with, but I said no. Granddad asked me if I wanted a drink. I asked him if they had any Cremola Foam or Irn-Bru, but all they had was milk. Then he remembered they had something called ginger ale in the drinks cabinet so he poured me a glass. It tasted like lemonade, but with a fiery kick that burned the back of my throat. It was utterly bogging, but I pretended to like it. When Granny asked me if I wanted more, I refused.

The doorbell rang, and everyone breathed a sigh of relief that some minor distraction had broken the monotony. Granddad went to answer it and he returned with Sandy, one of their friends who had dropped by to return a book that he had borrowed. He provided a welcome diversion for Granny and Granddad who, because of the presence of an outsider, I was now obliged to call Vera and George.

Vera introduced me to Sandy as Christine's youngest child, and he proffered a cursory smile, before embarking on an appraisal of the merits and demerits of the book. Needless to say, the conversation meant less than nothing to me, but I was pleased that there was someone else in the room to draw the focus away from me.

After about half an hour, and two cups of tea, Sandy got up to leave. Vera and George pressed him to stay for another cup, or a whisky or dinner, but he said he needed pipe cleaners and he would have to hurry down to the tobacconist's on Byres Road before it closed. After he left we sat in barely punctuated silence again until Granny suggested that I might like to go outside to play.

She led me out onto the cobbled lane that ran along the back of their garden. A group of boys, about my age, were playing commandos and she summoned them over. They eyed her suspiciously – I got the impression they weren't exactly on intimate terms with Granny – but when she presented me to them, they welcomed me into their group with good grace.

After Granny had gone back indoors, we made our proper introductions. They spoke with posh accents that sounded more English than Scottish and they had fancy names like Marcus and Piers. Their clothes were neat and unblemished, and they had shiny, floppy hair – not the brutal, down-to-the-wood crewcuts inflicted on most of my friends. I asked them if they went to a Pape or a Proddy school. Jasper was the only one who went to the local school, which was Proddy. The rest said they went to private schools that had Catholics and Protestants.

They asked me if I wanted to join their game of commandos, so I said yes. They asked me what my regular gun noise was, and I told them it was 'rat-a-tat-a-tat-a-tat' but that was being used by Jasper so I was told I'd have to choose another one. I asked if anyone was using 'pyow-pyow-pyow-pyow' but Piers had bagsied that one. They said 'pchoo-pchoo-pchoo-pchoo' was still up for grabs, as was 'tarrow-tarrow-tarrow-tarrow'. Neither was a particular favourite of mine but I opted for the former. The only rule they had was that the main road was out of bounds, so we split up and took our positions in the field.

The other players had an advantage over me because they knew the area. I felt my best option was to occupy a holding position on high ground to give me an overview of the terrain, so that I could assess the likely hideout positions of the other soldiers. I climbed onto the top of a garage and lay flat on my stomach.

As I scanned the rows of gardens it occurred to me how different the area was from the back courts of Govan. These were the communal gardens of townhouses, yet bicycles and items of garden furniture stood untethered, inviting theft that never came. Lawns were flat and finely manicured, and there wasn't a scrawl of graffiti or a dog shite in sight.

Suddenly I was caught off guard. I heard the rat-a-tat-a-tat of Jasper's Thomson sub-machine ring out. He had scaled the garage and was standing over me. I had taken a head shot and I was down. I had to wait until everyone else was dead for a new game to begin, by which time two others, Jeremy and Ben, had joined in.

The next time I managed to get down to the last three before being killed. I should have progressed further. I had spotted Marcus emerging from a rhododendron bush and caught him with a direct hit to the body, but he refused to go down, claiming he was wearing a bullet-proof vest. I tried to tell him that I was using a high velocity rifle and there wasn't a flak jacket in the world that would cushion the impact of a magazine load from one of those babies, but while I was arguing Jeremy floored me with a rocket propelled grenade.

After the second game of commandos everyone was bored, so Ben suggested we go to the university and see if there was anything worth nicking from the bins. They explained that the engineering department was always throwing out lots of disused equipment, and its bins were a treasure trove of great stuff. They said it wasn't far – and there was no sign of any immediate resolution from Granny and Granddad's house – so I agreed to join them.

It was just a short walk over the hill. The boys were really nice, all competing for my attention, giving me tips and offering advice. Piers told me to tuck my trousers into my socks because sometimes there were rats and they might try to run up your trouser leg. Jeremy had a packet of Tutti Fruttis he handed round, but he asked me to choose my favourite flavours first. I took an orange and a lemon one. I left the best ones – the raspberries and the blackcurrants – for the others, in case they thought I was abusing their hospitality.

On first impressions there didn't seem to be anything of much value in the bins. Ben said that, quite often, you found clocks and measuring scales and other gadgets like that, but the only stuff on offer today appeared to be some rubber bungs and tubing and a cracked glass beaker.

Then Marcus called over from another bin in which he had found strips of coloured perspex. When you held them up to your eyes it made the world look that particular colour. We snapped off bits and stood looking at things in different colours, everyone shouting whenever they discovered something new and exciting. The best bit was when you looked at the sky. Because it was dark, it was like a scene from a science fiction film with the stars and the moon glowing pink and purple.

We divvied up the strips – the boys all insisted that I should have my pick but I just took a couple of small ones – and then I said I should be getting back. As we walked back over University Avenue, the boys asked me whose house I was visiting. I told them it belonged to my Granny and Granddad, but that my mum had been staying there because she'd had a big fight with my dad. I told them the story of the blazing row over Tony and how I'd woken in the morning to find Mum had left home. I also told them about Sophia being arrested for demanding money with menaces and about Tony threatening to batter Dad.

The others walked alongside me, captivated, occasionally

trotting to catch up or asking me to repeat a word or two lest they should miss any minor point of detail. As I spoke, it occurred to me that, without having to make up anything, or even to exaggerate, I was holding their interest. With every word I spoke, they gazed open mouthed and incredulous, waiting for the next exciting development.

It was all the truth. The scenes I described, with all their dubious glamour, represented an honest account of my life and yet it could almost have come from a film or a television drama. Finally, it seemed, there was excitement in my life, so why did I feel so rotten about it all?

When I finished talking, everyone pitched in with stories about their parents. Jasper told how one day he came home from school to find his dad shoving a hairbrush down his mum's throat. He tried hitting his dad on the back to make him stop, but he didn't, and eventually Jasper had to throw a cup of hot tea over him. The police came round later and made him tell them everything that he had seen. Now Jasper lived with his mum and a man called Clive who wasn't his dad.

When I got back to Granny and Granddad's house, they were sitting with Mum and Dad at the kitchen table, drinking coffee. I went to the toilet, and, as I passed through the hallway, I saw a holdall with all of Mum's things packed in it, sitting by the doorway. I knew then that she was coming home, but I didn't let on when I returned to the kitchen and waited for her to tell me, making out like it was a big surprise.

She said she'd agreed to come home on three conditions. The first was that Dad accepted the offer of a loan from Granny and Granddad to get back on his feet, with his new business venture. She made buying and selling watches and radios from Shaheed's sound very high powered. Dad smiled and nodded. The second condition was that Tony would return to school to sit his Highers and then he would go to university.

– And the third condition, Mum said, as she kissed me on the forehead, is that we all have a truly happy Christmas.

Dad collected Mum's holdall and took it out to the van while we said our goodbyes to Granny and Granddad on the doorstep. Granny gave Mum a long, tight hug.

– Are you sure you know what you're doing? she said.

Mum nodded. Granny kissed her on the forehead, then we drove home.

18

Christmas without Santa was a bit like *Jaws* without the shark, but Mum and Dad promised that this year was going to be the best ever. After all the recent discord and upset, they said we deserved a special celebration.

Now that I knew presents came from department stores in exchange for money, rather than being delivered gratis by a benevolent patriarch with a beard, Mum thought it would be a good idea if I embraced the seasonal spirit and used my pocket money to buy gifts for members of the family. She told me, with no hint of irony, that it was better to give than to receive. It was one of those expressions favoured by adults that appeared to have no grounding in reality and served only to reinforce my conviction that she had started early on the egg nog.

I spent an entire morning with her in town, trawling the shops, trying to make fifteen bob stretch four ways – but no matter how I cut it, it was always going to look as if I had got everything free with petrol. My final selection included a bottle (the smallest) of Nulon hand cream for Mum, a pocket torch for Dad, a hairband for Sophia and a pack of playing cards for Tony. I was feeling pretty pleased with my budgeting skills until Mum tossed Granny and Granddad into the equation. I hadn't banked on having to widen my generosity to include extended family as well.

– Why do I have to buy presents for them anyway? I demanded in an ill-tempered, high-decibel outburst that made our fellow customers in the Lewis's perfumery wince with middle-class panic. They're *your* parents.

– They're *your* grandparents and they're always very generous when they buy presents for you, Mum pointed out.

– But they're old. They've got nothing else to spend their money on.

The other major consequence of not believing in Santa was the sudden imposition of financial reason. In previous years I had been able to demand the sun, the moon and the stars – along with a top-of-the-range selection box – in the certain knowledge that none of it came at a price. The only implication of adding a Waddington's compendium to my already extensive list of demands was that the old man in the red coat might have to crack the whip a bit harder if his elves started slacking.

Knowing now that my material whims would have to be financed by the blood, sweat and tears of my parents made me think twice about asking for a Raleigh Chopper – especially since I hadn't yet outgrown the Tomahawk I'd been given last year – but I decided to ask for one anyway. The fact was that I simply couldn't continue to go through life without a Chopper. It was *the* must-have acquisition of 1975. Being Chopper-less meant I was now in the minority among my friends, and people were beginning to talk.

Wally could get away with not having a Chopper because everyone knew his family was too poor to afford one. And therein lay the ethical dimension to my present-asking policy which convinced me of its worth. If I got a Chopper, I would give my Tomahawk to Wally.

Since Dad and Tony had almost come to blows, I had decided that I needed to do more to boost the credit side of my soul. It's not that I believed I was intrinsically a bad person. If someone – other than Sophia – suffered a misfortune, then, on the whole, I tried not to laugh. But my near death experience – the real one in the living room with Dad and Tony, not the fabricated one in the orchard with the Goddess of Glencairn Drive – had convinced me that I needed to do more to escape the advancing clutches of purgatory.

I had two options. One was to bite the bullet and get 'confirmed' or whatever it was that Father Byrne had said would qualify me for a regular bite of his wafers. That would allow me to go to confession and say all the Hail Marys and Our Fathers that were necessary to get my ticket to heaven. If I could get my Grade Two survival badge, I was pretty sure I could pass whatever test the Catholic Church set for me, but the truth was I was enjoying being lapsed too much for that. Now that I had been to mass once, I found that I could legitimately drop into conversation – apropos of nothing and with a sneering disregard for my own spiritual wellbeing – how long it had been since I had last been to mass.

That is why I decided on option two, which involved generally trying to be a better person – stealing less, giving more, and being more sympathetic to those less fortunate than myself. It was also a handy way of being able to offload a bike I had grown bored with months ago and of acquiring a higher spec model with a clear conscience.

In any event, the family's money worries had been eased considerably in recent weeks, after Dad had agreed to borrow money from Granny and Granddad, allowing him to replenish his stock from Shaheed's and sell it at the markets in the run-up to Christmas.

The first sign of a crack in the newly negotiated détente between Mum and Dad came when she told him he would have to phone Aunty Betty and break the news to her that she couldn't come over for Christmas. Mum had only been home for a couple of weeks, and already they were rowing, but she refused to back down. She said that, after all we'd been through, it wasn't too much to ask for us to have some time on our own.

Aunty Betty had spent every Christmas with us since Grandma died, and, with each passing year, her presence became more contentious. Last year she yacked loudly all the way through *The Great Escape*, ruining it for the rest of us. Whenever a German soldier appeared on screen she asked if he was a goodie or a baddie, and she spent the entire escape scene expounding her theory that City Bakery mince rounds were getting smaller.

She was always going on about how she wasn't a drinker and how she had the appetite of a bird, yet she ate twice as much as the rest of us and she always managed to work her way through the best part of a bottle of Harvey's Bristol Cream. Then she sat down to the Queen's speech in Dad's chair, where she remained until *Late Call*, sucking loudly on an unbroken succession of Pan Drops which she kept secreted in her handbag and defended with the gun-toting vigilance of a chain-gang guard.

Betty was distantly related to us on Dad's side, though even he couldn't remember precisely how. She was a spinster who lived on her own in the Newmains flats – although she claimed to live in neighbouring Bonkle because it was more upmarket – and there wasn't a blade of grass that moved in the village without her knowing about it. Mum and Dad met her for the first time at Grandma's funeral when she spent most of the wake telling Mum how the last funeral she'd attended was Bobby Fullerton's, Bonkle's longest serving butcher who'd traded sexual favours for links sausages during the war when there was rationing.

As Mum and Dad were leaving after the purvey, Mum said to Betty, out of politeness, that she must come to visit sometime. Three months later, two days before Christmas, Betty phoned to take her up on the offer and she'd done so every Christmas since.

It's not as if she came laden with expensive presents as a quid pro quo for us having to put up with her incessant prattling. We always got the same things: a bottle of bubble bath for me – about as much use as a nuclear reactor – with the Co-op price tag still on; a bottle of Hai Karate aftershave for Tony; and a book of scraps for Sophia.

Dad complained about Betty as much as the rest of us, but he didn't want her to have to spend Christmas Day on her own. In the end the matter was academic because, when he phoned to give her the bad news, she pre-empted him by telling him she was sorry, but she would be spending Christmas with Uncle Frank and his family that year. Dad made out that he was disappointed and said there would always be next year, but I could tell he was secretly delighted.

I ran upstairs to tell Tony. He was studying in his bedroom, where he'd spent most of his time since Mum's return. I thought he would be happy – Betty wound him up more than any of us – but he just shrugged and got on with his revision. I told him I wished he would lighten up, that it was nearly Christmas when he should be enjoying himself.

– What's to enjoy? he asked in a sarcastic tone. The only thing I'm going to enjoy is getting out of this stinking shithole.

– What do you mean? I asked.

– I mean, the minute my exams are over, I'm offski.

– Where will you go?

– A flat, a room, a railway tunnel – anywhere to get me away from that pair of wankers downstairs.

– You'll never go, I said.

– Just watch me.

I never thought I'd feel like this, but I missed the old Tony, complete with his bad jokes, his wise cracks and his tall tales whose sole purpose was to expose my gullibility. He hadn't made up a story in weeks. Instead he just sloped about with a sullen expression and the weight of the world on his shoulders. And yet, the thought of not having him around made me fraught with fear.

Ever since Mum's walk-out, he'd been distant and unapproachable, and it exposed just how dependent I was on him for guidance and knowledge, and how lost I'd feel if he wasn't around. Ordinarily I would have quizzed him about Kane's sister and whether it had anything to do with the ladder, but after his altercation with Dad, I felt wary around him. His reaction had been so out of character. I couldn't believe he was serious about leaving home, knowing that he would be abandoning me when I needed him most. I would be starting at the secondary the year after next and I had a whole stack of questions that needed answered.

Following close on the heels of the Aunty Betty saga, there was another blazing row between Mum and Dad. It transpired that, in their protracted negotiations over her homecoming, he had omitted to mention Sophia's recent brush with the law. What with everything else that had happened, I could see how Dad might regard dropping the bombshell that their fourteen-year-old daughter was a potential felon as one for the backburner.

The first Mum heard about it was when a brown envelope dropped through the letterbox bearing a 'Glasgow Procurator Fiscal Service' postmark. She opened it to discover that Sophia would be required to attend a hearing of the children's panel on 30 May.

Dad had to explain what had happened, and, with my lurking presence in the room temporarily overlooked, I was privy to the full, unvarnished sequence of events. Cumbo, it emerged, had been offered two tickets for the Bay City Rollers concert by a friend of a friend of a boy with whom he sold match programmes outside Ibrox stadium. Cumbo agreed to buy them – one for him and one for Sophia – and suggested to her that, in order to pay for them, they prise the money from younger secondary pupils as they queued for their lunch outside the Crit.

Sophia collected 'donations' from the more pliant ones while those who resisted were dragged into Clifford Lane by Cumbo who administered more persuasive methods of parting them from their cash. When one of their 'clients', Degsy Munro (whose wee brother, Stephen, was in my class at the primary), returned home with a black eye and an empty stomach, his parents phoned the school who phoned the police.

Dad tried to present the revelation in a positive light. The letter didn't say that Sophia would definitely be facing criminal charges and was, therefore, good news, he argued. But Mum didn't see it like that. There followed a voluble exchange, during which Mum pointed out, not unreasonably, that it would have been nice to learn that her daughter was a suspected racketeer from her husband or, at a push, from her daughter and not from Ronald Snoad, assistant clerk to the juvenile criminal division.

By Christmas Eve, the family appeared to have weathered these setbacks. At least, we had resolved not to allow them to ruin the festivities. Mum, in particular, seemed determined to make Christmas a success. For the first time we had a real tree – the wilted, silver tinsel stick that had served every Christmas since I could remember was consigned to the dustbin, and the new model stood proud and resplendent with shiny baubles and decorations, exuding a fragrant, Scandanavian freshness.

Mum spent all of Christmas Eve cleaning the house from top to bottom so that it would be spotless for Christmas Day. Sophia, who had barely uttered a civil word since Mum had banned her from ever seeing Cumbo again, was roped in to vacuum the carpets, and I dusted all the surfaces and polished the lamps and ornaments.

Mum insisted that we all attend the watchnight service at the kirk – all except Dad who was working late at the Barras, flogging Shaheed's finest to last-minute Christmas shoppers. As a special treat, she said we didn't have to wear our Sunday best. She made tasty treats – mulled wine, mince pies and a baked, spiced ham – for when we returned. I hadn't seen her so happy and relaxed in months.

We walked to church in the darkness, our feet crunching on the frosty pavement below. The night was cold, but perfectly still, without a hint of wind, and the black sky was peppered with bright stars. I was expecting the service to be dull as hell, but Reverend MacIver's sermon was actually quite amusing for a change. He said that if Jesus was born today he would probably be a rock star like Elton John, only with more hair. Then he went through the lyrics of Elton John songs, showing how they were related to scenes from the gospels.

At the end of the service he invited everyone into the church hall for mugs of hot cocoa and Santa-shaped shortbread, baked by members of the Women's Guild. As we milled around trying to avoid eye contact with Mrs Yuill, Reverend MacIver came over to talk to Mum. He smiled at me and asked if I was looking forward to Christmas, and I felt a crushing sense of betrayal, knowing that I had forsaken him for the iconic glamour of the Catholic Church.

But, true to form, he didn't even mention my recent absences from Sunday school. He just said he hoped to see us all next Sunday and moved on. I couldn't help liking Reverend MacIver but he was his own worst enemy. I hadn't been to Sunday school in weeks. I had been moonlighting at St Bernadette's and he hadn't given me so much as a mild rebuke. I thought he needed to take a leaf out of Father Byrne's book when it came to ecclesiastical strong-arming. A bit less carrot and a bit more stick would soon see his attendances rise.

As we walked back home along Sherbrooke Avenue, I could see our house in the distance, its darkness broken only by the twinkling of the fairy lights on the tree. Although this was my first Santa-free Christmas, there was still a magical sense of anticipation – a feeling that something special was about to happen.

Sophia and Tony walked on ahead while I meandered slowly with Mum, happy to have her all to myself. She was keen to hear everything that was happening at school and with my friends. I told her what everyone was getting for Christmas. Chabs and Bifter had both asked for Choppers. Cuddihy had been given a Chopper for his birthday so he wanted a pogo stick, while Jukebox wanted Super Striker with diving goalkeepers and an Action Man with gripping hands. Wally had been conspicuously silent on the subject of Christmas presents, and no-one ever asked Johnny Nae Da what he was getting to save him the embarrassment.

I hadn't had a conversation like this with Mum for ages, just talking about me and my life. It felt great that things seemed to be back to normal. I told her the house hadn't looked so spick and span since Vivienne had been round to clean it. The moment I said it, I realised my mistake. I'd promised Dad I wouldn't tell anyone about Vivienne's visit, but it was out there now and there was nothing I could do. I thought Dad had been much too sensitive about the whole issue and I couldn't see that Mum would have that much of a problem with it. But she pounced on the revelation like a Serengeti cheetah on a dozing wildebeest.

– When was Vivienne in the house? she shot back.

– Oh, it was while you were staying at Granny and Granddad's. I shouldn't have told you. Dad said it was our little secret.

– Oh, did he indeed?

– Yeah, it was no big deal. She came over to give him a hand with the housework. She made us a steak and kidney pie as well. It was really nice of her.

The next morning I was awake first, at six o'clock. In previous years 'Santa' had always left my presents at the foot of my bed, but this year Mum said that, since I was a big boy and I knew the truth about Santa, I could open my presents in the living room with the rest of the family.

The problem with that was that I had to wait for the rest of the family to get out of bed, and there didn't appear to be any great sense of urgency about that. I shook Mum awake, but she told me to go back to bed until it was a reasonable hour. I lay back down and shut my eyes tightly, my heart racing with anticipation at all the surprises that awaited me downstairs. I dozed for what seemed like a couple of hours, but when I looked at the clock again, it was barely a quarter past six.

I woke Mum every fifteen minutes until half past seven when, finally, she relented and agreed to get up, but even then, I had to wait until everyone had put on their dressing gowns and used the bathroom. Finally, we congregated in the downstairs hall, and Dad made a sound of a dramatic drum roll before opening the door to the living room.

The presents were stacked around the base of the tree and filled stockings surrounded the mantelpiece, draped with tinsel and streamers, making the room look like a fairy grotto. Pride of place was my bike – not a Chopper but a Top Hopper, the Shaheed budget alternative. I could see Dad scanning my face for any hint of disappointment but I was delighted. It was pillar box red with big, sloping, silver handlebars and a pink-and-white, candy-striped, cushioned seat. I tried it out for size. It had glamour and character, and I knew immediately it would draw admiring glances out on the streets.

I also got a chemistry set, with the instructions written in Czech and half the parts missing, and a selection box made by a company called Maher's, full of sweets that I had never heard of, which tasted like they were made from cooking chocolate. Sophia got a Binatone tape recorder and a cassette called *Pop Paradise*, a compilation of chart songs sung by session singers with a picture on the cover of a lady dressed in hot pants, holding a puppy.

Tony had asked for money to buy clothes in the January sales, so he got an envelope with fifteen quid inside. He opened it with an inscrutable look on his face and there was a moment of unbearable tension when I thought he was going to hand it back, but he just smiled sheepishly and said thanks.

Dad had bought Mum a silver necklace, which she opened and put to one side without saying anything at all. Then she started opening presents from other people and when she got to my bottle of Nulon hand cream, her face broke into a big smile, and she leant over and kissed me on the head.

Mum had bought Dad a pasta-making machine and a couple of cookery books. He made a big deal of them, passing them round and telling everyone how great they were, but Mum just ignored him. He kept asking her if she liked her necklace, but she didn't answer. I knew she was pretending not to hear because I was further away from Dad and I could make out what he was saying perfectly well.

I was desperate to take my new bike out for a spin, but Mum insisted that I wait until we had eaten. Dad was in expansive mood as we sat around the breakfast table, talking about how much money he had made at the Barras the night before. Business had been booming in the run-up to Christmas, and he'd had to replenish his stock at Shaheed's a couple of times over. He'd made enough profit to be able to repay some of the cash he'd borrowed from Granny and Granddad.

Mum served up plates of bacon and French toast, and as she passed Dad, he tried to grab her arm playfully, but she pulled it away. He asked her if she was all right, but she just ignored him. As we ate, he talked confidently about how the last month was only the beginning and that he had big plans for the future. He knew January and February would be quiet months but, once things started to pick up in the springtime, he would diversify into other product lines, and, if things went according to plan, he might even be able to open a shop. Throughout it all Mum sat, thin-lipped and expressionless.

When everyone had finished eating, she began to clear away the dishes. Dad continued to hold court, saying how he'd heard the milk snatcher on the radio the other day. She was the new leader of the Tory party and she was talking about how, when she became prime minister, she was going to make it easier for people like Dad who owned their own businesses. When he said he was thinking about voting for the milk snatcher at the election, Mum burst out laughing.

– Oh, Christ, I've heard it all now, she said, as she marched into the kitchen and slammed the plates down onto the draining board.

Dad followed her in and closed the door behind them. Sophia and Tony exchanged glances and shook their heads in unison.

– A Tory as well as a twat, Tony said. Bollocks to this, I'm not hanging around listening to them.

– Me neither, Sophia said, and they both disappeared to their bedrooms.

I decided to stay behind to see if I could hear what they were talking about. Their conversation was conducted in stage whispers so all I heard was the occasional muffled word or phrase. Things became increasingly ill-tempered until, suddenly, Mum raised her voice.

– In my house, Robert. Did you really have to bring her to my house? she shouted.

Then I heard Dad tell Mum to keep her voice down. He said it wasn't like that, and there followed another muffled exchange when I couldn't make out anything. A few moments later, the kitchen door opened and I pretended to be deeply engrossed in my Czechoslovakian chemistry set. Mum was doing her best to smile, but she kept sniffing and wiping her eyes.

– Right, let's get this show on the road, she said. We have a big day ahead of us.

After I'd helped to clear away all the presents and wrapping paper, I took the Top Hopper out for its maiden ride. I manoeuvred it onto the driveway and rolled it into the street, scanning the area to see if any of the neighbours were watching. I was bursting with pride and as I mounted it, my legs were shaking. I cycled round the block then down to the bottom of Gower Street, over the railway bridge and onto the Paisley Road, reclining in the seat with my head cocked back against the foam rest, doing my best to look like Peter Fonda in *Easy Rider*.

Among the Top Hopper's features was a stand, a headlight powered by a dynamo and a gear mechanism with three separate gears, operated by a joystick. Despite it being a bright, crisp morning, I cycled around with the headlight on and periodically I dismounted to tie my shoelace to make full use of the stand. Whenever I hit the slightest incline I flicked the joystick to run through the gears. As it was Christmas Day, the streets were empty, and there was no-one around to witness my conspicuous show of wealth.

On my return home I freewheeled down the railway bridge, crossing Maxwell Drive which was deserted. As I began the ascent of Gower Street, I flicked the joystick from third to first but, as I did so, I felt a clunking sensation beneath my feet and the pedal resistance remained as stiff as before. I shifted back into third and then down to first but nothing happened. I tried going through the gears individually but the bike remained stuck in third. I'd had barely thirty minutes of Top Hopper use and already the gear mechanism was broken.

Back home the atmosphere was thick with tension, and I decided that, in those circumstances, news of my gear-related difficulties could wait until a more opportune moment.

– How was the bike? Dad asked enthusiastically.

– Great, I replied.

He was in the kitchen – as usual he was cooking Christmas dinner – and Sophia was watching *Top of the Pops* to find out if 'Bohemian Rhapsody' was the Christmas number one. Mum and Tony were upstairs in their bedrooms. When the Queen's speech came on telly, Dad called for everyone to come and watch it, but Tony refused to leave his room.

Dad went upstairs to coax him out, but it ended in a shouting match with Tony saying the only reason they ever watched the Queen's speech in the past was because of Aunty Betty and that he wouldn't piss on the Royal Family if they were on fire. Dad lost his temper, ordering Tony to show some respect for his head of state, at which point Mum emerged from her room and told Dad to stop being a pompous arsehole. She said Tony didn't have to watch the Queen's speech if he didn't want to.

– I just thought it might be a nice thing to do as a family, Dad shouted as he marched back down the stairs

– That's what Christmas is supposed to be about, after all – family?

– That's a good one coming from you, Robert, Mum shouted after him.

It was dark when we finally sat down to eat. Dad had laid out the good cutlery and crockery which we hadn't used since last Christmas, and the table was decorated with streamers and crackers. Each place setting had more than one lot of cutlery because there were several courses and we all had a wine glass.

As a starter there was prawn cocktail, served with a slice of lemon for everyone except Sophia who didn't like fish, so she had a boiled egg, sliced in two and covered with mayonnaise. She told Dad she didn't like mayonnaise so he scraped it off and replaced it with salad cream. Then there was soup made with the giblets from the turkey which Sophia refused to eat unless Dad told her what a giblet was. When he told her, she still refused to eat it and so did Tony.

By the time the main course was served – turkey with all the trimmings – Dad was frazzled and Mum hadn't uttered a word since the shouting match about the Queen's speech. Dad piled everyone's plates high but he told us not to start eating yet. He disappeared into the kitchen and returned with a bottle of wine. He made a big deal of uncorking it and then he poured a glass for himself, Mum and Tony. Sophia and I had lemonade.

– Before we start, I'd like to propose a toast, he said, raising his glass.

Mum glanced at the ceiling and sighed. Dad shot her a dirty look but he pressed on.

– I'd just like to say that this hasn't been an easy year for us. I lost my job and Tony and Sophia have also had their problems. But throughout it all we kept faith with each other and we managed to pull through. It's going to be a tough year ahead. Tony has his exams and Sophia isn't out of the woods yet with her troubles. But, whatever happens, I want you children to know that I'll always be here for you. I'll always be your Dad.

At that point Mum stood up and threw her napkin down on the table.

– Christ, I can't take any more of this, she said, pulling away from the table. What's all that about, Robert, getting your excuses in first?

– I'm just trying to tell my children that I care about them, Dad replied.

– I can't do this. I can't sit here playing happy families, Mum said, slipping effortlessly into the shipping forecast.

– But we agreed, Christine.

– I know we agreed, but I can't pretend.

– Don't do this, Dad said in an admonishing tone. Don't ruin their Christmas. If you do that, I'll never forgive you.

– *You'll* never forgive *me*? Christ, that *is* rich.

As they argued, I glanced through the living room window and spotted Wally hanging about in the Proffy. The park was in darkness, but his silhouette was visible beneath the yellow street light. As accusation and counter-accusation flew, I wondered if there would be a natural break in proceedings when it might be politic to ask if I could go outside to show Wally my new bike.

– Is that what this charade has been about – ensuring that we all have a jolly Christmas? Tony asked scathingly. Do you think we're stupid or something?

– It was your father's idea, Mum said. I thought you deserved to know the truth.

– The truth? You'd have to be demented not to know the truth, Sophia scoffed. We've known the truth about you two for months.

My food was getting cold so I decided I might as well start to eat it. This altercation had all the makings of an occasion when I would be dispatched to my room, so I figured that, if I had an empty plate, it might improve my bargaining position when I asked to go out to play with Wally. As the verbal volleys flew over my head, I tucked into my turkey and stuffing, sprouts and roasties.

– Well, you can't blame me for trying to maintain an image of family togetherness, Dad protested.

Mum exploded.

– Oh, is that what you've been doing? Maintaining an image of family togetherness? If anyone has been holding this family together in the last few months, it's been me, while you've been off gallivanting with your fancy woman.

There followed a prolonged silence, broken only by the sound of me chewing on an overcooked chipolata. I decided to take advantage of the momentary break in hostilities to ask Dad to pass the cranberry sauce, which he did. I expected the others to round on him after the last contribution, but, instead, Sophia turned her attention on Mum.

– You've hardly been a saint in all of this, she said. I seem to remember you buggering off in the middle of the night to live with Granny and Granddad when the going got tough. Dad has his faults but at least he stuck around.

– That's not fair, Sophia, Mum protested. I went away because I wasn't prepared to stand by and watch Tony's life being ruined.

– Oh, it's all Tony, everything's about Tony. He's all you care about. You don't give a shit about the rest of us.

– That's not true, Sophia. I care about you all, but Tony has the chance to make something of himself. He could be a successful lawyer and that was being taken away from him. I couldn't watch that happening without taking a stand.

Tony shook his head vigorously.

– You're not bothered about me at all. This is about you and what fits in with your plans.

– How can you say that, Tony?

– You've never asked me what I want.

– Well, I know you didn't want to spend the rest of your life with Theresa Kane.

My ears pricked up at this. Her name hadn't been brought up since the day Dad and Tony almost came to blows, which was fine by me as the whole ladder issue seemed to have died down. I'd become increasingly convinced that her visit to the house couldn't have been related to the ladder and this appeared to confirm it. Why Tony would want to spend his life with Kane's sister, however, was anyone's guess.

– How do you know that? Tony demanded.

– You couldn't have. You're so much better than that. You've got so much going for you.

– Have a word with yourself, Mum, for Christ's sake. You're just the same as Dad. You just express your prejudices in a different way. I don't even want to be a fucking lawyer. This is all about you, making up for what you missed out on. You just assume that what you want is best for me. Well, let me clear things up for you, it isn't. I want to make my own decisions.

Sophia threw her napkin down as well, to indicate that she wasn't prepared to go through the sham of a happy Christmas dinner.

– Oh, listen to you all. You're such victims, she said witheringly. Dad's a victim because Mum's trying to turn him into something he's not. Mum's a victim because she got a family when what she really wanted was a career. Tony's a victim because he's put upon and misunderstood, and no-one will give him space to be the irresponsible wanker that he really wants to be. I thought I was a victim because no-one gives a toss about anything I do until the shit hits the fan. But I'm not really because I wouldn't want sympathy or understanding from any of you lot, anyway.

– Sophia, Mum said pleadingly, trying to put a comforting arm around her, but she pulled away.

– Well, let me tell you, the only real victim in this house is Steve, Sophia continued, pointing at me. The only consolation is that he's too young and too dim to have the first idea what the fuck's going on.

– Who are you calling dim? I retorted.

Wally was sitting on the electricity box when I cycled across the road towards him on the Top Hopper. He affected a look of disinterest, but I could tell from the way he cast his eyes over the bike's features that he was impressed.

– So, you didn't get the Chopper, then? he said, I thought, a little too snidely.

– Nah, I didn't want one anyway. I wanted one of these, I replied breezily.

He scanned the name, printed in glittery, silver letters on the crossbar, which was just visible in the glow of the street light.

– Top Hopper, never heard of it.

– It's big in the States, I lied. They don't even know what a Chopper is over there. Dad had to get it specially imported.

Wally didn't say anything. He just shivered in his thin denim jacket. Then he pulled a crumpled packet of Players from the pocket of his jeans and removed a half-smoked cigarette which he lit with a match.

– That's what I got for Christmas – ten fags – and only because I managed to blag them from the old bastard.

I laughed.

– Nah, seriously, what did you get? I asked.

– I am serious, he said.

He explained that his old man had been sent into town two days ago to buy Christmas presents and a turkey. He eventually returned late on Christmas Eve, pissed, having drunk and gambled away all the money. There followed a blazing row with his old dear, after which she got pissed as well, and they both collapsed in a drunken heap in the early hours. It was now late afternoon, and they were still in bed, comatose, with no prospect of them waking. All Wally's brothers had left to spend the day with friends and girlfriends. Suitcase had given him money to buy his dinner from the Chinese takeaway at Cessnock when it opened.

Wally's problems made mine seem inconsequential, and I felt guilty that I had flaunted my new bike in front of him. He looked gaunt and forlorn, sitting alone in a deserted street on Christmas Day with nowhere to go and no-one to look after him. I said I'd ask Mum if he could have some of our leftovers, but he said he didn't want them. I didn't push it, largely because I didn't want to expose him to the ugly atmosphere in our house.

I wanted him to have my Tomahawk there and then but I knew that if I offered it as a gift, he would see it as charity and refuse. So I said that I was going to put an advert in the hardware shop window to sell it, but in the meantime, he could borrow it if he wanted. I made out like it was a reluctant offer for a couple of days, and only if he promised to take care of it and not to leave it unchained in the backyard.

He accepted grudgingly and promised to return it the day after Boxing Day. We walked over to my garden, and I lifted it out of the shed. I'd taken good care of it, and, apart from a pair of balding tyres and a dirty back mudguard, it was in good condition.

As I unlocked the padlock and removed the chain, Wally was midway through a story about how the social workers had been round at his house the other day. One of the neighbours had spotted him sleeping in the middens and had reported his parents for neglect. The social workers were always round at his house, usually because of his chronic truancy, but he thought this time was different. Wally was not normally given to relaying the detail of his family's travails so I knew it must be serious.

– There's a family case conference in the New Year.

– What's a family case conference? I asked.

– That's when all the pen pushers from the social work department get round a table and decide if they're going to put me in a home.

– They wouldn't put you in a home, would they?

– No, because I'm not hanging around to let them.

– What do you mean? I asked.

– I'm off my mark. I'm running away. First chance I get.

19

The Prof. died. His body was found on a bench in Bellahouston Park. He had thirteen pence in his pocket, and the only other possession he left, other than the clothes he was wearing, was his rusty old bike, which was lying next to him. I cried when I heard. It was funny because I didn't cry when Dad left home to live with Vivienne. I really wanted to but I just couldn't will the tears to come. Then, when Jukebox Durie told me about the Prof., it was like something just clicked in my head. The floodgates opened, and I couldn't stop sobbing. Jukebox stood staring at me like I was mental.

The Prof.'s death – alone, outside, in the dead of winter – was too sad to bear. I knew I was crying tears of guilt because of all the times I'd taken the piss out of him while he blabbered on his usual shite about the war and stuff. It didn't seem right that someone could be left to freeze on a park bench with no-one around to lift a finger to help. If only I'd been there, I could have done something to save him. But Mum said he was just an old man whose time had come. He'd lived that way for years and the tragedy wasn't his death, it was his life.

At first Dad didn't let on that he'd moved in with Vivienne. When I asked him where he was living, he just said he was staying with friends until he got a place of his own, before quickly changing the subject. He came by the house every couple of days to see me, Sophia and Tony, but it wasn't the same as having him live with us and I missed him. It was weird hearing him ring the bell of his own home rather than just letting himself in, and there was a tense atmosphere whenever Mum was around. Mostly we just sat in the living room with the telly switched off, not saying much.

After that he suggested it would be better if we went out and spent the day somewhere. He picked us up in the van, and we drove to different places to eat. The first couple of times we went to Gino's for pancakes and milkshakes, but then Dad said we really should try somewhere different so we went to a Berni Inn where I had had deep fried scampi and chips with tartare sauce served in little individual sachets. The waitress brought a whole bunch of them to the table, but I only used two so I stuffed the rest in my pocket when no-one was looking, figuring I could probably swap them for something in the playground.

Sophia had a gammon steak with a pineapple ring on top, and Tony had a mushroom omelette with chips. Dad just ordered a coffee because he said he would have his dinner later, when he went home. Sophia said he must have nice friends, if they were prepared to cook his meals as well as offering him accommodation. Dad smiled and then asked everyone what they wanted for pudding.

The following weekend was half-term, and he promised he would take us to Largs on the Monday when there was no market. Largs was a fading holiday resort on the lower Clyde, long favoured by Glaswegians for daytrips during the summer months when it still drew crowds in sufficient numbers to exude a kiss-me-quick, end-of-the-pier vibrancy. Off season, when the Big Wheel was mothballed and the hot dog stands were boarded up, activity on the front was restricted to a pensioner walking his dog and a collection of local hoods breathing malicious intent around the entrance to the single penny arcade that remained open.

It was a cold, grey day with heavy clouds hanging low in the sky. A gusting wind whipped in off the sea, drenching the deserted promenade in a shroud of salty spray. We sought shelter in Nardini's, the famous art deco café which stood defiantly against the irresistible tide of downmarket populism that had engulfed the rest of the town. With its gold wicker furniture and its smart waitresses dressed in starched, white, monogrammed pinafores, it retained a proud elegance, in contrast with its seamier surroundings.

On previous visits to Nardini's I'd been restricted to a glass of milk or, at a push, a milk shake, but on this occasion I ordered the most expensive Knickerbocker Glory on the menu, without a word of reproach from Dad. I had observed a strange and welcome phenomenon since Mum and Dad's break-up. During these outings with Dad, whatever I requested, within reason, I was granted – sweets, bottles of ginger, chips, even a Mitre football when we stopped off at the petrol station to fill up the van. Tony and Sophia denounced such gifts as 'blood money' – Dad's way of salving his conscience – and they refused to accept them, but I took everything that was going. I knew it wouldn't last forever and I was determined to milk it for all it was worth.

The Knickerbocker Glory was layered, in ascending order, with two scoops of Nardini's home-made ice-cream, tinned fruit cocktail, chopped nuts, more ice-cream and raspberry sauce, and it was capped with fresh cream and hundreds and thousands. It had two wafer funnels sticking out of the top and it was served with a long-handled teaspoon.

The three minutes and forty seconds it took me to destroy it were the most deliciously opulent of my short life. I cocked my head back and tipped the glass until it was completely inverted, draining the last of the raspberry and ice-cream residue from the bottom, before reclining in my wicker chair and wondering if Dad's conscience would stretch to another. It didn't.

However, he did give me ten pence to spend in the penny arcade. Penny arcades were another illicit institution whose windows bore my breathy imprint. Despite showy, colourful distractions like the one-armed bandits and the pinball machines, with their flashing lights and ringing bells, I was fascinated by the penny waterfall, which I regarded as a licence to print money. I noted that its title was a blatant misnomer – it should have been called the two pence piece waterfall. Piles of coppers gathered on a series of sliding platforms, and above them was a row of coin slots into which you dropped your two pence pieces, hoping to dislodge the piles below.

I handed over my sweaty ten pence piece to a bored-looking woman in the change booth in exchange for five twos and made my way to the machine. It seemed I had arrived at exactly the right moment. Dozens of coins were perched with impossible precariousness on the edge of the platforms. All it would take was my modest contribution to send a cascade of cash crashing into the payout trays below. I didn't see how I could lose. I did.

It was still daylight when the van chuntered out of Largs. Everything we'd had to say to Dad had been said, and so we proceeded home in silence. As we drove through Paisley, darkness rushed in like a speeding train, and, by the time we pulled into Gower Street, it was night. Dad said he had a busy week ahead – he was going to try out two new markets, in Alloa and Bathgate – so it would be Thursday before we would see him again. He asked where we wanted to go for tea, and Sophia suggested we come and visit him in his new house.

Immediately Dad said that wouldn't be possible because he didn't want to impose any further on his friends who were putting him up. Sophia asked who these mysterious friends were, but Dad just said they were people he knew through the restaurant and we wouldn't know them.

– We know you're living with Vivienne, Dad, so why don't you just admit it? she said matter-of-factly.

Dad's face turned scarlet, and his mouth must have been bone dry because, when he tried to swallow, he choked.

– I suppose it was your mother who told you, he said ill-temperedly. I knew she couldn't keep her mouth shut.

– Actually, Mum didn't tell us, Tony said calmly. We managed to work it out for ourselves. It was fairly obvious.

It may have been obvious to him and Sophia, but it came as a shock to me. I knew Dad was friendly with Vivienne, and she made a very decent steak and kidney pie, but I couldn't see why he'd want to live with her and not with us. When I asked Mum about it later, she said I was old enough to know the truth about what had been going on.

She said sometimes mums and dads didn't always spend their whole lives together. Sometimes they realised they didn't love each other in the same way they used to, and in those circumstances they often decided to go their separate ways. That's what had happened with her and Dad. They had known for some time they weren't getting along, and when Mum went to stay with Granny and Granddad after the argument about Tony's future, it was the culmination of a lot of things that convinced them both the time had come to live apart.

The day Dad and I went to collect her, when they'd had their long chat in Granny and Granddad's lounge, they resolved then to remain together until the summer, because they didn't want a major disruption ahead of Tony's exams, but Christmas had brought things to a head and, in the end, they both agreed they couldn't see it through.

– But it won't be forever, you and Dad living apart, will it? I asked.

Mum's mouth curled, doing its best to break into a smile, but the rest of her face refused to co-operate.

– I'm afraid it probably will be forever, she said. I know it's difficult to understand, but things change, and people don't always feel the same way about each other as they once did.

– Do you still love Dad? I asked.

– He's my husband and the father of my children, and I'll always care about what happens to him, but, no, I don't love him in the way I used to.

– Does he love you?

– I think he probably feels the same way, Mum said. Besides, he's got Vivienne now.

It hadn't occurred to me until that moment that Dad could have a relationship with Vivienne similar to the one he'd had with Mum. Vivienne was a barmaid who was good for a free bottle of Coke and a hand with the cleaning. Beyond that, I couldn't see what was in it for Dad. But then marriage break-up was an unknown quantity to me. The only reference point I had was Johnny Nae Da, and a shiver ran down my spine at the thought that my life had become even remotely similar to his. I quickly reasoned that the two situations were vastly different and that you couldn't sensibly compare them. Johnny Nae Da's dad lived with a new family in the East End. My dad had simply left home and was living with a woman he used to work with. You could hardly call that a new family.

– Does Dad love Vivienne? I asked Mum.

– I don't know the answer to that. You'd have to ask him.

– Will they get married?

– I don't know that either.

– Do you hate Vivienne?

– No, I don't. I hope they do love each other and that they'll be happy. Your dad's a good man. He works hard and he wants to do what's right by his family. He deserves to be happy. He just couldn't be happy with me.

– Will you marry another man?

This time Mum managed a convincing smile.

– Let's just say I have no firm plans to do so at the moment.

After learning about Dad and Vivienne, and then with the news about the Prof.'s death, I was really miserable, so to cheer me up, Dad agreed to take me to one of the markets. I'd been lobbying for months for him to let me help out on the stall, but he kept saying it was a place of work, not a playground. Eventually I managed to convince him I'd take it seriously and I wouldn't be a nuisance, so he relented.

As it would have to be at the weekend, I had the choice of Saltcoats or Paisley. I opted for Paisley, one of the biggest outdoor markets in Scotland, drawing crowds of shoppers from all over the West Coast. Dad arranged to pick me up early on Sunday morning. He said we could go back to his house later on where Vivienne would cook us our tea.

I was excited about going to my first market, but I felt that, by entering Dad and Vivienne's 'love nest', as Tony called it, I would be betraying Mum. I told her about the arrangements, and she quickly put my mind at ease, telling me not to feel guilty. She said Dad and Vivienne were now a fact of life and we had to get used to it. She was determined that all of us – me, Sophia and Tony – should have a close relationship with Dad because she'd never had one with her father.

We arrived at the market shortly before eight o'clock. At that time of the morning it was a scene of quiet industry as traders busily erected their stalls, from a jigsaw puzzle of metal poles, wooden boards and nylon tarpaulins, and set out their products on display.

Within an hour it had turned into a buzzing palladium as loudmouthed vendors volubly competed for the attention of the thousands of customers who'd flooded into its narrow aisles.

This was Shaheed's writ large, with row upon row of discount merchandise and factory seconds, where quantity was more important than quality and everything cost something ninety-nine. Half-price PVC sandals fought for airtime with over-ripe fruit and veg, shop-soiled electrical goods and six tea towels for a pound. The stench of boiled hot dogs and sweating onions mingled with the odour of manure from the nearby sheds which, on weekdays, played host to a cattle mart.

Men with microphones offered unbelievable bargains at knock-down prices, today and for one day only. In the shops this set of machine washable, polyester bed sheets with matching pillow cases would set you back eleven ninety-nine. They weren't even looking for ten or nine ninety-nine. They didn't want eight, seven or even six ninety-nine. If they were asking five ninety-nine, people would be entitled to think they were getting a great deal, but they didn't even want that. Ladies and gentlemen, these sellers didn't bandy superlatives about lightly, but what they were offering was the bargain of the century.

Stocks were limited, and it was first come, first served. They weren't interested in time wasters so genuine buyers should show their money now, while there was still time, because, make no mistake, ladies and gentlemen, everything must go today. Before they had sold a single item, the punters were six deep at their stalls, frenziedly waving five-pound notes above their heads.

Dad's stall was positioned close to the entrance and was artfully assembled to present each item in its most favourable light. Clearly, he had learned a lot in the months since our first visit to Shaheed's, and I saw, for the first time, his astute business sense. He was charming and persuasive, and he knew precisely how to handle each individual customer. Those who approached the stall with little or no intention of buying often found themselves walking away with an instamatic camera or a fifteen-pound car radio.

Dad placed a small foldaway table in the centre of one of the busiest aisles, from which I was instructed to sell one particular line of stock. Throughout the morning he kept changing the line, knowing instinctively which customers would be passing at a given time and what they would buy. Early in the morning, when the housewives were up for their farm fresh eggs and the cheapest cuts of meat, it was imitation capo di monte ornamental roses. At ninety-nine pence a piece or two for one eighty, they sold like hotcakes. Later, when the families started to arrive, it was cushioned deck chairs at a fiver a pair and, for the amateur handyman, forty-piece alloy socket sets at three ninety-nine.

It turned out to be one of the busiest days since Christmas, and Dad was in jubilant mood at all the money we were making. I had so much fun that the hours flew by and, when I thought it was only lunchtime, it was already half past three. Dad suddenly realised that we hadn't eaten so he tossed ten bob in my direction and told me to go and buy a couple of hot dogs.

I wandered around, marvelling at all the wares on display. There were lots of record stalls selling singles cheaper than they were in the shops, and posters and badges of the latest pop stars like David Essex and Donnie Osmond. Sophia would have a field day. I was sure Tony would also be impressed at the number of stalls selling cheap high-waisters, tank tops and Simon shirts. I couldn't wait to tell them.

I hung around the toy stalls, inspecting their footballs, cricket bats and tennis racquets. They weren't of the greatest quality, but they were cheap enough to afford if I saved up my pocket money. One stall had piles of trump cards, most of which I'd never seen before – drag racers, American trucks and Formula 3000. Trump cards were the new craze at school, fast replacing football cards as the must have collector's item. Sleek and shiny, they were smarter than football cards and came in a plastic box, but, at ten bob a pack, it was an expensive craze to get into.

With four packs, Angus Dickie had the biggest collection in the school, including British classic and Formula One cars, commercial aircraft and speedway bikes. I had none. As I scanned the stall's rich pickings, I was overcome with a feeling of envy and an urgent desire to own one of them. I had to have a pack of trump cards. While the toy seller was busy with another customer, I slipped the box of drag racers into my trouser pocket.

If I had fled the scene immediately, I would have drawn attention, so I picked up a plastic trumpet and pretended to examine it. I held the mouthpiece to my lips and blew, as though I was testing it, then I shook my head to denote that I was unimpressed and placed it back on the stall.

The other customer departed, and the toy seller turned towards me. He was fat and sullen, and he couldn't have been much older than Sophia so I figured he was more likely to be the toy seller's assistant. I was self-conscious because of his close attentiveness and pretended to look at some of the other toys. When I made to leave, he picked up the trumpet and called me back.

– This thing's covered in your spit. Are you going to buy it?
– Nah, I don't fancy it, I said as casually as I could.
– It's five bob, he said as though he hadn't heard me.
– I don't want it.
– Well, I can't sell something that's covered in your spit.

I took it from him and wiped the mouthpiece with my sleeve. I inspected it and then wiped it some more before handing it back.

– What's in your pocket? he demanded.

I flushed with panic. I looked down and I could see that the outline of the trump card box was clearly visible through my trouser pocket. There was no point in denying it. I thought about making a run for it, but the aisles were packed with shoppers and I knew I wouldn't get very far. I smiled. I don't know why, it was a wholly inappropriate response, but it was instinctive – I was trying to ingratiate myself. I reached into my pocket, retrieved the box and placed it back on the stall.

– I was only kidding, I said, flashing an obsequious grin. I was going to put it back.

It was a ludicrous proposition, which I didn't expect him to believe for a moment, but I was cornered, and my only recourse was appealing to his sense of disbelief. His face contorted into a snarl.

– Yer a filthy wee thief, he spat.

– I'm not, pal. I was going to put it back, honest. I was just trying to wind you up.

– Yer a liar and a thief.

People were beginning to stare so I tried to walk away, but he grabbed my arm.

– Where do you think you're going, thief?

I tried to wriggle free, but his hand was like a clamp.

– SOMEONE CALL THE POLICE! I'VE GOT A THIEF HERE!

A group of shoppers was now gathered in front of his stall and some of them were laughing. One of the other traders shouted that my hands should be cut off like they did in Arab countries, and the laughter grew louder. Someone else shouted that hanging was too good for me. The more I struggled, the more the fat assistant seemed determined to hold onto me, and the more ridiculous the scene became.

He wrestled me to the ground and sat on me to prevent my escape. It was a humiliating spectacle, but I was too scared to be embarrassed. At that moment I would have said or done anything just to get away. Suddenly I heard the voice of a man behind us, asking what was going on. The fat assistant stood up but retained his tight grip on my arm.

– I caught him trying to pinch a packet of trump cards, he said.

The man had a money belt around his waist and he was carrying two polystyrene cups of tea. I figured he must be the toy seller.

– I wasn't. It was just a joke. I was going to put them back, I protested.

The toy seller walked around the back of the stall. He didn't seem interested in me.

– What should we do with him? asked the fat assistant.

– Let him go.

– *Let him go?* The fat assistant repeated incredulously.

– You're making a scene. It's bad for business, the toy seller said, before turning his attention to me.

– Bugger off, ya wee toerag. If I see you round here again I'll scrub yer arse.

The fat assistant released his grip, and I fled, barging into shoppers as I ran. I felt conspicuous, with hundreds of eyes on my back and I had to find a secluded spot to recover my composure. I made my way to the toilets at the far end of the market and locked myself in a cubicle. The toilets were filthy, and the smell of piss and shit was overpowering, but I didn't care. I crouched down and plunged my head into my hands, praying that my heart rate would slow down. My legs trembled, and I felt as though I was going to burst into tears.

I remained there for about ten minutes, but I knew I'd have to return to the stall otherwise Dad would become suspicious. I forced myself out of the cubicle and weaved the long way round the vast market to avoid having to go anywhere near the toy stall. Several times I got lost and had to retrace my steps to get my bearings before trying again.

Eventually I found what I was sure was the right way back. I felt sick with dread. There was no way I could have eaten anything, so I bought a hot dog for Dad and told him I had already eaten mine while I was looking round the stalls. I said I was tired and asked him if I could sit in the van for a bit. I wanted to keep out of sight. I was terrified I might be spotted by someone who had witnessed the incident, who might tell Dad. The market was due to close in less than an hour so Dad agreed, but said I would have to help him pack up.

The market emptied as quickly as it had filled and, when Dad summoned me from the van, suddenly I felt utterly exposed. I reckoned the toy seller and his fat assistant were less than fifty yards away and the only thing standing between them and Dad was the cover of a couple of dozen stalls which were now being dismantled at an alarmingly quick rate. Ours seemed to be one of the slowest to be cleared. Every watch, lighter and radio had to be carefully returned to its packaging before being packed into larger boxes and loaded into the van. I willed Dad to speed up, but he proceeded at a laborious pace.

Then it occurred to me that we were on the only exit route out of the market. In order to leave, every trader would have to pass our stall. The thought had barely entered my head when I saw the toy seller drive past in a red Toyota van. His fat assistant was in the passenger's seat and, for a split second, our eyes met. The Toyota continued, and I breathed a sigh of relief, but then it stopped and slowly began to reverse. My heart leapt, and I dived into the back of Dad's van for cover.

Through a gap in the back doors I watched the Toyota pull up in front of our stall. The toy seller and the fat assistant got out. They had a short conversation with Dad, then I heard him calling my name. Reluctantly, I climbed out of the van. The game was up. I felt like a prisoner on death row, making the final walk to the electric chair. Refusing to make eye contact with the toy seller or his assistant, I approached Dad.

– Is this true? he demanded.

– What? I said, feigning ignorance.

– Did you try to steal a pack of cards from these men?

– No, I lied.

– He fucking well did, said the fat assistant.

– I didn't, Dad, honest.

– Yer a thieving, lying wee shite and I ought to boot yer baws up and down . . .

– That's enough of that, said the toy seller.

Dad put his hand on the toy seller's shoulder and led him away.

– OK, look I'll deal with it, he said. I'm sorry, I had no idea.

– It's not a problem, pal, the toy seller replied. He never got away with anything but I thought you should know, given the problem everyone has with shoplifters.

We finished packing in silence. The tension was unbearable. I'd rather Dad had exploded on the spot than delay the inevitable. The matter would have to be addressed sometime, and this was only allowing his anger to fester.

I braced myself for a furious onslaught, similar to the one meted out to Sophia when she was caught demanding money with menaces. I grimaced in anticipation of the inevitable battery of recrimination – how I was stupid, untrustworthy and immature, how I had humiliated him and let him down. Mum would have to be told, of course, which would mean another roasting. That was an unexpected and unwelcome consequence of separated parents – suffering punishment twice.

But, as we drove home, Dad acted as if nothing had happened. He talked about the volume of traffic and wondered aloud what Vivienne had made for tea. He even stopped off at a café in Paisley and bought a big tub of ice-cream with raspberry sauce which, he said, we could have as a special treat for pudding.

He returned to the van and sat for a few moments with his hand on the key, as though he was about to turn it, but then he sat back in his seat and turned to face me.

– I'm only going to ask you this once. Did you try to steal a pack of cards from that man?

He was staring me in the eye, but, no matter how hard I tried,

I couldn't hold his gaze. My eyes darted nervously from the car key, to his forehead, to a boy in a snorkel parka on the other side of the road, kicking a tennis ball against a wall.

– Yes, I said, eventually. I did. I'm sorry.

My mind was already racing, as I tried to anticipate what my punishment would be. Petty theft was a relatively serious misdemeanour and could result in a grounding of up to four weeks or indefinite suspension of pocket money. Yet, against all expectation, Dad's tone remained equable. Instead of the predicted volley of abuse, he simply asked me why I had done it. I'd never been asked that when I had done something wrong and I was stuck for words. I had perpetrated an act of petty theft. What did he care what my motives were?

– It's a simple question. Why did you steal the cards? he repeated.

– 'Cos I wanted them, I replied.

– We all want things we can't have. It doesn't mean you go around stealing them.

– But it was only a pack of cards. It wasn't a big thing like, eh, I don't know . . . a ladder.

– A ladder?

– Yeah, a ladder. It only cost ten bob.

– Have you ever tried earning ten bob?

He knew I hadn't. I'd never had a job. I didn't know if he expected an answer. I thought probably not. I wasn't used to this – Dad trying to reason with me.

– Well, have you? he demanded.

– No.

– No. You haven't. Well, let me tell you, it's not easy. Earning any amount of money is hard. These traders are doing their best to earn a living to clothe and feed their families and to keep a roof over their heads.

His voice had become fractionally louder and more passionate, but he stopped momentarily and took a breath. When he resumed his tone was measured again.

– I have to work with them. They trust me. How do you think it makes me feel when I bring my son along and he tries to steal from them?

By this time I had enough of a handle on the conversation to know that he expected an answer.

– Bad, I replied.

– Yes, very bad and embarrassed. You need to understand that when you do things like that, it reflects on those around you. Are you happy for those people to think that I've done badly as a father?

– But you haven't.

– When you go around stealing, it looks like I have.

– That's not fair.

– No, it's not.

To my surprise, Dad said he wouldn't be telling Mum. He admitted that he didn't want her thinking he had allowed me to run riot and get into bother. More surprisingly, he said there would be no punishment. He said I'd suffered enough and, if I learned from the experience, then that was more beneficial than being reprimanded.

– Thanks, Dad.

– Don't thank me, just don't do it again. I want to be proud of you.

I should have been punching the air – I'd been caught stealing and got away with it – but the thought of making my dad ashamed of me made me feel terrible. I also felt responsible that, if Mum ever found out, she would think it was his fault for not looking after me properly. I knew that wasn't true. It had nothing to do with him. It had been my own stupid fault.

The biggest regret I had was that I'd taken Dad for granted. I saw him infrequently enough and I wanted those occasions when we were together to be special, because there wasn't enough time to make it up to him. I wished that Sophia and Tony felt the same. He was the only dad we had, and we were the only family he had.

We pulled into the street where Vivienne lived. It was full of council houses that were older and smaller than the one we lived in. Her street wasn't as smart either. Bins overflowed in gardens, and rusty cars sat on piles of bricks at the side of the road. I couldn't understand why Dad would want to leave our nice, comfortable home to live here.

Dad let himself into the house with his key and called out Vivienne's name. She came to greet us, dressed in an apron and carrying a wooden spoon. A comforting smell of home cooking drifted into the hallway. She kissed Dad on the cheek and said hello to me. Then she led us into the living room.

Sitting on the floor, watching television, was a boy who, I guessed, was a couple of years younger than me. He was skinny with fine white hair and a look of panic etched into his face. Dad walked up behind him and ruffled his hair, just like he used to do with me.

– This is Curtis, he said. Vivienne's son.

Wally's family case conference was due any day now, and he continued to insist that he was going to run away from home and hide out in barns, like the guy in *Whistle Down the Wind*. I didn't believe him. That sort of thing only ever happened on TV and in films – I'd never known anyone do it for real. He kept asking if I wanted to go with him. I didn't say no because I didn't want him thinking I was a shitebag, so instead I asked lots of questions, trying to pick holes in his plan.

He said he was going to steal a car and drive to the Highlands. I asked how he would start it without a key. He said one of Holdall's mates had told him how to hotwire a car and it was a piece of piss. I pointed out that he'd never driven a car before, but he said he'd pick it up soon enough – it was just like riding a bike.

I asked how he'd get the money for petrol, and he said he'd steal a car with a full tank. I pointed out that it would have to be a big car to get him all the way to the Highlands, so he said he'd steal a Rover or a Morris Oxford from one of the posh houses in Pollokshields. I suggested a ten-year-old boy driving a Morris Oxford might raise an eyebrow or two, but he said he'd only drive at night.

I asked how he'd buy essentials like food, clothes, sweets and comics. He said he'd stop off at places on the way and do odd jobs like washing cars or running errands. He reckoned you could charge a bob a car – enough to buy a bag of chips. Two cars a day would get you lunch and dinner, and anything on top of that was pure profit.

The atmosphere between Mum and Sophia and Tony was still

tense, but I didn't think it had reached a sufficient pass that I needed to run away from home. After the disastrous Christmas, Mum was doing her best to comply with Sophia's wishes to treat us all as equals and Tony's desire that she should respect that we were individuals with feelings and opinions.

No-one seemed concerned to find out if I was harbouring any unmet requirements. Tony's exams remained the main focus of attention, and everything was geared towards making sure nothing interrupted his studies. Sophia's appearance before the children's panel also hung over the household like a spectre.

No-one seemed to be bothered that Dad was living somewhere else with a new family. Sophia and Tony had both met Curtis, when they went to Vivienne's house for lunch, and they both thought he was a nice kid. I couldn't help thinking they were missing the point. They didn't share my concern that we were now fatherless. It never occurred to them that Curtis obviously had something we didn't that made Dad want to live with him and not with us. They didn't appear troubled by the possibility that we had driven Dad away with threats of violence, demands for money with menaces and by stealing trump cards from his colleagues.

Mum wasn't much help when pressed on the matter. She said he was, and always would be, our dad no matter what we did or what house we lived in. He would love us just the same. We were his only children, and, even if he and Vivienne got married, Curtis would only ever be his stepson. That only made things worse – giving the snotty little brat a formal title; knowing that he was any kind of son to my dad.

Word of Mum and Dad's break-up hadn't come out at school yet, but I knew it was only a matter of time. Sophia and Tony seemed to have no compunction about telling anyone who would listen that our parents had separated, including many of the elder brothers and sisters of people in my class at the primary. When it did become common knowledge, it was certain I would be assigned a 'Nae Da' title just like Johnny Nae Da. It wouldn't matter that, unlike Johnny Nae Da, I knew where my dad lived and saw him every other day.

Suddenly, I had an irrational hatred towards Johnny Nae Da. He was so fat and smelly and unpopular – the very notion that I might have anything in common with him was laughable. That I could be ostracised alongside him as a fatherless outcast was too disturbing to contemplate. Yet at the same time, I felt instinctively drawn towards him, hanging around with him in the playground and walking him home after school. I knew that I risked drawing attention to myself – openly befriending a friendless pariah – but I couldn't help myself. I believed that, somehow, he held invaluable clues about the future direction of my life. He was a lock that I had to unpick.

I asked him about his relationship with his father, about the last time they had met, and about the rumours that he had brothers and sisters living in the East End, whom he had never met. Of course, I never let on that, like him, I too was a 'Nae Da'.

He was glad of my company and flattered by the attention, but he was guarded and suspicious, and he stuck to his story about his dad serving life in Barlinnie for murder. He kept trying to steer the conversation onto more prosaic topics like what was on telly last night and the goal he nearly scored in the Papes v. Prods match.

Finally, after some sustained badgering, he agreed to tell me the true story about his dad, but only if I swore on my eyes that I'd never reveal it to another soul – and if I bought him a jumbo sausage supper, with a pickled egg from the Crit. He stood behind me in the chip shop queue, ensuring the order was fulfilled to his satisfaction, leaving me with only enough money to buy myself a penny caramel. Then he sat on the low wall behind Cessnock underground station, chomping through his battered sausage as he laid bare his family's darkest secrets.

He barely remembered his father because his parents separated when he was three. They split up because his dad kept battering his mum. After a particularly savage beating, the neighbours called the police, and his dad was jailed for common assault. While he was in prison, Johnny Nae Da and his mum packed all their things in supermarket carriers and fled. They moved in with his granny, but when his dad got out of jail he found out where they were and turned up drunk, shouting violent threats. They had to call the cops to have him taken away. Then his mum went to court and got a judge to ban his dad from coming near them.

They moved into a tenement flat in Ibrox and they hadn't seen his dad since. The last they heard, he had married another woman and had three kids, two girls and a boy. Johnny Nae Da didn't know their ages.

When he was eight, his mum asked if he wanted to meet his old man. She said she was terrified of him and she never wanted to see him again, but, if Johnny Nae Da really wanted to meet him, then she would make contact. Johnny Nae Da said he appreciated the offer but he didn't want to.

– Why do you want to know all this? he asked, through a mouthful of chips.

– No reason, I'm just interested, I replied.

I asked him if he thought he'd ever want to meet his dad, maybe when he was older, but he said he wouldn't.

– As my ma says, if he really was interested in me, he would've come round to see me when he was sober. She reckons he's not bothered about us any more. She says he's the biggest shit she's ever met.

That wasn't what I wanted to hear. It made me think that maybe Dad would forget all about us and wouldn't want to see us again. Despite what Mum said about him always being my dad, I was sure that, deep down, she couldn't care less if I ever saw him again. Whenever I asked about him, like when I was worried about him living with Vivienne and Curtis, Mum always said he was a good man who deserved to be happy and that he would always be my dad.

But then, in everyday life, she seemed to forget all about that and her attitude hardened. Like, for example, when he came to pick us up to go on one of our outings, they would stand apart, awkward and silent. After sixteen years of marriage, they couldn't think of a single thing to say. Then, if he was late bringing us home, she would lose her temper, saying how that was typical of him and that he couldn't be trusted to do the simplest of things.

I seemed to be the only one who still cared about Dad. Tony had his own life – he would be moving out of the house and going to university soon – and while he and Dad had patched up their differences, he didn't care where Dad lived. Sophia would probably also be leaving home in a few years and she wouldn't care either.

I asked Johnny Nae Da if he missed his dad, but he said he didn't remember having one and you don't miss what you've never had. I asked what the worst thing was about not having a dad.

– Being the only one, he said without hesitation. It's not easy being different. If there was even one other person in our class who didn't have a dad, I wouldn't feel so alone.

I watched him sitting on the wall and I thought about the Prof. I pitched forward, imagining Johnny Nae Da growing old and facing the same fate – living and dying, cold, forlorn and alone. That was my cue. I could have told him he wasn't the only one in the class without a dad and that he would never have to feel isolated and persecuted again. I could have revealed my own parents' break-up and, in doing so, possibly altered the future direction of his sad life. But as I watched his fat, ginger-topped face bite into a pickled egg and its mangled remnants clinging to the blackened stumps of his teeth, I couldn't bring myself to do it.

The shows came to Bella. The entire south side of the park was transformed overnight, from a barren expanse of grass into a bustling, neon-spangled metropolis of carnival rides, tombola stands, candyfloss stalls, fortune tellers' tents and shooting galleries.

The excitement was uncontainable. The shows were the one occasion when we felt like something truly significant was happening in our lives, when our unsung corner of the world became the centre of the universe for a weekend, when thousands of people flocked from far and wide and queued for hours to bring some exhilaration to their lives.

The people who worked at the shows were called Pikies – swarthy, unusually hirsute people who spoke with an indeterminate accent and had more tattoos than anyone I had ever seen. I found this itinerant race, who lived in caravans and lit unfeasibly large bonfires, exotic and terrifying. I stood at a safe distance, watching with rapt fascination as they loitered around the entrances to the local pubs and bookmaker's shops with their wild-looking Alsatians and their even wilder children.

Mum thought everything about the shows was common and she forbade us from going anywhere near them. She would rather have seen me in a pair of bell bottoms, buying chips with a bunch of Catholics from Maryhill than come within a mile of a Pikie. But this year I decided to take a stand.

– All my friends are going, and, besides, there's nothing wrong with the Pikies. They're just ordinary folk trying to earn a living, like the market traders who work with Dad. Only with wooden teeth.

Mum laughed, and then she did something she'd never done before. She agreed with me.

– You're right. They are just ordinary people. All right, you can go but make sure there's a crowd of you and don't spend all your money. And don't go on anything that looks dangerous. And keep away from the Alsatians.

I'd helped Dad out on the stall on the two previous Sundays, and he'd agreed I was now old enough to be paid – five bob a day – which meant I had ten bob to spend at the shows.

Chabs, Cuddihy and Bifter dogged school on Friday afternoon so they could beat the rush. The word was there was a new rollercoaster this year that looped the loop twice and was the fastest ever seen in the west of Scotland. They reckoned that if we waited until after school, we'd have to queue for four or five hours to get on it, so they slipped out of the playground at lunchtime, taking their chances with Wutherspoon. She'd never believe they'd all suddenly been struck down with a mystery illness the weekend that the shows just happened to be in town, and it would almost certainly mean six big ones on Monday morning.

They asked me to join them, but I declined the invitation. They thought it was because I was scared of getting the strap and accused me of being a big shitebag, but I just let them believe that. The truth was, I didn't want to go with them. I had plans of my own.

Lyndsey Cummings lived in one of the brown brick houses on Maxwell Drive. People from our estate looked down on the folks who lived in the brown brick houses, which were older and shabbier than our own. Faded paint flaked from the rotting frames of their grimy windows, and their gardens were grubby and unkempt. Abandoned chassis of old motors and redundant white goods lay strewn chaotically in their driveways, and sinister-looking weeds exploded volcanically from every surface.

I spent most of Saturday morning sitting on a wall across the road from Lyndsey's house. There was little sign of life, and I began to fear that she might be out, but then, shortly after eleven, the door opened, and she appeared, followed by her mum, dad and Cumbo. They all climbed into the family car, a rusty old Ford Prefect, parked in the driveway.

Lyndsey didn't see me, and I was too embarrassed to call out her name, so instead I sat, helplessly silent, as doors slammed shut and the car reversed out into the street. It was about to pull away when Cumbo spotted me. The car halted, and I could see a heated verbal exchange taking place inside.

I sat making a none-too-convincing attempt at indifference until eventually the rear passenger side door opened and Lyndsey emerged sheepishly. As she walked across the road towards me, I could hear Cumbo catcalling and cooing.

– Just ignore him, Lyndsey said, but I could tell she was morti-fied. What do you want?

I had spent most of the last few days preparing my speech, settling on a precise form of words which, I was confident, would combine assertiveness, humility and charm, but as I stood facing her, my mind went blank. I panicked. The seconds ticked by, the silence filled with Cumbo's humiliating jeers.

– Hi, lover boy, I heard him shout, and I knew I had to fill the void.

– Do you want to go to the shows? I blurted out.

– When? she asked, unfazed.

– Tomorrow afternoon.

– OK, she replied, without hesitation.

It was as simple as that.

I stood at the main gates of Bella overcome with a feeling of paranoia that I was being watched, that something in my demeanour betrayed the truth – that I had arranged to spend the afternoon with a girl. I'd chosen Sunday afternoon because I knew that, by then, all my friends would have been to the shows already. There was still a small chance that I could be spotted by someone who knew me, but it was a risk worth taking.

Though I would never have admitted it on pain of torture, I enjoyed Lyndsey's company, but I had another reason for inviting her. My tête-a-tête with Johnny Nae Da had not been a success. Being privy to his experiences had, in the end, been of no benefit. They did nothing to enlighten my own circumstances because, when it came to the crunch, I couldn't confide in him.

Sophia, Mum, even Tony had proved no help, perhaps because they were too close to the situation. I needed an objective assess-ment, and, for reasons I couldn't properly explain, Lyndsey seemed the natural choice. I'd only spoken to her on a couple of occasions, but there had been an intimacy that convinced me she would be sympathetic and helpful.

She arrived ten minutes late. She was wearing a pair of jeans with a dragon embroidered on one of the legs with red and yellow silk thread, and an orange sloppy joe T-shirt with a glow worm on it. Her hair was tied in a ponytail, and she had a clean, freshly washed smell.

I felt a pang of guilt that I had not taken such care over my appearance, and so I offered to pay for all her rides. I had worked out that ten bob would get us on four rides as well as a hot dog and a stick of candyfloss. She said she couldn't let me pay for everything, so I said she could pay for the candyflosses.

On a normal Sunday afternoon, the park was peacefully windswept and all but deserted, the silence broken only by the sedate thwack of iron on plastic from the pitch 'n' putt course and the occasional dog bark. Today, it was a heaving mass of bodies, their excited chatter punctured by loud staccato gunfire from the shooting galleries and the shrill tinkling of carousel music.

It had been raining heavily, and thousands of eager feet had churned up the soft turf, so by the time we arrived it was a slick mud track. The stallholders had laid out flattened cardboard boxes as improvised walkways, but it hadn't taken long for them to become saturated and to meld into the muddy, squelchy gloop.

We picked our way gingerly through the bog, between the attractions, deciding which one to go on first. We settled on the dodgems. I insisted on driving, hammering the pedal to the floor and swinging our cab around the track as fast as I could, then swerving on a pinhead, whacking into every vehicle within range. Lyndsey was thrown back in her seat, but she laughed and whooped at my heroics, and I knew she was having a good time.

She yelled with unalloyed pleasure on the waltzers as a tooth-less Pikie whirled our booth through a thousand and eighty degrees. On the ghost train, she screamed with fright every time a skeleton or a ghoul appeared unexpectedly. When a light flashed suddenly, revealing a mad axe murderer – his blood-tipped blade poised ominously above our cowering heads – she unleashed an ear-piercing shriek and grabbed my arm.

It was the first physical contact I'd ever had with a female who was not a member of my family, and I was overcome with a shuddering sense of betrayal, like I was doing something I shouldn't – grassing on my best mate or cheering on a goal for Rangers. But I stayed with it, refusing to yield to an irresistible instinct to pull my arm away. I closed my eyes and eased into a pleasing new comfort zone. I felt a glow of wellbeing, and my chest puffed with pride. She clasped my arm tighter, and I moved towards her, feeling her warmth and breathing in her sweet smell.

The moment was over as quickly as it arrived. Our tiny carriage chugged to its inevitable, benign stop, and we were back in the light. The connection between us had lasted only a few seconds, but in that instant all the sadness and fear of the past few months had evaporated, and I felt good about my life.

We went for a hot dog and then wandered around, marvelling at all the exciting attractions. I tried to have a go on the shooting gallery to impress Lyndsey with my marksmanship, but the Pikie refused because I wasn't with an adult.

Instead I had a go at the snooker challenge. A pile of coins was balanced on top of a red snooker ball which sat on the table inside a white circle. The idea was you had to hit a white ball from one end of the table and cannon into the red, dislodging the coins but making sure they landed within the circle. You had three goes.

I chalked the end of the cue, trying to look like I knew what I was doing, and leaned over the table. On my first shot I struck the white ball cleanly but with too much pace, and it crashed into the red ball, sending the coins splaying across the table, miles outside of the circle. On my second attempt, I hit the white more gently, completely missing the red, and my face burned with embarrassment. Lyndsey said I was unlucky, but she was just being kind.

On my third and final attempt, I was so nervous at the prospect of making an arse of myself that I tensed up and completely mis-cued. The tip of the cue skidded off the surface of the white, which trickled at a grindingly slow pace along the baize. Somehow it managed to reach the white circle and nestle up to the red before coming to a halt.

The hairs on the back of my neck stood up as I watched the pile of coins rock back and forth on the top of the red in agonising slow motion. Finally, they collapsed, and, miraculously, landed inside the circle.

Lyndsey jumped up and down, whooping and yelling, then she threw her arms around my neck and hugged me tight. Caught up in the excitement I hugged her back before I realised what I was doing in public and pulled away.

As a prize, the Pikie offered me the choice of a small, silver plastic trophy the size of an eggcup with the word CHAMP printed on it, or a white furry gonk wearing a tartan bonnet. I hesitated.

– Och, don't be a rotten shite. Take the gonk fur yer burd, the Pikie said.

I grabbed the cuddly toy, more to silence him than anything else, and handed it to Lyndsey who blushed and turned away.

It was six o'clock, and the shows were closing. I made the pretence of wanting to go on the rollercoaster, but when Lyndsey said she'd rather not, I was actually quite relieved. Instead we spent the last of our money on candyflosses and then we left the park. It was getting dark as we walked home, and the sky was starting to cloud over again. We wandered at a snail's pace, taking the long way through the Cunyon, exchanging stories and anecdotes.

I don't remember how I engineered the conversation round to my family problems, but I found myself in the middle of a detailed description of Mum's walk-out, Dad's fight with Tony and his departure to live with Vivienne and Curtis. I didn't have to think about what I was saying; it all came instinctively. Throughout it all she listened, nodded, smiled and frowned in all the right places.

– It's all right for families to live apart, she said, as she picked another sliver of candy floss from her stick (I had finished mine half an hour before).

– Is it?

– Of course it is. My aunty and uncle are divorced and they live in separate towns. My cousins only see their dad once a week. Sometimes not even that because he's a lorry driver and he works away. Sometimes they don't see him for weeks at a time.

– God.

– Yeah. So you see, you're not so badly off after all. And as for the wee boy, what's he called?

– Curtis.

– Yeah, Curtis. As for him, where's his real dad?

– I don't know.

It was true, I didn't know. It hadn't occurred to me to ask, and Dad had never mentioned it.

– No, you see, he doesn't have a proper dad like you. Your dad is just this guy his mum's met who has come to live in their house. Did you ever think about it like that?

– No.

I hadn't.

– No, maybe poor wee Curtis is more miserable than you because his mum's got a new fancy man who's got his own kids and who doesn't give a shit about him.

– No, Dad's not like that. He would give a shit about him. He likes kids. He wouldn't just barge in and ignore Curtis, he . . .

We had reached Lyndsey's house. She had a grin on her face as she picked the final strands of candyfloss from her stick. She had made me think about things in a new way. Not even Mum had been able to do that.

– Thanks for paying and all, she said.

– That's OK.

We stood facing one another, and, for the first time that day, an awkward silence descended.

– No, thank *you*, I said.

– What for? she asked.

– I don't know . . . you know . . .

– No, what?

– You know . . . just . . . I don't know . . .

She leaned forward and kissed me on the cheek.

– So was the Pikie right? I asked. Are you my burd?

She blushed.

– If you like, she replied.

I walked to school the following morning buoyed by a euphoric sense of danger, a feeling that I had shared in something illicit and wonderful. Even being in the company of a girl was taboo – far less touching and being kissed by one – but I began to understand for the first time what had motivated Mark Crawford, the disgraced Woolworth's Lothario, to risk such humiliation. I would never go public about what had happened with me and Lyndsey, that was for sure, but I was equally certain that I couldn't wait to see her again.

I hung around the school gates, hoping to catch a glimpse of her. We'd made a pact that, if we saw each other at school, we wouldn't acknowledge the other's presence, but we worked out a series of signals so we could communicate. Scratching your nose meant 'Hi', rubbing the back of your neck meant 'See you after school' and putting your hand up to your mouth as if to cough meant 'I've got something I need to tell you'.

I saw Samantha Henry and Joanne Moffat crossing the road, but there was no sign of Lyndsey and my heart sank a little. Inside the playground the usual suspects were playing in the Papes v. Prods football match. One or two of them had spotted me, and they were pointing. I didn't know why. They started to walk towards me just at the moment when the girls passed.

– Sorry to hear about your mum and dad, Samantha Henry said with mock sincerity.

– Must be shite not having a dad, Joanne Moffat added, stifling a giggle.

I froze. Chabs, Cuddihy and Jukebox Durie were coming towards me, but I was paralysed by terror and a crippling feeling of betrayal. I didn't know whether to scream with rage or to cry. I grabbed my schoolbag and bolted. I headed along St Andrews Drive, running faster and faster until my body ached and my lungs felt like they were about to explode. I kept going, along Maxwell Drive, onto Nithsdale Road and up to Sherbrooke Avenue. I didn't know why I was running or where I was heading. I was driven by an instinctive need to get as far away from the school as possible.

I stopped when I reached the Cunyon and sat in the clearing, my back resting against the giant trunk of a horse chestnut tree. I stayed there for most of the morning, not because I had a lot to think about, but because I couldn't trust my legs to support my weight. Eventually, I got to my feet. I knew what I had to do. I had to find Wally, before it was too late.

I knew he wouldn't be at school, so I scoured all the haunts he visited when he was dogging – Bella, the disused railway station, the motorway site, round the back of the Co-op. As a last resort I went down to the Cunyon and found him, pretending to be Evel Knievel on the Seven Hills. I asked him when he was going to run away.

– Dunno, tomorrow maybe.

– Make it today, I said.

– Why?

– 'Cos I'm coming with you.

His face lit up. He asked me why, and I just said someone had let me down. I told him I had some conditions: we would go on our bikes, not in a stolen car; and we would go to Largs, not to the Highlands. I knew Largs and I figured we could find work at the amusements – just like the Pikies.

He wanted to go there and then, but I said we'd need to leave it until later on. If I wasn't home for tea, Mum would raise the alarm, and that wouldn't give us enough of a head start. Better to slip away after everyone was asleep. Besides, we'd need some basic provisions to keep us going. And there was one final thing I had to do before leaving.

I stood on the pavement outside Lyndsey's house and looked at her dad's rusty car sitting in the driveway like a flea-ridden old sleeping dog. Her dad worked nights at the shipyard so I knew he'd be in the house at this time of day.

I knocked on the front door, and a few moments later he appeared, unshaven, wearing a towelling dressing gown which, at one time, would have been white but was now dishwater grey. It flapped open to reveal a large belly, partly concealed by a coffee-stained vest. His thinning, flyaway hair was stuck up at the back, giving him the appearance of having been caught in a sudden gust of wind. Between his lips was a half-smoked cigarette and he was clutching a mug which said WORLD'S GREATEST LOVER.

– Lyndsey's still at school, he mumbled through the fag, before I had a chance to speak.

– Aye, I know. Can you give her a message?

– Aye, whit is it? he asked.

– Tell her she's chucked.

His face remained deadpan.

– Any reason?

I thought for a moment.

– Nah, tell her just 'cos.

21

I picked at my tea. Mum had been late home from college and had opened a tin of baked beans with mini Frankfurters, which she served on toasted pan bread. It was one of my all-time favourite meals, but I had no appetite, knowing that within a couple of hours I would be a fugitive. Mum kept asking why I wasn't eating and she didn't seem to believe me when I said I was full up.

– You've hardly eaten enough to make a gnat feel full up, she said.

When I volunteered to do the washing up I caught another glint of suspicion in her eye, but it was such an unexpected rarity that she didn't question me further. I wanted her out of the kitchen so that I could squirrel away some food to provide nourishment when I was on the run. Mum hadn't been to the shops at the weekend and there wasn't much in the cupboards but I grabbed what I could.

Mum, Tony and Sophia were watching *Nationwide* on telly. They were laughing at a feature from Plymouth about a dog that could bark along to '*La Marseillaise*'. I strolled through the living room as nonchalantly as I could with a tin of pilchards in tomato sauce, four Weetabix biscuits and a half-finished jar of Marmite stuffed down the front of my trousers. I said I was going upstairs to my bedroom to do my homework, which provoked another look. I hardly ever volunteered to do my homework and certainly never before *Nationwide* was finished.

– Are you feeling all right? Mum asked.

– Fine, I said, skipping out of the room as a Weetabix biscuit slipped down my trouser leg.

– That boy's up to something, I heard her say as I made my way upstairs.

Once inside my bedroom I jammed a chair under the door handle to make sure I wouldn't be disturbed; then I began laying out a list of provisions I thought I might need out in the wilderness. As well as the food I had liberated from the kitchen, I set aside a toothbrush, a facecloth and a spare pair of underpants; my football card collection; my top-rated conker and my spud gun – in case of a sudden attack by wild animals.

I lifted my mattress and retrieved my *Warlord* survival kit, which I always kept at the ready in case of such an emergency. It comprised a list of items recommended by Lord Peter Flint – king of all British secret agents – for living in the wild. As a fully paid-up *Warlord* agent, I was on a state of permanent alert, ready to respond to a threatened attack by anti-*Warlord* forces.

In the most recent issue of the comic, Lord Flint had warned – 'Fraid the news I have for you this week isn't very good! I received a letter from the leader of an anti-*Warlord* group informing me that his organisation had taken over control of two *Warlord* HQs. They are intending to attack two more HQs within the next couple of days. So I'm warning you all now to tighten up your security! Who knows? It could be you!

While my situation bore no relation to an impending attack by anti-*Warlord* forces, it was just the sort of emergency for which Lord Flint might regard his survival kit as being necessary. It included a heliograph, a secret agent stamp, a camera, binoculars, a water bottle, a piece of string, a magnifying glass, a compass, four teabags, a candle and a magnetised needle.

I had the secret agent stamp – it came with the *Warlord* wallet and the *Warlord* badge that you got through the post when you sent off five bob to the comic company to become a *Warlord* agent. I also had the string, the teabags, the candle, the compass, the magnifying glass and the water bottle – actually, it was a discarded malt vinegar bottle that I had retrieved from the bin.

But I didn't have the camera (Dad had forbidden me from using his Box Brownie) the binoculars (Who in the name of God owns a pair of binoculars? Mum had asked) – and I didn't know what a heliograph was – or a magnetised needle.

I laid a white handkerchief on the carpet and laid everything on top of it. The aim was to then pull the corners together and tie them to the end of a stick – a technique I was borrowing from last year's Christmas panto production of *Dick Whittington* at the King's. But the hanky was too small to carry even a fraction of the things. It was clear I needed something bigger.

I crept into Mum's bedroom and rummaged through the drawer in which she kept her gloves and headscarves, eventually settling on a large beige and black silk square with a picture of a swan printed on it. It was the biggest piece of material I could find, but even it wasn't big enough to contain all of my possessions. It was obvious some would have to be jettisoned. I ditched the most dispensable items – the toothbrush, the face cloth and the spare pair of pants – but still there was not enough room. Something else had to go.

I conducted a forensic audit of the remaining items, assessing the suitability of each and its likely necessity in the wilderness. It came down to a straight choice between the football cards and the Marmite. I ditched the Marmite.

I had arranged to meet Wally round the back of the Crit at eleven o'clock, which meant I'd have to be out of the house by a quarter to. The plan depended on Sophia being in bed and asleep by then. Fortunately Mum had insisted on early nights so she was asleep by ten.

A short time later I heard Tony and Mum coming upstairs. They brushed their teeth in the bathroom and kissed one another goodnight, before retiring to their respective rooms. I heard the click of the landing light, and the house was in darkness.

Beneath my bed sheets I was fully clothed. I kept a close eye on the clock at the side of my bed, and when the hands reached ten forty, I eased myself off the mattress and put on my duffle coat. I could tell from Sophia's laboured breathing that she was out for the count. Then I crept downstairs, through the house and let myself out the back door.

It was colder than I expected and raining heavily, and I wondered if I should have worn a jumper. But it was too late now. I was in the garden by then and I couldn't risk returning to the house in case I woke someone. I manoeuvred my bike out of the shed, nosed it down the path, onto the pavement, and cycled down Gower Street for the last time.

Holding the pole of my Dick Whittington sack over my shoulder meant that I could only keep one hand on the handle bars which made steering difficult, and on more than one occasion I nearly fell off. When I reached Clifford Street, I was forced to dismount and walk.

– Well, fuck me, look who it isn't. The wee Proddy poof, said a voice ahead of me.

I halted and looked up. Kevin Kane stood in the darkness, surrounded by a yellow fluorescent halo effect, created by the streetlight. He was flanked by two burly henchmen. Chilled droplets of rain trickled down my forehead and bounced off the end of my nose like lemmings from a cliff. I nodded limply and tried to walk around them, but the henchmen blocked my path.

– Wherr dae ye think you're gaun, fanny baws? Kane asked.

I wiped the rain from my eyes to get a clearer view. From his tone, I was expecting a look of aggression, but instead he wore a relaxed, mocking smile. Despite the detached expression, I knew this was the Waterloo moment I'd been dreading for months and I wasn't going to escape unscathed. I was Tony, cornered by the Sharks in *West Side Story*. I was Butch and Sundance, surrounded and outflanked by the Bolivian army.

In the circumstances, I decided the best form of defence was denial – craven, snivelling and obsequious denial.

– It wisnae me that lost yer da's ladder, big man, by the way, I protested.

Despite being taller than me, Kane was not, objectively, a 'big man'. He was squat and heavily built, with a protruding forehead and dark, deep-set eyes, but I thought the moniker might appeal to his sense of vanity.

– Aye, ye did.

Clearly it hadn't.

– Naw, ah didny, honest.

Speaking in his own vernacular was another attempt at ingratiation.

– Aye, ye did.

That too failed.

– Aye, OK, ah did, I conceded. But it wisnae jist me (I was not alone). Therr wiz others therr tae (I acted in concert). Ah wiz jist the last wan tae go (I left last). Ah tried tae get the ladder back, but the wummin that lived therr (the female resident) said her man (her husband) hud gied it tae the clennie (had given it to the cleansing department).

– Fuck the ladder, he replied angrily. Ah couldnae gie a shite aboot the poxy ladder (the ladder is a trifling matter).

I was stumped. If he didn't give a shite about the ladder, then why were we having this conversation? What had I done to upset him? I racked my brain for clues. He was always referring to me as a wee Proddy poof, but surely that couldn't be it? If he stopped to batter every Protestant who crossed his path, he'd never make it to the end of the street.

Perhaps he had just taken an irrational dislike to me. Perhaps I exuded some objectionable quality that brought out the worst in him. As I pondered that possibility, another thought occurred to me, one that might just have proved to be my salvation. Whether Kane liked me or not, we had something in common. We had a family connection that might be some pretext for our conciliation.

– Ma brother knows yer sister, by the way, I blurted out.

The sinister smile dropped from his face. His head turned, almost imperceptibly, and he gazed at me with a studied bewilderment. The cold was clearly getting to his henchmen, who shuffled from foot to foot, wiping the white drizzle from their faces. Kane's silence unnerved me. Perhaps the point needed elucidating.

– Tony. Ma brother, Tony. He knows yer sister. Theresa, is it?

Suddenly he ordered his henchmen to leave. They prevaricated long enough for him to lose his temper.

– GO ON, FUCK OFF! he shouted, pushing them away.

– Awright, keep the heid, said one of them as they turned and walked away.

Now it was just the two of us, one on one, a straight showdown between Kane and me. It was Clint Eastwood against Lee van Cleef in *For a Few Dollars More*. I was done for.

– Ur you for fucking real? he asked, his face etched with rage.

– What?

– UR YOU FOR FUCKING REAL?

I panicked.

– Look, what's the matter, big man? All I said was that my brother knows your sister.

– AYE, AH KNOW HE DOES. HE KNOWS HER A BIT TOO FUCKING WELL. THAT'S THE PROBLEM. THAT'S WHY I'M GONNAE KICK YER HEID UP AND DOON THIS STREET.

The situation was spinning out of control, and I didn't know how to stop it. Tony's friendship with Kane's sister had always confused me. I'd no idea why it commanded the status it did, why it had sparked such ructions within our family. Of course, it had occurred to me that she was the girl I'd caught him with at the Cunyon. But why should that have prompted such a huge debate about him leaving school, getting a job and spending the rest of his life with her in miserable penury? Why should her visit to our house have prefaced such a violent stand-off between Tony and Dad? I couldn't recall for that moment where the idea had originated, but I believed Kane might know the answer.

– Does this have anything to do with shagging? I asked.

The directness of my question took him by surprise. His eyes widened, and he stared down at me, witheringly and incredulously.

– Yer some piece of work, wee man. Ah'll gie ye that.

That wasn't a proper answer. That was a shipping forecast answer, and it was getting me nowhere. There was something about shagging that people weren't telling me. I knew instinctively that it was wrong because it involved the removal of clothes, but there was more to it than that. But what? Just when it appeared I was getting close to a proper explanation, people always started to talk in riddles or to clam up. Everyone seemed to be involved in a conspiracy to prevent me from knowing the truth. Now I had the opportunity to find out, albeit from a source intent on beating me senseless, but I wasn't prepared to let it slip by.

– HAS IT GOT ANYTHING TO DO WITH SHAGGING! I shouted.

Kane recoiled.

– Of course it's to do with shagging, he said. The bastard knocked her up.

I stared at him blankly.

– He got her pregnant.

Still there was no flicker of recognition from me.

– He gave her a baby.

– What, by shagging her?

Kane's face screwed into a contorted ball.

– OK, very fucking funny, wee man. Think yer a clever bastard, dae ye? Well, yiv hud yer fun, now yer gonnae get yer baws skelpt. See how fucking funny ye think that is.

And that's how it happened. That's how I learned about the facts of life – shortly before bearing the full force of a clenched fist in the middle of my face. I felt the grinding crunch of Kane's knuckle against the soft frame of my nose and breathed the smoky, soporific aroma of pain. My knees buckled, and I was swept into the gutter like a sapling uprooted by a hurricane.

I felt my head bounce off the pavement and I looked down to see a thin streak of blood curdling in the muddy rainwater. My first instinct was to stop myself from becoming drenched, and so I staggered to my feet, but I quickly felt the weight of another pile-driver against the side of my head. I rolled with the punch and managed to remain upright, but then another, harder punch landed slightly above my cheek and I was down again.

I blacked out. I don't know for how long. It could have been a second, or it could have been a minute. When I regained consciousness, I felt plump droplets of perspiration force their way through my head and roll down my bruised face. I was soaked through, though I didn't know how much of it was rain and how much was sweat and blood.

Kane stood over me, his fists clenched. He kicked me hard in the stomach and ordered me to get to my feet so that he could hit me again. Then I heard a voice behind us.

– Hoi, leave him alone.

Kane frowned.

– Look pal, this isnae your fight, he pleaded. What's it to you?

– He's my mate, the voice insisted. And if ye don't leave him alone, I'll batter you.

The voice was slightly nasal and familiar. I sensed it moving closer, and Kane backed off. There was a fearful look in his eyes.

– Aye, all right, big man, ahm gaun, he said, before turning on his heel and running off.

I rolled over onto my back and looked up to identify my saviour. My blackened eyes had already started to close over, and I had to squint through the rain and the darkness, but I just about managed to make out the ungainly, imposing figure of Daft Davie.

22

There was majesty in Govan, but you had to know where to look. In the summertime, shards of bright sunlight filtered through the long arms of the shipyard cranes, casting elegant shadows on the red neo-classical columns of the town hall. The air was filled with the sweet scent of honeysuckle and geraniums that grew abundantly in the deep terracotta pots that surrounded its entrance.

It was an oasis of beauty against a backdrop of grim hardship and an incongruously benign setting for an event that had taken on the significance of Judgement Day for Sophia. For months, this moment had been cast with black portent, when she would be called to account for her misdeeds.

A letter addressed to Mum and Dad announced that, because she had committed an offence, she would be required to appear before three panel members who would decide whether 'compulsory measures of supervision are needed for your child and what these measures should be. This could include steps taken to protect, guide, treat or control your child.'

Mum was in a fractious mood. She and Dad had spent most of the morning sparking off one another like warring scorpions. She kept talking about how affronted she was at the position in which Sophia had placed her, where her parenting was being questioned by some faceless bureaucrats. Dad said there was plenty of time to be embarrassed after the hearing, and, in the meantime, they had a daughter who needed their help and support, not bitterness and condemnation.

– Don't talk to me about being a good parent, Robert.

– All right, Christine, give it a rest.

The fact that Dad was obliged to wear a suit and tie for the first time since he'd left the restaurant exacerbated his anxiety and he pulled at his shirt collar like a child with a rash.

We arrived at the town hall with plenty of time to spare. Sophia entered the building with the resigned, hangdog look of an Asian bride, and I felt genuinely sorry for her. It hadn't been an easy time these last few months.

A grey-haired, crisply starched commissionaire instructed us to sit on a row of orange plastic chairs which had been lined up outside a door with a hand-written sign on it which said 'Children's Panel'. There were only three seats so I opted to wait outside, on the Govan Road, where I spent the time throwing stones down a stank until the commissionaire came out and told me to stop.

I had another reason for wanting to be outside. I knew Cumbo's hearing was on the same day and I was hoping that I would catch sight of his family arriving and that Lyndsey might be with them. She hadn't spoken a word to me since the day I told her dad she was chucked. Not unreasonably, in my opinion. But she hadn't given me the chance to explain why I had done it – that I had got the wrong end of the stick.

I thought it was Lyndsey who had told Samantha Hendry and Joanne Moffat about my parents' break-up. In fact, Joanne Moffat learnt about it from her big sister who was in Sophia's class at the secondary and who had heard it from her. It was a simple mistake, and I was sure Lyndsey would understand if she only knew the truth. Even if she didn't understand initially, I'd work on her. Eventually she would.

I thought Sophia would be in for hours, but fifteen minutes later she emerged with Mum and Dad, wearing a smile, and I knew things had gone well. When I asked what had happened, Mum tried to explain, but she used so many big words that I was none the wiser.

– She got a slap on the wrist, Dad said.

– Don't trivialise this, Robert, Mum barked. She didn't get a slap on the wrist, she got a very serious warning.

– I'm not trivialising it. I'm just trying to make it understandable for the boy.

– She was told in no uncertain terms that if she ever did anything like this again then there would be very serious consequences, Mum explained.

Sophia remained silent, staring down demurely at her black patent leather shoes.

– Do you hear me, young lady? Mum asked. I don't want you to think that you have got away with anything here because that is most definitely not the case.

– Yes, Mum, I hear you, Sophia replied.

Mum had already meted out her own form of punishment, banning Sophia from ever seeing Cumbo again. Sophia feigned upset and victimhood, but she continued to see Cumbo in secret. I knew this because I had seen them snogging round the back of the Co-op, but that was a nugget of intelligence I planned to wield at a more opportune time.

After the hearing, Dad offered to take us all out for lunch. Mum agreed as long as it was understood by everyone that it wasn't a party. The fact that Sophia had not been given a more stringent punishment should not be a matter of celebration but reflection. I wanted to go to Gino's, but Dad said we should go somewhere a bit more upscale.

We drove to the Glynhill Hotel in Renfrew in Dad's new Rover 2000. It was the first time Mum had been in it, and she pretended it was no big deal, but I caught her running her hand over the walnut dashboard, and I could tell that, really, she was impressed.

There was a cold lunchtime buffet in the bar, but Dad insisted that we eat in the proper silver service restaurant, from the à la carte menu. Dad had been more lavish with his cash since he'd opened his new shop in town. Trade was booming, he said, and even Mum had to admit that he had a flair for business.

He kept saying how he wished he'd become self-employed

years ago but he'd been held back by silly notions about where people came from and their proper place in the world. I didn't really understand what he was talking about, but I just nodded my agreement anyway.

Sophia said the reason he was being so flash was because he had no-one else to spend his money on now that he'd split up with Vivienne. I got really excited when I found out that they'd gone their separate ways, because I thought it would mean he'd get back together with Mum, but she just laughed and said that's not how things worked in the real world.

– Your dad and I are both very different from the people we were when we met and got married. It's best that we get on with our own lives, she said.

I thought I'd be more upset than I was but actually I felt OK, especially when Dad said he agreed with Mum. After having gone through their break-up, I felt better placed to handle the disappointment. Things were never going to be the same again, and I just had to get used to it.

Life at home was much easier, and I was glad that I'd decided not to run away, after all. Though I'd never have believed it at the time, Kane actually did me a favour. After his battering, I returned home and climbed back into bed. When Mum woke me in the morning for school she wanted to know where I got the black eyes from. She didn't believe I'd fallen out of bed in the middle of the night.

In the end I was forced to tell her and Dad the whole story – about the ladder, the Cunyon and my showdown with Kane. Dad went round to Kane's house for 'clear the air' talks with his parents, and they seemed to patch things up. Apparently, Kane's old man was really decent about the whole thing. He was furious that Kevin had given me a doing and refused Dad's offer to pay for the missing ladder.

Later Mum took me aside and said it was time I knew about the 'birds and the bees'. I didn't know what she was talking about and when she started banging on about penises, I didn't know where to look. I thought she was winding me up, but when I asked Tony about it later, he said she was telling the truth.

The week after Sophia's hearing we all gathered around the front door waiting for Tony's exam results to drop through the letterbox. We were wired with excitement, especially Mum who paced the hallway, quietly uttering affirmations to herself. Tony was the coolest person in the house.

Of course, he did better than anyone had hoped for – straight As in all subjects – and he spent the next ten minutes beneath a mountain of bodies, smothered in kisses and congratulations. He got more than enough to get into any law school in the country, but he'd already decided he was going to study English because he wanted to be a writer. He opted for Glasgow University and agreed that he would continue to stay at home for his first year. After that he would think about moving into digs.

I was relieved and delighted because it meant he'd still be around when I was going up to the secondary, at least for the first few months. After that, I was sure I'd be able to cope on my own. The secondary didn't hold the same fear for me as it had. I figured that if I could survive the events of the past year, then I could survive a change of schools, even if the frequency with which I acquired stiffies seemed to be increasing at the same time as my ability to control when and why they occurred was correspondingly diminishing.

The bigger surprise was when Mum told us that she'd also been accepted by the university, to study psychology. We didn't even know she'd applied. We were all delighted, and even Dad wished her well, saying she deserved it after all the hard work she'd put in at college.

After that, Mum and Dad seemed to get on much better. Mum phoned Dad when she had a problem with the bank, and he told her how to get it straightened out. Then, when Dad's washing machine broke down, he brought his laundry round, and she washed it for him.

The only outstanding problem I had was Wally. He was hacked

off at being left round the back of the Crit in the pissing rain when we were supposed to be running away together. After hanging around for two hours when I failed to show up, he decided to go on his own. He got as far as Dumbarton Road where he was picked up by two cops in a panda car, who wanted to know what he was doing roaming the streets at two in the morning, wet through. They drove him back home.

At his family case conference it was decided that he should be taken into care, but then Suitcase volunteered to look after him in his new flat in Clydebank. It was agreed that he would stay with his brother on a trial basis under social work supervision.

It meant he'd have to start at a new school on the other side of the city, and, after consulting with his teachers, it was decided that he should repeat Primary Six because he'd missed so much of the work. He said he didn't mind doing that as no-one knew him at the new school and they wouldn't know he was repeating. He said he was really excited about going and that he was determined to make a go of school.

The night before he left for Clydebank, we cycled to the Cunyon one last time, using the Seven Hills as stunt ramps. He got to be Evel Knievel because he'd bagsied it first, which meant I had to be Eddie Kidd, which was rubbish. I hated being Eddie Kidd. The early summer sun was setting over the high flats and it was growing dark, so we cycled back, stopping at the top of the railway bridge.

– I'll chum you back to your house so that I can drop the bike off, Wally said.

It was the first mention of the Tomahawk since I'd 'lent' it to him at Christmas. I sensed he knew I wasn't expecting it back but felt he had to make the gesture.

– That's all right. You can hang onto it for now, I said. I'll get it another time.

It was getting late, but he seemed in no hurry to depart. He told me about how Handbag was getting a new Kawasaki 100 when he started work at the shipyard and that he'd promised to give him a backy. Then he launched into a story about an argument he'd had with one of Handbag's mates who was trying to tell him that a Honda 250 Dream was a better bike than a Yamaha RD 200. I offered him no encouragement to continue, but it didn't halt his flow and eventually I interrupted him.

– Look, I have to be going, Wally. My tea will be getting cold.

He stopped in his tracks. A crestfallen look came over his face, and I felt guilty.

– I'll see you later, OK? I said, doing my best to sound reassuring, but in that moment I think we both realised it would be the last time we'd see each other.

– I don't want to go to Clydebank, he said suddenly. I won't know anyone. I want to stay here with you.

I smiled at him and patted him on the shoulder.

– You'll be fine, I said. And we went our separate ways.

Wally was my best friend, and I knew I'd miss him, but I no longer wanted to be like him. Things always seemed to happen when Wally was around, but after the events of the past year, I began to think that sometimes it's better when nothing happens, when life just grinds along at the same slow and predictable pace. I was happy being part of my own family. I was happy being me and I knew it was time to move on.